Both Ends
of the
Night

Marcia Muller

Both Ends of the Night

WHEELER
PUBLISHING, INC.
ROCKLAND, MA

★ AN AMERICAN COMPANY ★

Published in Large Print by arrangement with
Warner Books, Inc. in the United States and Canada.

Wheeler Large Print Book Series.

Set in 16 pt Plantin.

Library of Congress Cataloging-in-Publication Data

Muller, Marica.
    Both ends of the Night / Marcia Muller.
        p. (large print) cm.(Wheeler large print book series)
    ISBN 1-56895-463-8 (softcover)
    1. McCone, Sharon (Fictitious character)—Fiction. 2. Large type books.
I. Title.
[PS3563.U397B68 1997b]
813'.54—dc21   97-21391
                                                                    CIP

In memory of Collin Wilcox,
who urged me to take to the skies,
and for Peggy Bakker,
who kept me up there

Many thanks to:

The folks at Petaluma Municipal Airport and Aeroventure, who made an inquisitive writer and fledgling pilot feel welcome;

Bonnie and Mike Fredrick and Tiffany Knight, my Arkansas connections;

Victoria and Ted Brouillette, in Minnesota;

Bob Gardner, CFI, whose gift of *Say Again, Please* made radio communication explicable;

Melissa Ward, extraordinary researcher;

And Bill, who never for a moment doubted that I could learn to land Cessna 7232S.

Night means the time between the end of evening civil twilight and the beginning of morning civil twilight, as published in the American Air Almanac, converted to local time.

—Part I.I, Federal Aviation Regulations

But there's so much more that the regulations *can't* tell you...

Both Ends of the Night

Three Years Ago

"*Well, how about that, McCone? You've lost your engine. Now what're you gonna do?*"

"*There's nothing wrong with the engine, Matty. You pulled back on power, that's all.*"

"*I'm the instructor. If I say you've got no engine, you've got no engine. You have an emergency landing place picked out?*"

"*...No.*"

"*Better find one.*"

"*There. Right there. That pasture. Brownish green. Cows to the east side.*"

"*So take me there. Where're you gonna put it down in relation to those cows?*"

"*As far away as possible.*"

"*Why?*"

"*Ranchers don't like you landing on their stock.*"

"*Right. What's the other reason?*"

"*...I don't know.*"

"*Well, suppose you'd borrowed that tail-dragger of your boyfriend's. Nice little cloth-covered Citabria, nice big price tag. You land near those cows, take your time calling for help, and you're likely to be missing a wing when you get back.*"

"*Why?*"

"*Cows just love to munch on airplane fabric.*"

"*God, Ripinsky'd kill me!*"

"*Maim you, anyway. Full power now, and take me home. You get the point of this exercise, don't you?*"

"Yes: Always have an emergency landing place in mind."

"I can't emphasize it enough: Emergencies can happen. They will happen. Always planning for the emergency can save your life."

PART ONE

November 22–23

One

Landing at Los Alegres Municipal Airport felt like coming home.

I angled in on the forty-five toward mid-field, turned downwind, and pressed the button on my headset. "Los Alegres traffic, Cessna four-four-two-five-Whiskey, downwind for landing, two-niner."

The 150 I'd rented at Oakland was identical to the plane I'd trained in. Los Alegres was where I'd learned the ABC's of flying. And somewhere below, watching with a critical eye, was my former flight instructor, Matty Wildress. I'd sooner exit without a parachute than make a clumsy landing in front of her.

I pulled on the carburetor heat, slowed the aircraft down, and added a notch of flaps. As I turned onto base I could hear Matty issuing orders: "Keep that airspeed under control. Look for other traffic. *Look!* Another notch of flaps now. Turn for final." She'd always claimed that her words echoed in students' minds years after they earned their licenses, and I was living proof of that.

On final now. Focused. I was used to flying Hy's tail-dragger rather than a tricycle type of plane like this, and the technique of touching down was somewhat different.

Please, I told myself, don't hit the tail skid. You'll never hear the end of it.

"Keep it straight," Matty's voice commanded in my mind. "*Straight!* Level off. Eyes on the far end of the runway now. The *far end*. Hold it off. Keep holding. Keep..."

I held the Cessna in a nose-up attitude as it settled. Then the wheels touched and I was rolling along the runway. Soft and smooth and straight.

You'd *better* be watching, Matty.

I spotted her as I turned off and taxied toward the visitors' parking: tall and slender, leaning against the counter at the fuel pumps, long brown hair blowing in the breeze. While I maneuvered between the tie-down chains, she walked toward me, hands thrust into the pockets of her loose blue jacket. By the time I stepped down, she was hooking the chain to the tail section.

"Nice landing, McCone," she called. "At least one of my students turned into a good pilot."

I grabbed the right chain and attached it to the ring on the strut. "I thought all your students turned out splendidly."

"Some better than others." She secured the right chain, then motioned toward the stucco building that housed the fixed-base operator—aircraft rentals, maintenance, and the flight school—and the Seven Niner Diner, so named because the field was seventy-nine feet above mean sea level. "Let's get a bite to eat."

Now that I moved closer to Matty, I was startled by what I saw. Her tanned skin held a sallow tint, and her gray eyes were deeply shadowed; fine lines etched by forty-some years of hearty laughter pulled taut, as if she were in pain. I hadn't seen her in over a year, but this was too profound a change for even that length of time. Something wrong here, very wrong.

She'd called me out of the blue the day before, claiming it was time for the flight review that the FAA requires every two years of all pilots. Why not fly up to Los Alegres for it the next afternoon? she suggested. The barely concealed note of urgency in her voice struck me as strange, particularly since my review wasn't due till next March, and it wasn't like Matty to get her dates mixed up. But when I told her that and tried to put her off, the disappointed silence that followed made me mentally shift appointments and agree to meet her at the airport for lunch. Now I was glad I had.

She caught me studying her and looked away, walking quickly toward the gate where a sign jokingly welcomed arrivals to Los Alegres International. "There's old Max," she said, pointing toward the small terminal building. "He's still hanging in there."

Max, the airport manager's yellow Lab, lay on the patch of lawn. He heard his name, looked up, and yawned at us. The dog purportedly had been on his last legs for years, but to tell the truth, he looked a hell of a lot better today than Matty. I called out, "Hey, Max," and followed her across the parking lot.

"Matty—"

She must have sensed the question that was coming, because she interrupted me and began chattering in a quick voice that was underscored by nervousness. "Listen, McCone, I meant it when I said some of my students turn out better than others. Take this hotdog I soloed last month; I never should've gotten out of the plane. The other day he's here shooting landings. A bunch of us are hanging around by the gas pumps, and Mark—you remember Mark?"

I nodded.

"Well, just as the guy crosses the threshold, Mark goes, 'Now, *there's* an accident waiting to happen.' And bam! Before anybody can say anything, the hotdog's put it into a ground loop."

"He get hurt?"

"Bruised some, especially his pride, but you want to see one screwed-up prop and nosewheel, check out the 152 in the hangar." She shrugged. "Can't say as I didn't try to drum it into his thick head: Just because you're on the ground—"

"Doesn't mean that you can stop flying the plane."

"I taught you well."

"Damn right you did."

We climbed the steps to the diner and made our way among the plastic tables and chairs on the deck overlooking the field. A lunchtime crowd of pilots, mechanics, and workers from the nearby office park were gathered there, and many called out greetings to Matty. She stopped to speak to one woman, waving for me to go on and get us a table.

A popular individual, Matty, and also something of a local celebrity in this small town forty-some miles north of San Francisco. Besides being the flight school's best and only female instructor, she was an aerobatic pilot of national reputation, and if all went according to her own fine-tuned plan, by this time next year she'd be the new U.S. Aerobatic Champion.

My association with Matty went back over three years, to shortly after my fifth ride in the Citabria belonging to my lover, Hy Ripinsky. Far above the Sierra Nevada he'd put the tiny plane into a precision spin, and then and there I'd decided to become a pilot myself. But Hy, who has his instructor's rating and occasionally takes on students at Tufa Tower Field near his ranch in Mono County, refused to teach me. I was, he claimed, stubborn and often disinclined to accept criticism—particularly from him. Before I was able to remind him of his own stubborness and disinclination to accept criticism, though, he offered to put me in touch with an old buddy of his who owed him a favor and would give me lessons at below the going rate.

I was surprised when the buddy turned out to be an attractive, willowy woman with thick brown hair that fell nearly to her waist. Initially I wondered, almost to the point of obsessing, about the nature of their long friendship, but after my first lesson I put my questions aside. Why, I reasoned, let what might or might not have happened between them cloud what promised to be a great student-teacher relationship? And even though I still wondered from time to time—wondered now, as I watched her talking animatedly, her slender hands describing loops and rolls in the air—I never regretted the decision. Matty had a magical way of transferring her skill to her students; under conditions unnerving to a novice, she was calm and supportive; her enthusiasm for even the most mundane aspects of flying—and there are many—was infectious. She'd made me the pilot I was today.

The student pilot–instructor relationship is a special one, fostered by a classroom situation that is far less than ideal. Several years before I met Matty, I'd had a few lessons from a naval aviator I dated; more recently I'd been flying with Hy. But as I belted myself into the left seat of that Cessna for the first time, I became acutely aware that I was placing my life in the hands of a stranger.

Over the course of the long hours we spent together in the cockpit, I learned a great deal about myself—and about Matty. Both of us were reserved women. We didn't speak of personal matters, we didn't trade in emotions. Even when a strong crosswind reduced me to a mass of Jell-O on landing, I stifled my gasps and concentrated on putting the plane into a sideslip. Even when my fear of relinquishing the controls in a tricky situation tried her patience, she didn't lose her temper. We were, I later realized, keeping each other at an arm's length in a space that was barely an arm's length to begin with.

Still, at such close quarters, the person beneath one's skin communicates in ways more subtle than words. By the time I'd earned my license, Matty and I could reach each other in a single glance.

And today I was reading her easily. She might be doing her damnedest to distract me from her nervousness and haggard appearance, but no amount of bright chatter could mask the obvious distress signals.

Now she left the woman she'd been talking with and came over to our table. As she sat down and put aside the menu, which hadn't changed in years, she said, "Former student of mine. She wants to take up aerobatics. More power to her."

"You going to teach her?"

"No, I'm not the best of instructors in that area. Fellow who taught me—you've met him, Jim Powell—is. I'm sending her to him." She regarded me for a moment, her eyes unreadable behind her sunglasses. "You ever think of taking it up?"

"Aerobatics? Uh-uh. Oh, I fool around sometimes—way up high, and under Ripinsky's supervision. But to be any good you've got to work hard at it; right now working hard at keeping my agency functioning is about all I can handle."

"Well, maybe someday you will. I'd like to see how you'd do. Of course, you always did hate stalls, so I'm not sure how you could handle, say, a Falling Leaf."

I smiled faintly. If we were to take a short ride in the Cessna this afternoon, Matty would find out about stalls and me.

She said, "So you're still flying that tail-dragger of Ripinsky's."

"Every chance I get."

"How come you don't have it today?"

"He's got it up at Tufa Tower, although he's coming down to the city later this afternoon. I had to rent, and I picked a 150 for sentimental reasons."

"Picked it because it was the cheapest rate

11

you could get, you mean. Although between the two of you, you and Hy can't be doing badly; last time I fueled at Oakland, one of the linemen told me you guys had bought a cottage on the coast. Mendocino County, isn't it?"

"Uh-huh. But we didn't really buy it; we paid a dollar to friends who had bad memories of the place."

"Nice deal. How is Ripinsky, anyway?"

She really was determined to play this scene out as if everything were fine with her, but I knew that sooner or later she'd confide in me. Sooner, if I didn't push, so I went along with her script. "He's fine. You've heard about his latest crusade?"

"The human-rights thing? Yeah. What got him started on that?"

"Oh, a while back he found himself in a bad situation, where he was helped out by people who were in pretty marginal circumstances themselves. It got him going."

"Going from tree-hugger to caped crusader?"

"Something like that."

She shook her head. "It's pure Ripinsky, all right: tough as nails, with a bleeding heart the size of Texas."

I smiled at the comment. Matty was a hard-line conservative; I was a mixed bag of viewpoints, both intellectual and emotional. Long ago we'd agreed not to discuss political issues.

The waitress came over and we ordered our usual: big burger for Matty, calamari sandwich for me, iced tea for both of us. A yellow Citabria, like Hy's except for the color, was on final; we watched as it did a touch-and-go. I twisted around so I could see it climb out, and when I

12

turned back to Matty, she'd taken off her dark glasses and was studying me.

Why? Out of habit, to assess my mood as she always had before lessons? To see if I'd changed in the time since she'd last seen me? No, neither. Something in her gaze tipped me off: she was trying to decide if she could trust me with her problem. And not because I was her friend but because I was a private investigator.

"Why didn't you just come out and ask?" I said. "Why'd you have to use the biennial as an excuse?"

"What?"

"You heard me. I reminded you that it's not due till March. You're in some kind of a bind, and you want to hire me. What is it?"

"Oh, God, McCone, you know me too well." She glanced around. "Let's not talk here, huh? Too many people."

"Where, then? When?"

"After we eat. You can take me up, check out our old haunts. I'll tell you about it in the plane."

I lowered the Cessna's nose to level flight attitude, let the speed accelerate, and throttled back to cruise RPM. "Now," I said to Matty.

She didn't respond.

I set my course due west toward the area where I'd so often practiced, above the farmland that stretched between the town and the coastal ridgeline. Matty slumped passively in the narrow seat, head bowed, eyes shut behind her dark glasses. Not the Matty who had once sat beside me, issuing orders while on the alert for every possible danger.

I checked for other traffic, then banked in a shallow turn. Relaxed pressure on the controls and let the plane fly itself. "Okay," I said, "start at the beginning."

The silence spun out. It told me her problem was serious, and very personal. Matty wouldn't equivocate this way about something to do with one of her students or the major-parts manufacturer that underwrote both her expenses for aerobatic competitions and her quarter-million-dollar customized plane.

Finally she sighed deeply and opened her eyes. "Okay, here it is. You know that I've been living with somebody?"

"You mentioned him in your note on my birthday card."

"Oh, right. Well, it's been nearly eleven months now, since the week after New Year's. His name's John Seabrook, and he owns a Christmas-tree farm right over there." She pointed toward the base of the hills, where there was a large tract of heavily forested land.

I rolled out of the turn and began a medium-banked one in the opposite direction. "And?"

"He's disappeared."

"Since when?"

"A week ago yesterday."

"You file a missing-persons report?"

"No."

"Why not?"

Shrug.

"Why not, Matty?"

"...You'd have to know John to understand. He's got a real thing about his privacy, and he doesn't talk about his past."

"At all?"

"No."

"That still doesn't explain why you didn't file a report."

"Oh, shit!" She bit her lower lip and looked out the side window.

I concentrated on completing the turn. Giving her time. My eyes swept the sky for other aircraft, but I didn't spot any. In spite of its being a beautifully clear November Friday, there had been little traffic on the way here or at either airport. Again I rolled out and brought the Cessna straight and level, taking in the way the watery sunlight put a glow on the browned hills.

When it seemed Matty was closing off again, I said, "You didn't file a report because you think John disappeared voluntarily and will be angry with you when he comes back, for calling police attention to him."

"...Something like that."

"And you think the disappearance has its roots in this past he never speaks of."

"Yeah, I do."

"Why?"

"Just a feeling."

"What were the exact circumstances of his leaving?"

"Damned if I know. I was away, had flown a couple of businessmen down to Monterey on a charter."

"You're taking on charters as well as instructing?"

"Sure. It's a good way to pick up extra cash, and the routes're so familiar I could fly them in my sleep. I haven't been on a cross-country

15

to unfamiliar territory in ten months; I've probably forgotten how to plot a course. Not that I'm complaining; I enjoy being home."

"So you were in Monterey the day John disappeared."

"Yes. When I got back, he wasn't home and one of the trucks was gone. It was late, but I didn't think anything of it, just went to bed. But in the morning I got worried—he never stayed away all night—and took a good look around. His shaving stuff, duffel bag, back-pack, and some of his clothes were gone. One of the guns, too—a forty-four Magnum."

"And he gave you no indication whatsoever that he would be going away?"

"Well, maybe. A couple of days before, he was supposed to have lunch with me at the diner, but when I got back from my eleven-o'clock lesson, he was very nervous—upset, really—and said he had to cancel. A problem at the tree farm, he claimed, but he wouldn't go into it. Then he wasn't around much till the night before I was due to fly to Monterey."

"And that night?"

"Just an ordinary night at home, except he was... well, more loving than usual."

"As if he was saying good-bye?"

She compressed her lips and shook her head, unwilling to consider that.

I put the Cessna into a steep-banked turn, thinking to head back toward the airport. "Okay, exactly what do you know about John's background?"

"Very little. He came to town ten years ago with his baby son and bought a half interest in this failing tree farm.

He says trees are one of the few things he really understands, and he must understand them pretty well, because the farm's turning a good profit and he bought out his partner last year."

"Back up a minute—he has a son?"

"Zachary. He's eleven."

"Is he with you?"

"Uh-huh. He's a good kid, we get on. And I guess John trusts me to look after him." She paused, reflective. "Zach hasn't had an easy time of it the past few years. He's curious about where he was born and what his mother was like—normal, at his age. But John won't talk about it, and it's driving a wedge between them at a time when a boy needs to be close to his father. There're no family photos; John doesn't get letters from relatives—or anybody else. It's like he's trying to erase his entire life before he came here."

"And you haven't asked him why?"

"No."

To most people it might have seemed curious that a strong, outspoken woman like Matty Wildress wouldn't have confronted the issue. But she was talking to the right person: I had avoided a similar confrontation with Hy during the years he'd remained stubbornly silent about the ugly things he'd seen and done as a charter pilot in Southeast Asia.

Matty added, "I figured if I gave him some space he'd eventually tell me."

I'd figured the same with Hy, and he'd finally unburdened himself. But John Seabrook had left Matty without a word.

I asked, "Where was Zach when his father left?"

"Staying with Karla and Wes Payne, our neighbors. Wes used to be John's partner. That's another thing that tells me he planned to leave; a couple of days before, he arranged for Zach to sleep over at the Paynes' that night."

"Does Zach have any idea where John might've gone—or why?"

"He's as puzzled as I am. Hurt, too."

"I'd say you're pretty damn hurt yourself. And you're afraid you're involved in something you can't handle."

She'd been looking at the ground as I continued to turn. Now she whipped her head around, nostrils flaring. "Hey, McCone, that's getting too damn personal. Back off!"

At last I'd caught a glimpse of the old Matty—the woman who did not passively accept the blows life dealt her, the woman who fought back. But the old Matty could also be closed off, prickly, and quick to take offense. She'd have to unbend if I was to work for her.

Instead of backing off, I rolled out of the turn and began pulling back on the yoke.

"What the hell?" she said.

I kept pulling back, raising the Cessna's nose higher and higher.

"McCone!"

I grinned at her. Kept pulling till I felt the controls go mushy. The stall horn squealed, the plane shuddered, and the lift went out from under the wings. The Cessna plummeted wildly, yawing to the left.

And I took my hands and feet off the controls.

Matty grabbed my arm and shouted, "Yes!"

I folded my hands in my lap as the Cessna pitched nose downward. Hills and pastures and trees and ranch buildings flashed past the windows at unnatural angles. Then, slowly, the plane righted itself. Its nose tipped upward and it began to fly without any help from me.

Matty was laughing now. "God damn, you sure did get over hating stalls!"

"Yeah, I did." I got back on the controls, brought us to level flight again.

Suddenly she was serious, studying my face. "You've changed, McCone."

"Sure I have. Now, how about you? You've always hated talking about anything personal. It's time you changed, too."

Two

The tidy rows of Douglas fir started beyond the drainage ditch beside the country road and spread up the hillside, parting like a forked river around a white frame farmhouse, then reconverging. Here and there branches brushed the sides of Matty's van as she steered it along the potholed driveway. Even with the windows closed, the trees' scent was strong, and it gave me a flash of childlike anticipation. With surprise, I realized Christmas was only five weeks away.

"Let me go over what you wrote me in my birthday card," I said. "You met John at the airport last September, on the day the pilots' association gives rides to raise money for charity."

19

"Right. Zach read about it in the paper and begged John to let him go up. I took him in that old 150 you trained in."

"John didn't want a ride, too?"

"God, no. He hates to fly, says he'll never set foot in a light plane." She pulled the van under an apple tree in the weedy front yard, where leaves and deadfall fruit lay on the ground. The house was one story, with a dormer attic window and a deep wraparound porch. Fuchsia plants, leggy now, hung from the eaves.

"Nice place," I said.

"Thanks. The yard could do with some work, and the house was kind of run down when I moved in. John had just bought out his partner and was putting all his energy into the tree farm, and besides, he's not good with stuff like painting and carpentry. I am, so he gave me free rein."

We got out of the van and crossed to the wide front steps. "Okay," I said, "you gave Zach a ride..."

"While John ate lunch at the diner. After that, he started hanging around the airport. He claimed it was the Seven Niner burgers that kept calling him back—one of the few things we've got in common is love of a good burger. But I knew it was really me."

"And he courted you throughout the fall and the holidays, till you moved in after New Year's."

Matty fumbled with her keys and inserted one in the lock. "Courted! That's one hell of a... what d'you call them?"

"Euphemisms?"

"Right. What he did was go after me with all the subtlety of a bull moose in rutting season. We had a damned good time together, and I decided I'd be a fool to let him get away, especially at the start of a cold, wet winter."

The hallway she led me into was narrow and wainscoted. Its hardwood floor gleamed, and above the paneling the freshly painted white walls were covered with enlarged color photographs. I stopped to look at one of Matty in the cockpit of a sleek yellow monoplane with a red sunburst pattern on its low wings. The canopy was open, and she was grinning widely, looking straight into the camera's lens.

"This isn't the plane you used to fly," I said.

"No, it's new, last year. Stirling Silver Star 360, customized to my specifications. Manufactured by Stirling Aviation in Arkansas. They're one of the top aircraft-design firms, got into a lot of trouble some years back, but have turned around beautifully. This plane is one of the best there is. Very low drag, performs like a dream in those upward rolling maneuvers that impress the judges. Has unlimited capability, really." She touched the picture frame lightly, straightening it.

"What does John think of you flying competitively?"

"He cheers me on."

"I'd've thought a man who hates to fly would be afraid for you."

She shrugged. "He's got confidence in my abilities and not a great deal of imagination when it comes to what might happen. I don't

21

have much myself. You can't, or you'd scare yourself right out of the cockpit."

And there was the reason I'd never be very good at aerobatics; my imagination was always several steps ahead of me, and often tripped me up.

"Hey," she said, "I know what you're thinking. Sure, there's risk involved. But simply living's a risk. My mother was a very fearful person; the whole time I was growing up, it was always 'You can't do that. What if something happened to you?' I used to listen to her and think, Jeez, what if *nothing* ever happens to me? The way I see it, life's about accepting risk, meeting it head on. Otherwise you might just as well sit in a glass bubble the whole time, waiting to die."

I nodded, recognizing it as a rule that I too had more or less lived by. Then I began moving along the hall, examining the other photos until I came to an eight-by-ten of Matty, a tall man, and an adolescent boy.

"This is John and Zach?"

"Yes." She glanced at the picture, and her lips tightened. Wordlessly she brushed past me, heading for the back of the house. I stayed where I was, taking a close look at the missing man and his son.

John Seabrook was big, the way a quarterback is, with powerful muscle development and not an ounce of fat. His light brown hair was longish, falling in a thick shock over his high brow, and his skin had the deep tan and weather lines of a man who has spent most of his life outdoors. Zach had a similar body type, but his hair was blond, his eyes a striking shade of blue. The facial resemblance was obvious, though: father and son shared the same square jaw, high cheekbones, and aquiline nose. No mistaking the relationship.

After a moment I went the way Matty had gone and found her in an old-fashioned kitchen, sorting through the mail she'd grabbed from the box beside the road. She saw me looking around at the warped green linoleum and cabinets coated in numerous layers of paint. "Not much I could do to improve this room," she said. "Calls for a complete remodel, and we can't afford it."

"I know how that is. You should've seen mine before I scraped together the cash to have it redone."

"Cash—that's always the problem." She grimaced and set the mail down. "Everybody thinks flight instructors make big bucks, and we would if we worked forty hours a week, fifty-two weeks a year, which we don't. And aerobatics is even worse: There's no prize money for winning a competition, and I've never earned more than six thousand for flying in an air show. If it wasn't for my corporate sponsor, I'd be out of the game."

"But the tree farm—you say it's profitable?"

"Now it is. John started a wholesale landscaping nursery three years ago, so it's not as seasonal a cash flow. Eventually we plan to redo this whole house. Not that I care what shape the place is in, so long as I get John home safely. What matters to me is that we're a family—what I've always wanted."

"Really? I wouldn't have thought family life fit your plans."

"Well, maybe not a traditional family life. God

23

knows I've never had that. First there was my own family, which didn't work for a variety of reasons. Then there was my marriage, which also didn't work, but for different reasons. When that busted up, all I had was my flying, which is more than a lot of people have, but still not enough. And now I'm afraid… shit, McCone, you don't need to hear it. You want to get started looking through John's stuff?"

Actually, I wished she'd talk more about herself; I'd never known about the marriage or the dysfunctional family. But time was getting short, and I was due at a dinner party in the city at seven, so I nodded and followed her upstairs to the bedroom she shared with John Seabrook.

Unlike most investigators—including my operatives Rae Kelleher and Charlotte Keim—I'm not at all comfortable intruding on other people's personal space. It strips the individual, who isn't there to protest, of precious pretense and privacy; it leaves me feeling only one rung higher than a voyeur on the ladder of disgusting practices. But a person's choice and treatment of his or her possessions can provide valuable information, and over the years I've become expert at reading others by the things with which they surround themselves.

John Seabrook's clothing, for instance: it told me he was very much the outdoorsman that his photograph suggested. Wool shirts, tees, jeans, cords, down vests and jackets—and there wasn't a suit or tie in evidence. He was an orderly man who arranged everything by type, so he probably possessed an orderly mind. When I asked Matty what he'd taken with

24

him, she was able to be specific: a blue down jacket, a couple of changes of his heaviest clothing, thermal underwear, a knitted cap, gloves, and hiking boots.

The dresser drawers were filled with neat piles of the usual stuff, except for the bottom one; that was dedicated to keepsakes and the kind of items we all hang on to because they've been given to us and we don't know what else to do with them. Seabrook's collection included an unopened bottle of Old Spice, two boxes of monogrammed handkerchiefs, a pair of silver cuff links, a shoeshine kit, a manicure set, and a gold-plated fortune cookie—all in their original boxes. He attached sentimental value to three silver dollars; a California scratch-off lottery ticket that, had he claimed it, would have netted him two dollars; a Clinton-Gore campaign button that told me one more thing he and Matty didn't have in common; a sand dollar; and a champagne cork. And in a blue velvet box I found a man's wedding band.

I took the ring out and held it up to the light. It was plain but scratched and had nothing engraved inside it. I looked at Matty and raised my eyebrows questioningly. With a shrug, she turned away and began straightening the rumpled bedclothes.

I held the ring in the palm of my hand, closing my fingers around it. Foolish to think its weight and shape might communicate something to me, and yet...

When Matty told me John wouldn't talk to Zach about his mother, I'd assumed bitterness on Seabrook's part, perhaps stemming from an ugly divorce or abandonment. But this ring—not just tossed into the drawer but preserved in its box among other mementos of apparently happy times—spoke of love and caring. I knew, because Hy also had a wedding ring preserved in his dresser drawer. Two years ago he'd shown it to me because it was of an original design created by an artist friend of his, and the expression on his face as he held it had unsettled me, because it gave away how much he still loved and missed his dead wife, Julie Spaulding.

After a moment I replaced John Seabrook's ring and said to Matty's back, "Anyplace else in the house where he keeps personal things or papers?"

"Not really. There're some books in the bedside table drawer and downstairs—outdoor adventure and thrillers, mostly. I've already checked them for anything he might've stuffed inside. His papers're over at the sales office."

"Where's that?"

"Down the road a piece. We can get to it in about five minutes by a trail through the trees. Do you want to take a walk over there?"

"Yes. There're a number of details I need to get started on this, including his Social Security number."

The Christmassy scent was nearly overpowering as Matty and I followed a well-worn path through the fir trees. It put me in mind of the list I'd drawn up of gifts I'd yet to buy, and of the plans Hy and I had made for Christmas Eve. No—"plans" wasn't the right word. Plans were things you thought out and agreed on and, in most cases, looked forward to. But these particular arrangements had descended on me like a flash flood, and, caught by surprise, I'd allowed myself to be swept away. Now I was looking forward to the event as much as I would to death by drowning.

On Christmas Eve, Hy and I were supposed to arrive with arms full of presents and hearts full of good cheer at the Seacliff district home that my friend and operative Rae Kelleher shared with my former brother-in-law, Ricky Savage. A year before, had anyone attempted to foist this scenario on me, I'd have pronounced the person quite insane. But since last July Rae and Ricky—who, if the charts were to be believed, was currently the hottest country singer in the nation—had been an item. And my sister Charlene was living in Bel Air with her new husband, international financier Vic Christiansen.

All of which added up to six confused and disillusioned Savage offspring.

Mick, my computer jock, was dealing best with the split and realignment. But that was to be expected: he was nineteen, caught up in his work and his own relationship with an older woman, and trying hard to act worldly. Still, his relations with Rae were somewhat strained, and recently he'd moved out of the office he'd shared with her and set up shop in a room that previously had been devoted to storage.

Mick's eighteen-year-old sister, Chris, was a freshman at U.C. Berkeley, and she'd found that the events of the previous summer, which had been fully documented by the gossip columns and tabloids, gave her a certain cachet among her new circle of friends. She visited the Seacliff house often with one or more of them in tow, obviously basking in reflected celebrity status. But she always called first to make sure her father was there; if he was in L.A. tending to his record label's business or at his recording studio in the Arizona desert, Chris kept her distance.

As for the younger children, ranging in age from fifteen to nine—their behavior could only be described as atrocious. They defied Charlene at every turn; they resisted any overtures from Vic, who badly wanted to be a good stepfather; and they'd each spent exactly one weekend with Ricky, who still became tight-lipped at the memory of those visits.

Frankly, I was on the kids' side. Their world had been shattered under unusually unpleasant and public circumstances, and they were fully entitled to act out their feelings in ways that justified their collective nickname—the Little Savages. At least, I was on their side until I considered what havoc they were going to wreak upon my Christmas....

Charlene and Vic had married after her quick Caribbean divorce in October, but deferred their honeymoon to the holidays. On December twenty-third they would fly up to San Francisco with the kids, turn them over to Ricky at the airport, and head off for a week in London. Ricky was upbeat about the long visit, but he tended to be upbeat about most things since he'd been with Rae, and I feared he was in for a crushing disappointment.

Rae, on the other hand, was plainly appalled at the prospect of playing a starring role in what could easily turn into the best horror show of the season. Thus Aunt Sharon and honorary uncle Hy had been cast as supporting actors in a drama that I was certain had been scripted by a writer with a monstrous imagination.

Christmas Eve, my absolute favorite night of the year, was going to be hellish beyond belief....

Matty's voice saved me from contemplating the opening scene of my personal holiday version of *A Nightmare on Elm Street*. As we approached the rear of a large red-and-green frame building, she said, "That's the sales office. We're supposed to open the day after Thanksgiving."

One week away. "Can you, if John isn't back by then?"

"We have to, so we will."

To the left of the building was cleared land where cut trees were already stacked; the live firs crowded in on the other side, as if jostling for first place in the line to be chopped down and taken home. Wide double doors in the center of the building stood open, giving access to the parking lot out front, and just inside them a man knelt, fluffing the branches of a white-flocked tree. He heard our footsteps and looked up.

The man's curly hair and beard ringed an apple-cheeked face with blue eyes under thick brows; had they been white instead of gray, he'd have been a dead ringer for Santa Claus. "Hey, Matty," he said, getting stiffly to his feet.

Nodding to me, he added, "Goddamn sacrilege, these things."

"The flocked trees, you mean?" she asked.

"Yeah, the flocked trees. In thirty-five years I never let a one of them in here, but ol' John didn't waste any time once he bought me out."

"Well, a lot of people like them."

"People like all sorts of things that're just plain unnatural. Trees is trees, young lady, and they shouldn't be dressed up like some prissy little girl in a pinafore." He winked at me and said, "Don't mind me. I'm an old curmudgeon. Ask my wife, if I haven't already convinced you." Then he stuck his hand out. "Wes Payne, former owner and pinch hitter for John."

I introduced myself, giving only my name, because I wasn't sure how much Matty had told Payne about John's disappearance.

Apparently she'd entrusted him with the whole story; she explained, "Sharon's a former student of mine, and a private investigator. I've hired her to try to get a line on John."

Payne sobered. "Still no word?"

"None."

"Not like him, Matty. I'm starting to think the worst."

I asked Payne, "John didn't say anything to you about going away for a while?"

"Not a word. We last talked... when? Two days before, when he asked me to come back and help out during the selling season."

"Wasn't that short notice?"

"Yeah, it was."

"I understand he also asked if Zach could stay with you and your wife the night he left. What explanation did he give?"

"Said Matty would be out late on a charter, and he had things to do."

"Did he ask in person or call?"

"In person. He came over to my place; it's down the road to the north."

"Did he seem his usual self?"

"Well, now, Matty asked me that too. And at first I said yes, but I've been thinking on it, and... You know, I'm not good at figuring people out. Trees're more my kind of thing. But I did pick up on a... Oh, hell, I'm not much with words, either."

"Take your time."

"Well, if I had to put a name to it, I'd say he was keyed up. Like he knew something was gonna happen, and he wasn't a hundred percent sure he could handle it."

"Afraid?"

"Yes and no. It was like... You've never been in combat, of course, but maybe you can understand. Beforehand, you're scared, sure, but you're up for it, too. You're psyched, and you want to go out and get the bastards. That was the feeling I got off of John that day, only on a much lower level."

I'd never been in combat, but I'd survived some very dangerous situations, so what he described was perfectly clear to me. There's a push-pull element in danger, and, at least in my case, the pull has a seductive quality that overcomes the push. If Payne had read John Seabrook correctly, he might by now be in very serious trouble.

Matty, no stranger herself to the push-pull mechanism, was frowning, apparently having reached the same conclusion.

31

I asked Payne, "Do you recall anything else unusual about the conversation?"

"Not offhand, but if something does occur to me, I'll let Matty know."

"Or you can call me." I gave him my card, and then Matty and I started for the office. Wes Payne knelt and returned to fluffing the tree, telling it that it was "a silly little poodle dog of a Doug fir."

Matty led me around the sales counter, where sample wreaths hung on the wall, and into a small room beyond it. It was cold there; a quartz heater of the sort that had been all the rage in the eighties stood unplugged in a corner. Silently she indicated the personal drawer of the file cabinet and perched on the edge of the metal desk. I sensed she was closing off again, weary and for the moment unable to face further discussion of Seabrook's disappearance.

I made short work of my search, noting both his and Zach's Social Security numbers as well as the numbers of bank accounts and credit cards. The files contained the usual items: back income-tax returns, the purchase agreement on the tree farm, receipts for current bills, a ten-thousand-dollar life insurance policy naming Zach as beneficiary, several gun registration forms, and pink slips on three vehicles. I asked Matty, "Which of these trucks did he take?"

"The Dodge."

I copied its license-plate and vehicle-identification numbers as well as the serial number of the .44 Magnum, and kept searching. In the last file I found two birth certificates: Zach's, showing he'd been born to John and Wendy Adams Seabrook at Beaumont Hospital in Royal Oak, Michigan, and John's, issued by Harper Hospital in Detroit. I copied down all the information, including the attending physicians' names.

When Matty and I left the office a few minutes later, Wes Payne was delivering a lecture to another flocked tree. "What," he demanded, "would your momma think if she could see you now?"

Matty and I spotted the rolled-up sleeping bag on the back porch of the farmhouse at the same time. Her mouth went slack with surprise and she bolted toward the steps.

John's back, I thought. I won't even have to open a file.

But then she called, "Zach? Zach, what're you doing here?"

The boy I'd seen in the photograph appeared in the open doorway: taller and thinner, after one of those sudden spurts of growth they experience at his age. He moved awkwardly, as though he wasn't yet comfortable in his new body.

Matty asked, "How come you're not at Kevin's?"

"He's sick. His mom called off the sleepover." Zach's lips pushed out defensively, as if he was afraid she'd think it his fault.

"Shit!" She smacked the porch railing with the palm of her hand and whirled, her back to the boy, fighting for control. Zach flinched.

Matty closed her eyes and moved her lips, forming the words *What next?* I frowned, puzzled at her extreme reaction to the boy's change of plans.

She took several deep breaths, then turned and put her arm around Zach. "It's not you, kiddo," she said. "Honest, it's not."

He resisted for a moment, then leaned against her. "I know—it's Dad you're mad at."

"No, I'm not mad. I'm worried, and I want him back here with us."

"Me too." But something in Zach's eyes said he wasn't accustomed to getting what he wanted and didn't hold out much hope of this wish being granted.

Matty must have realized that. She brought him over to me and said, "Hey, you remember last night when I told you I was going to talk to somebody who knows about stuff like this? Well, here she is—Sharon McCone, my former student and a private investigator. She's going to find your dad for us."

Zach looked me over without replying to my greeting, his gaze skeptical.

"And now," Matty said, "we've got to work on the problem of where you're gonna stay." To me she added, "I'm doing an air show up north of Sacramento tomorrow. I've got to fly there tonight."

Zach said, "I already called all my other friends. No go. What about Uncle Wes's?"

"He and Aunt Karla are driving down to their daughter's in Danville for the weekend." Matty bit her underlip, thinking.

"I'm old enough to stay alone—"

"No. Not because I don't trust you, kiddo, but till your dad's back, I don't want to leave you by yourself. He'd have my ass if he thought I hadn't taken good care of you."

Of course that wasn't the whole reason. She

34

was afraid that someone might harm Zach because of whatever his father was involved in. And Zach knew that; the kid wasn't stupid.

Suddenly I was afraid, too—for Matty. With all this weighing on her mind, how could she fly tomorrow—performing snap rolls and Whifferdills and Cuban eights at high speeds and low altitudes within a narrowly defined box of space?

I said, "Maybe you should skip the show."

"Can't. I've committed to it. It's the last show of the year, and I need the money. Besides, if I don't go up there and do it, I'll be letting this thing get to me. You start that, and pretty soon you lose all your confidence."

I understood altogether too well; I'd had a near miss in a rented twin-engine Beechcraft earlier that year and almost lost all my confidence. Almost.

"Well," I said, "why not take Zach along?"

"You saw the picture of my plane. Where's the passenger seat?"

"Oh, right." Suddenly I noticed her gaze had turned speculative. "What?"

She eyed me some more, beginning to smile. Zach glanced from her to me. Then he folded his arms across his chest and tried to ignore both of us. Matty nodded encouragingly at me. I scowled.

Dammit, I knew what she wanted. And the worst part was that Zach did, too. He was trying hard to act as if what I decided didn't matter, but it did. And I wasn't sure he could take yet another bruise on his already tender feelings. Still, how the hell was I going to get started on the investigation if... ?

Quickly I did a mental review of friends with children. Anne-Marie Altman and Hank Zahn, two of the oldest and dearest, had a foster daughter who was only a couple of years younger than Zach. Maybe the kids would hit it off—or at least tolerate each other for the weekend.

"Zach," I said, "I understand you like to fly."

Three

Pier 241/2, where I'd moved my offices the previous summer, was on San Francisco's Embarcadero, next to the SFFD fireboat station and directly under the span of the Bay Bridge. Not an ideal location if you're into quiet contemplation, but splendid if your goal is to keep the rent payments low. I'd heard of the vacant suite from an architect client whose firm was located there; fortunately he and the leasing agent from the Port Commission's Tenant Services division had engaged in a conspiracy of silence—the only silence I'd ever be likely to associate with the pier— until I went to look at it.

When I saw the generous size of the rooms opening onto the catwalk on the north side, I convinced myself that the overhead roar of the bridge traffic was really a distant rumble. The whoop of the fireboat's siren didn't faze me as I stood in what could become my private office: a spacious tan-walled room where a huge arched window at the very end of the pier afforded a view of Treasure Island. The suite was far too large for my agency, but that was no drawback, since I'd committed to sharing with the newly formed firm of Altman & Zahn, Attorneys-at-Law.

Anne-Marie and Hank were horrified when I brought them to view my find. How, they asked, could we concentrate in such surroundings? We'd develop chronic headaches, begin mainlining aspirin. How could we talk with clients on the phone or, worse yet, in person? We'd go completely deaf in months—weeks, even.

Not so, claimed Ted Smalley, former office manager for the now defunct All Souls Legal Cooperative, and soon to be our shared factotum. To get our hands on that kind of space we could adapt to anything. There was room for both firms to expand; we could have a library and a conference room; and he—praise the Lord—would at last have a large office all his own and a separate copy-and-supply room. Compared to such luxury, what was a little background noise?

At that exact moment the fireboat siren went off and Hank, who had been in Vietnam, almost hit the floor.

By the time he recovered, Anne-Marie was looking around with the same shrewdly appraising expression as Ted, and the leasing agent was rubbing his hands together in anticipation. Hank still balked, so the agent offered a twenty percent rent reduction because of the "unfortunate noise factor." We signed the lease on the spot, and ever since had bragged about how cleverly we'd fooled the agent into cutting the asking price.

When Zach and I arrived there at a little after

six that Friday evening, the shoreline boulevard and the nearby streets of the South Beach district were full of people heading for the many bars and restaurants that had sprung up with our waterfront area's recent renaissance. Inside, the pier was nearly deserted. Lights burned in the first-floor suite of a documentary filmmaker, and Ted's white Dodge Neon sat in its parking space, but the other tenants had left for the weekend. I pulled into my assigned place on the concrete floor where forklifts used to move and stack cargo.

Zach jumped out of the car, looking around eagerly. His interest in his surroundings eased some of my growing concern for him; up to now he'd resisted my attempts at conversation and had voluntarily spoken only six times since we left Los Alegres.

On the climb-out in the Cessna, he'd asked me, "Did Matty warn you not to fly over that yellow house where the guy who likes to shoot at planes just moved in?" Mercifully, she had. When I leveled off, he said, "Cruise speed for one of these is about a hundred, right?" Yes, I told him, it was. And on final at Oakland, he asked, "How come you flew out of here, when you live in San Francisco?" I was familiar with Oakland, I explained, and saw no reason to brave Class B airspace at SFO when Class C was less congested.

After that he didn't speak until we were on the bridge in my MG. "This is a really old model," he said. "Did you have to do a lot of work on it?" A rebuilt engine, body work, and a new red paint job. A few minutes later:

"This Habiba Hamid I'm supposed to be staying with—what is she, some kind of towelhead?" I replied that Habiba's father had been from the Arab emirate of Azad, and she wouldn't appreciate being called a towelhead. In response he asked, "When's Matty coming to get me?"

"Sunday afternoon." And it can't be too soon for all concerned.

But as soon as I mentally voiced the comment, I looked at Zach's wan face and felt a stab of sympathy for him. At eleven he'd been thrust into the hands of a stranger who was, in turn, about to thrust him into the hands of other strangers. His father was missing, Matty was about to fly in an air show while in a dangerous emotional state. And if anything happened to her, Zach's future would be very uncertain.

Besides, even taking into consideration the towelhead remark, his behavior was positively decorous in comparison to that of the Little Savages.

Now his interest in the pier drew him from his protective shell. As I got out of the MG, he asked, "You really work here?"

"Sure do."

"Cool."

"Want to explore while I check in with my office manager?"

"Uh-huh." He ran for the iron stairway leading to our catwalk.

I followed, patting one of the oleanders that sat in redwood tubs at its foot—purchased by Ted because, he claimed, they thrived on murky light and exhaust fumes. And indeed they must, because their robust health put the other tenants' ficus and citrus and ornamental evergreens to shame.

The door to Ted's office, located between my agency and the law firm, stood open. As Zach ran off along the catwalk, I knocked on the frame, stepped inside, and stopped—my way blocked by two cardboard boxes filled with fake garlands and tree lights and Christmas ornaments. Ted—a dapper, goateed man who likes to wear opulent vests and jackets with his faded Levi's—smiled up from behind a desk stacked high with paperwork.

"You're back!" he exclaimed, as if my arrival were a minor miracle. Ted had taken to obsessing every time I flew, certain that some evil force of nature or my own ineptitude would overcome me. I'd never be able to convince him that the twenty-minute flight from Los Alegres to Oakland had been blissfully uneventful, compared to the forty-minute rush-hour drive on the freeway and bridge.

"I'm back. Any messages?"

"Your sister Charlene wants you to call her. And Mick's still in his office, if you need him for anything."

"Okay, thanks. What's this stuff, anyway?" I nudged one of the cartons with my foot.

"Decorations that Neal and I culled from our respective collections." Neal Osborn was a used-book dealer and Ted's new partner; they shared an elegant apartment in an Art Deco building on Telegraph Hill.

"Why'd you bring them to the office?"

"I thought I might salvage some for the contest."

"What contest?"

He rolled his eyes. "Don't you ever read the memos I put in your in-box? The tenants are staging a decorating contest, and we, my dear, are going to take first place."

I glanced into the box at my feet. A demented-looking ceramic goat with a holly sprig in its mouth and little legs that dangled down from its chunky body leered up at me. "Not with this stuff, we aren't."

Ted ignored the comment. "Who's your young friend?" He motioned through the door, to where Zach leaned over the rail of one of the catwalks that crossed to the other side. In spite of the dizzying drop, the kid was relaxed, kicking one foot back and forth between the uprights and whistling tunelessly.

"Somebody I'm hoping to stash with Anne-Marie and Hank for the weekend."

"Bad timing—they left for Tahoe an hour ago. Habiba's stashed with Rae and Ricky."

"Damn!" Well, maybe Zach could stay there too. Hy and I had been invited to dinner tonight, to make plans for the Christmas Eve from hell, so I'd just bring him along. Which reminded me, I was running late. I handed Ted a photograph of John Seabrook that Matty had given me. "Would you mind dropping this with that photographer on Howard Street on your way home?"

"No problem. Duplicates?"

"A dozen."

"Will do."

"Thanks. Have a good weekend."

"Wait!"

"Now what?"

"About the contest—you're right; we can't

41

use most of this crap. So I'm taking up a collection to buy new stuff."

"I am not made of money, you know."

"Scrooge."

I sighed. "How much?"

"For the agency's owner, twenty seems reasonable."

"*Twenty!*"

"You want to uphold our honor, don't you?"

"If I give you twenty, you'd better buy some damned good decorations." I fished the money from my bag and reluctantly handed it over. "What's the prize for winning?"

"A contribution by the losers to our favorite charity."

I snorted in a manner that would have done old Ebenezer proud and went to see Mick.

"Sure," my nephew said, "I'll get started on the Seabrook business tonight." He was lounging on the base of his spine in his swivel chair, long legs propped up on his wastebasket, one hand resting on his PowerBook. I've always considered his relationship with what is, after all, only an assemblage of silicon chips and plastic to be quite unnatural, but I do appreciate the results he gets with the infernal device.

Suddenly it occurred to me that this was an unusually late hour for Mick to be at the office, particularly on a Friday. "How come you're still here?"

"Just haven't gotten around to wandering down the street yet." He subleased Rae's former condo at BayCrest, a short distance along the Embarcadero.

"You're not seeing Keim tonight?" Charlotte

Keim was my most recently hired operative, and the older woman in Mick's life—twenty-six to his nineteen, but he, as she put it, "played older."

His mouth twitched, and he looked down at the notes he'd taken on John Seabrook till all I could see was the top of his blond head. "Lottie's out with somebody else."

"Who?"

"How the hell should I know? She's her own woman, she does as she pleases."

"Mick, are you okay?"

"Get lost, Shar."

"No, really—"

"I'm okay—all right? If I made it through all the shit that came down on the family last summer, I sure as hell can make it through a little game playing on Lottie's part. Now get out of here so I can work."

"You'd be upset too," my sister said, "if your ex-husband had just walked in and made off with two of your kids."

"Charlene, calm down." Ricky, snatch the children? Why would he? He and Charlene had joint custody. "Tell me exactly what happened."

A hissing intake of breath, then silence. Charlene was smoking dope—something she'd vowed to give up, since Vic didn't indulge. I waited impatiently.

"Okay, he was in L.A. for most of the week, staying at the Zenith condo." Zenith Records was the label Ricky and two associates had formed earlier that year.

"And?"

43

She was sucking on the joint again. I tapped my fingers on my desk and smiled distractedly at Zach, who was sitting in the armchair under my potted schefflera.

"And," she went on, "he was too damn busy to see the kids. So this afternoon he shows up here, cheerful as can be, and says, 'Who wants to fly to San Francisco with me?' And the next thing I know, Molly and Lisa are packed and out the door."

"So why're you calling me? Do you want me to tell him to return them?"

"God, no! It's peaceful around here for a change. I just called up to bitch about how high-handed he was."

"Well, this way you and Vic can have a quiet weekend—"

"Vic's in New York."

"Ah." Now I understood. During her marriage to Ricky, my sister had spent entirely too much time alone while he traveled; with her new husband on the East Coast, she must have been experiencing an unpleasant sense of déjà vu.

She added, "I guess what really pisses me off is that Jamie and Brian wouldn't go too. Ever since she went up to visit Ricky in October, Jamie's been an absolute little... asshole. And Brian... well, Vic bought him a new computer—which he's yet to thank him for—and since then he's been out there in cyber-world. I don't think he even noticed his father was here. If only they'd gone along too, I'd be on a plane to New York right now."

Instead, she was feeling sorry for herself and

getting loaded on dope. I knew the impulse, only my drug of choice was white wine. "When's Vic coming back?"

"Tomorrow night."

"Well, then."

"I know, you think I'm making too much of this. But dammit, Shar, Ricky breezes in here, all happy because he's going home to Rae, and promises the kids a plane ride and fun things to do on the weekend, and in the meantime I'm just... stuck."

"It hurts to provide the day-to-day care and then get upstaged. All I can tell you is to hang in there." A divorce involving children, I was learning, was a complicated and sad proposition, no matter how satisfied the parents were with their new lives.

I set down the receiver and motioned to Zach. "We're out of here."

At least I now knew he was sure to be welcome at Rae and Ricky's, where one more child would scarcely be an imposition. And the property was equipped with a very good security system.

"...in my checking account. Seventy thousand more than I thought I had."

"What!" I transferred my cellular phone to my left hand and steered through the stone pillars of Seacliff. "Take it slowly, from the beginning," I said to Matty, glancing at Zach—who had gone silent on me again—and hoping he wouldn't intuit how upset she was.

"Okay, here it is: I was on my way to the airport when I realized I was low on cash. So I swung over to Lucky Store, where they've got a branch of B. of A., and hit the Versateller. I get a hundred bucks, the card and the transaction report come out, and I check my balance. There it was—seventy thou. I damned near died on the spot. Now, those machines, you know how you can take a look at your account activity? I did. Seventy thou, all right, deposited yesterday."

"How? By whom?"

"Don't know. If I were going to be here tomorrow, I'd go to my branch and find out."

"Where are you now?"

"The airport. Plane's all fueled and ready to go." She paused. "What d'you think, McCone? Does this have something to do with John, or is it just some computer glitch?"

"Hard to say."

"Is there any way you can look into it while I'm in Sacramento?"

"I think I'd need power of attorney."

"Well, no time for that; I'm supposed to be up there at eight for dinner with my corporate sponsors, and I'm going to be late as is."

"When will you be at the motel number you gave me?"

"After dinner. Eleven, latest."

"Let me think about this. I'll get back to you."

When I flipped the phone shut, I saw Zach watching me, his face serious and a little scared. "Something's wrong with Matty."

"Not wrong—she's just confused." I put my hand on his shoulder. At first he recoiled from my touch, then changed his mind and leaned into it. "Not to worry, kiddo," I said, automatically adopting Matty's term of address for him. "But since we're almost at my friends' house, I think I'd better warn you: try to look at this weekend as an interesting experience with a somewhat primitive culture."

High-pitched Little-Savage screams erupted as Hy opened the door of Rae and Ricky's red-wood-and-glass house on the bluff above China Beach. I'd suspected he'd already be there when I saw his Citabria in the tie-downs at Oakland, and the curbside presence of his ancient Morgan, which he garaged near the airport, had confirmed it. His wild-eyed, desperate look and the way he raked his fingers through his dark blond mane told me he wished he'd remained at his ranch.

I hadn't seen him in weeks, and I wanted to twine my arms around his neck and press close to his tall, lanky frame; wanted to kiss the lips that at the moment were pulled taut with displeasure beneath his shaggy mustache. Instead, I introduced him to Zach.

Hy shook the boy's hand and told him he was an old friend of Matty's. He was about to add something, but a shriek interrupted, and running feet thundered across the entryway behind him. Shortly after the sound faded, Rae appeared, leaning around him. Her freckled face was flushed, and her long auburn curls straggled down from a comb that was supposed to be holding them off her shoulders.

She said, "Little Savages is the name for them, all right."

Zach and I moved inside, and I managed to introduce her to him before two towheaded girls—aged eleven and nine—galloped in from the living room and through the arch-way to the kitchen, calling out to me as they passed. My nieces, Molly and Lisa.

Rae put a hand to her forehead and regarded Zach with alarm, as if she expected him to join in the chase. His quiet manner seemed to reassure her, and she said, "Lisa and Molly have discovered that the open floor plan makes a great racetrack. I've got a headache, and Ricky's into the gin, so you know how the evening's going."

"How's Habiba coping with all this?"

"Sitting very still and observing, as if it's her first trip to the circus and she's pretty sure she doesn't like it."

Hy had headed for the kitchen. By the time we got there, he'd opened a beer—and not his first, judging from the number of empties in the recycling bin. The room was spacious, with handcrafted tiles and a hardwood floor, centered around a butcher-block worksta-tion. Ricky leaned against it, clutching a glass that contained a generous martini. Habiba, who had adopted him as one of her father fig-ures, sat close beside him on a stool; when he moved to hug me, she reached out and hooked a finger through his belt loop, as if she was afraid he might go away. Beneath her slash of black bangs, her dark eyes were somewhat glazed.

Ricky's eyes duplicated Habiba's expression, and his thick chestnut hair was as disheveled as Rae's; his handsome features were set in long-suffering lines, and when a scream echoed in the living room, he shuddered. In spite of his discomfort, I couldn't help but smile. Mr. Savage, superstar, had apparently gotten himself into something he now regretted. I turned from him and hugged Habiba, who clung unusually tight.

Nine-year-old Habiba and I were good friends, sharing a closeness that transcended our thirty years' age difference. Sometimes that happens when you go through an ordeal with another person and learn what she's made of. The little girl was finely crafted of good, courageous stock—the best there is.

I'd just gotten Zach introduced all around when another wave of rampaging little girls broke on the kitchen floor. Hy, Habiba, Zach, and I winced.

Rae looked desperately at Ricky: *Do something!* He looked back so helplessly that you'd have thought he'd never fathered a child, let alone six. And then Rae threw up her hands and completely lost it.

"That's enough!" she yelled.

Lisa froze, one foot in the air. Molly, the elder and thus the leader, slid to a stop, planing on the polished boards. She slewed around and demanded, *"What?"*

"I said, *that's enough!* You're driving us all crazy with that running. You're to stop it right now!"

Molly glanced at her sister. A dark look of complicity passed between them. Then she drew herself up in a haughty, naughty manner that brought back to me vivid images of Charlene at her age.

"*You* can't tell me what to do," she announced. "*You're* not my mother!"

Oh, hell, I thought, expecting Rae to burst into tears and flee the room.

But she surprised me—surprised us all. As

49

Ricky pushed away from the butcher block, intent on grabbing his daughter by the scruff of her neck, Rae motioned for him to stop and looked sternly at both girls. Then she drew herself up in an exact imitation of Molly and, from the slight advantage of her full five-feet-two, loomed over her.

"I may not be your mother, young lady," she said, "but I *am* the alpha woman in this house. And that gives me the right"—she paused ominously, raising her arms as if to pounce— "to torture you!"

Before Molly could move, Rae grabbed her by the shoulders and spun her around, pinning her arms. My niece doubled over, screaming in outrage. Rae held her so her feet were off the floor and kicking. Then the screams became interspersed with giggles; Rae was tickling her.

I glanced at Lisa. She had drawn back against the cabinet behind her, her face a study in betrayal and envy.

Rae noticed her reaction, too. "Come on, Lisa," she called. "Help me out here. She might"—she held out a hand and let go of Molly, who scrambled for the living room— "she might escape!"

For a second Lisa hung back. Then she grinned and grabbed Rae's hand. Together they set off in hot pursuit.

Ricky closed his eyes. "God help us all."

Three pairs of feet thundered across the living room. More shrieks and squeals filled the air. Then, from the room's far end, Rae announced, "Okay, I win! Downstairs with you—to the dungeon!"

More screams, and then a door slammed, muffling them.

Silence. Blissful silence.

"Dungeon?" Habiba said, eyes wide. Zach, I saw, was exhibiting similar horror.

Ricky ruffled Habiba's hair, grinning at Zach. "No instruments of torture, guys. Just the lower floor; it's soundproofed on account of my rehearsal studio. A good place for those two to have their bedrooms, don't you think?"

Habiba smiled self-importantly. When she stayed over, she got to sleep in one of the upstairs guest rooms.

Zach folded his arms and leaned against the butcher block next to Habiba, trying his best to act nonchalant. To me he said, "Primitive culture—yeah."

I went over to Hy and briefly rested my forehead against his shoulder. "So," he asked, smoothing my hair, "what's new at McCone Investigations?"

I knew he was wondering about Zach, whose presence I'd yet to fully explain. I shook my head, meaning I didn't want to discuss it in front of the kids, and said, "Not much." To Ricky I added, "Charlene called me earlier."

"To complain about me making off with Lisa and Molly, no doubt."

"More to complain about the others not going along too. She called Jamie a little asshole."

He smiled faintly. "Charly's never been one to mince words, has she? Jamie's taking the divorce harder than anybody, and I feel for her, but I've exhausted all the ways of getting through to her. That time she came up here

51

in October—you and Red were on that case up in Oregon—I offered her my American Express card, told her to buy whatever she wanted for her room. She said she didn't need any 'shit' because she was never coming back, and proceeded to sulk in front of the tube the whole weekend."

Hy asked, "And Brian?"

"Lost in cyberspace—his way of coping—and I can't reach him, either."

"Well, Molly and Lisa seem okay, even if they are a little... well..."

"Hy, you don't need to be tactful where they're concerned. They're absolute hellions, but I love them anyway. And, yeah, they will be okay, now that they're discovering Red isn't a wicked stepmother—or whatever you call your daddy's significant other. I sort of thought that would happen, which is why I'd hoped to get all four kids up here this weekend. It would've saved a hell of a lot of wear and tear on everybody at Christmastime."

While Ricky and Hy were talking, I'd been watching Habiba. An open jar of olives sat on the butcher block, and her hand moved stealthily toward it. She sneaked one, popped it into her mouth, and glanced up at Ricky. In a moment she sneaked another. He pretended to discover what she was up to, frowned fiercely, then winked. Habiba waited till he turned his attention back to Hy, then sneaked two and offered one to Zach. After a brief hesitation, he took it.

Suddenly I felt a rush of gratitude toward the man I still called Brother Ricky, who—even though he seemed temporarily to have forgotten what hands-on fathering was like—felt deeply for lonely and displaced children. There was nothing he could do to erase the bad, sad things that had happened to Habiba in her young life, any more than he could erase the hurt he and my sister had inflicted on their own kids. But he tried in small ways: he knew that olives were Habiba's favorite all-time treat, and he'd purposely left the open jar between them.

And Habiba apparently recognized loneliness and discomfort in others: she'd seen it in Zach and taken her small, tentative step to ease it. Encouraged by his acceptance of her gift, she climbed off the stool, olive jar in hand, and asked him, "Do you want to see something really cool?"

"Uh, sure."

"Is it okay if I show him, Ricky?"

"Why not?" He watched them cross the kitchen, then called, "But be sure to keep your clothes on!"

Habiba turned, putting one hand on a slim hip and wrinkling her nose in disgust. "Sometimes you can be so *gross!*"

When they were gone, I asked, "What was that all about?"

"She's taking him to see the hot tub." There was a Jacuzzi in the solarium off the master bedroom, from which you could see the Golden Gate, Marin headlands, and the Pacific. "Habiba's figured out that Red and I get in the tub together without, as she puts it, our swimsuits. She finds the practice dreadful—and fascinating."

Rae came back, checked something in the oven that smelled like lasagna, and took

Habiba's stool. "I parked them in front of the rec room tube with one of those tapes you rented," she told Ricky. "And for all our sakes, I promised them they could eat down there."

"Thank you for being so nice to my horrible children, Red."

"They're not horrible. They just don't know how to act around us yet."

"Well, they'd better learn fast, or we'll both be certifiable." He held his glass to her lips, but she bumped it with her hand and dribbled martini on her blue sweater. With the unconcern of one who suffers many spills, she flicked the droplets off, steadied the glass, and sipped. It put me in mind of the night they met, when she'd been so starstruck that she'd dropped a cup of Coke on her foot.

I glanced at Hy, saw him smiling at me, and knew what he was thinking. Last summer, when I'd been vehemently and outspokenly against their unlikely pairing, he'd insisted they'd be good for each other. A touch of the old I-told-you-so in that smile, Ripinsky.

"Okay," he said to me, "tell us what you're doing with Matty Wildress's boyfriend's kid."

"Well, you remember I said there was something odd about her reminding me of my biennial four months early. What she really wanted was to hire me, but, being Matty, she couldn't come right out and ask." I started to fill them in, but in the depths of the purse I'd set on the counter, my cell phone rang. The phone had been a fortieth birthday present from the office gang—a way of keeping me on a short leash, I suspected. For a moment I was tempted not to answer it, but then I fished it out and flipped it open.

"McCone?" Matty again.

"Yes. What's happening?"

"Plenty, but I can't talk about it now. I'm at the airfield where the show's gonna be held, about to catch a ride to the motel. There're all sorts of people from the aerobatics club around and... Do you think you could come up here?"

"Tonight?"

"If you wouldn't mind. I need to show you something I found in my plane. I could reserve you a room at the motel, cut short my dinner with my sponsors, and meet you there."

There was an edge to her voice that I'd never heard before—a note of panic, too. "Hold on." I covered the mouthpiece and turned to Hy. "How'd you like to fly to Sacramento so I can meet with Matty tonight?"

"Can't." He motioned with the hand that held the beer can.

"I'll pilot; I haven't been drinking."

"Well, sure. I'll be glad to keep you company."

I told Matty we'd both be there as soon as possible. Then I apologized to Rae and Ricky for cutting short our evening together and went to tell Zach I was leaving. When I came to the door of the solarium, I found him and Habiba sitting cross-legged on the wide ledge around the tub, the empty olive jar between them. They'd turned on the small overhead spotlights; the window glass reflected them as they inclined their heads toward each other, talking intensely.

Habiba was speaking swiftly and softly:

"...really horrible. First my mom, then my grams and my nanny, and then my dad. All *gone*. Every time I thought it couldn't get worse, it did."

Zach said something that I couldn't make out.

"Yeah, it was. But people helped me. Sharon and Hy. Anne-Marie and Hank. And now I've got Ricky and Rae, if I need them."

Again he spoke in a low voice.

"Yes, you do. You've got this Matty person. And Sharon's on your side; I can tell. That means you've got all the others. And..." She looked away shyly. "And you can always talk to me, if you want to."

I turned and left Zach in the capable hands of a little girl who was wise beyond her years.

Four

A *plastic windup toy.*

The comparison popped into my mind as Matty opened the door of her motel room for Hy and me. I tried to dismiss it—after all, this was Matty Wildress, one of the most self-possessed and dynamic women I knew—but the image wouldn't go away. Her fixed gaze, her masklike face, her constrained motions— they all suggested an automaton containing a spring-coiled mechanism that, if released, would send her jerking and teetering toward disaster.

To me she nodded curtly. She allowed Hy to hug her, but stood rigid in his embrace.

I sat down on a chair beside a small round

table and rummaged in my bag for my voice-activated tape recorder. Hy rarely hugged anyone but me, and I needed a moment to still my old questions about the two of them.

The motel was one of the sort that typically cluster around freeway interchanges, this particular exit being off Interstate 5 some miles northwest of the state capital. While its lobby exhibited some pretense to a Western theme—cacti and wagon wheels and peeled-bark furnishings—the decor of Matty's room was bland, and every object appeared to be either screwed down or attached to the walls. A place to spend the night when practically anything clean would do.

Hy saved me from contemplating a framed series of meaningless paint smears by joining me at the table. Matty sat on the edge of the bed. Her expression was so passive that for a moment I forgot the question I wanted to ask. "Okay," I finally said, forcing a reassuring note into my voice, "we're here to help. What do you have to show us?"

She reached into a duffel bag at her feet and pulled out a flat white woolly object; it had a black snout and legs, and a red satin heart appliquéd to its side. I stared, trying to fathom what it might be.

She attempted a smile. "Weird, huh? It's a hot-water bottle disguised as a lamb. You're supposed to fill it through a stopper in its silly little mouth. A present from my first aerobatics coach, Jim Powell. A joke, because he started teaching me in the dead of winter, and I was always cold."

"And this is what you found in the plane?"

"Yeah. A week or so ago it disappeared. I was upset, because I always kept it there—for luck, you know? Jim wrote me a list before he gave it to me, rolled it up and stuffed it inside. The kind of list I write for my students when they get their licenses, only having to do with aerobatics."

I remembered my own list well and still had it among my treasured possessions. In addition to practical tips and words of encouragement, Matty had included humorous items gleaned from early aviation handbooks: "Never leave the ground with the motor leaking"; "Aviators will not wear spurs while flying"; "It is advisable to carry a good pair of cutting pliers in a position where both pilot and passenger can reach them in case of an accident." And at its bottom she'd added, "You're a good pilot, McCone. Fly safe, happy, and often."

I asked, "So the lamb reappeared tonight?"

"I noticed it was stuffed behind the seat when I took my bag out after I tied. It wasn't there this morning. Naturally I checked to see if Jim's list was still inside. It was, but with this wrapped around it." She poked her index finger under the lamb's snout and pulled out a roll of paper, peeled the top sheet off, and handed it to me.

I smoothed the sheet out on the table. Hy leaned closer, and we both examined it. A letter, written in a spiky, crabbed hand.

Dear Matty,

I hope you never read this letter, but if you do, I'll have been gone over a week and won't be coming back to you and

Zach for quite some time—if ever. And never to Los Alegres.

The following is vitally important and must be followed to the letter. *It will save both your life and Zach's.*

I've arranged for a wire transfer of $70,000 to your checking account. Your branch manager, Jeff Collins, is a friend of mine, and he knows you're to have it in cash. I spun him a yarn about a lucrative investment opportunity, so just smile your pretty smile and act mysterious when he tries to worm the details out of you.

As soon as you have the money, take Zach and disappear. Don't say good-bye to anybody, not even the Paynes, and above all, don't tell anybody where you're going.

My leaving has nothing to do with us, Matty. You're a beautiful, strong woman—the best in every way. And that's why I know I can entrust Zach to you. Do whatever you have to, use assumed names, go someplace where you don't know anybody, keep a low profile. And raise my boy as I would—with love.

I can't explain what's happening—not now, and probably not ever. Please trust me. But if somehow, in some way, I survive this, I'll find you, no matter where you are. I promise I will.

Love,
John

I read the letter twice, then asked Matty, "Are you sure this is John's handwriting?"

She nodded, biting her lip.

"Why would he go to the trouble of hiding it inside the lamb?"

"Surest way of getting it into my hands when he wanted it to. He knows I have the show this weekend, and he also knows that I always read Jim's list beforehand."

"Okay, John could've put the letter in the lamb before he left, but how did it get back into your plane today?"

"He asked somebody at the airport to do it, I guess. I keep my plane in Hangar B; there're dozens of people in and out all the time. John could've convinced any one of them that the lamb was a surprise or a joke."

"Okay, about the money—where would he have gotten that much?"

"Don't know. He—"

"I'd say we've got a bigger problem on our hands than figuring out where John got hold of the seventy thou." Hy's voice was rough with anger. "He says it's vital that you and Zach follow his instructions—*to save your lives.* Matty, what the hell kind of guy did you hook up with?"

"A good man. I'm sure there's a reasonable explanation for all this."

"Right. He's such a good man that he involved you in something without warning you about it. A good man who took off without a word, leaving you and his son in danger."

"Okay, you've made your point."

But Hy wasn't content to stop there. "I'll tell you one thing," he said, "you're not flying tomorrow."

Her spine stiffened. "Oh, yes, I am. You are not giving me orders, Ripinsky."

"In this instance I'm giving them. You're going to—"

"Go on exactly as I have before. I will fly, and I will fly well. And I will not take John's money and disappear. I am not giving up my whole life just because he got himself into some jam and is running scared."

I said, "His letter made it sound more serious than running scared. Add that to what Wes Payne told us, and it appears that he went looking for a confrontation and may not have survived it."

"He can't be dead!"

"You've got to entertain that possibility. And if he is, you don't want yourself and his son to be the next victims."

"Great! Just great!" What was left of her composure crumpled, and once again I had a mental image of a windup toy moving in quick, jittery steps toward the edge of a table.

"Matty, it's only one show. This time only, won't you—"

"No! I told you earlier, I can't cave in to pressure. First I wouldn't fly. Then I'd have myself so spooked that I couldn't fly."

"I don't think it's that drastic—"

"Oh, it's drastic. It's drastic, all right! Who the hell does John think he is, doing a thing like this to me? How can he ask me to vanish? Jesus, if I do as he told me, I'll never be able to fly again! The first place anybody would look for me is at an airport. Besides, I couldn't change the name on my license without leaving a paper trail. What would I do? How could I live?"

"Seventy thousand will last a long time if

you're careful, but that's beside the point. I've already got an operative working—"

"Money! You think I'm talking money, McCone? I'm talking about *who I am*. And who I am is a pilot. Dammit, whatever possessed John to saddle me with this, to saddle me with his kid?"

She paused, out of breath and seeming to hear the echoes of what she'd said. "Oh, Jesus, I didn't mean that about Zach. I love the kid like he was my own. I've got to protect him. But how can I, when I don't know who or what to watch out for? Even if we did run, there'd be no guarantee we'd be safe."

Hy and I exchanged glances. His anger had diffused, and his frown indicated he was deeply disturbed.

I said, "Neither of us is suggesting you run. Zach's safe for the time being, and we'll see he stays that way. All either of us is asking is that you don't fly till we can find out what's going on."

"I can*not* back out of this show, McCone. It'd be like backing out of my life."

I could understand what she was saying, even if I didn't like it. We all have our ways of remaining strong in the face of emotional battering, our ways of remaining ourselves when circumstances contrive to rob us even of our identity. Matty's was to fly, and fly well.

Now Hy was stroking his mustache and staring contemplatively at her. "Okay," he said, "I'll make you a deal."

"What?" Warily.

"You fly—but only if you let me help you pre-flight the plane."

"My mechanic and I—"

"No, not this time. There's a possibility somebody may tamper with it, and if anybody can spot the evidence it's this old master mechanic."

She was silent.

"So how about it?"

"Jesus, you've been playing cloak-and-dagger games too damned long!"

"Just don't try to outdo me by playing ostrich."

I said, "He's right, Matty. You know he is."

"Oh, shit!" She threw her hands up in surrender. "Do what you want. All *I* want is to fly."

"Good call, Ms. Wildress." Hy stood, pulled her to her feet, and hugged her again. "Now, why don't you get some sleep. We'll head out to the field early tomorrow." To me he added, "Let's go, McCone. We've got some arrangements to make."

The motel's bar was crowded, but Hy and I managed to capture a corner booth. While I placed our drink orders, he scouted out the free hors d'oeuvres and came back with a couple of plates piled high with meatballs and taquitos, chicken wings and pizza rolls. It all looked to be of the frozen-and-microwavable variety—and a far cry from the home-cooked lasagna we'd missed at Rae and Ricky's.

Seeing my frown, he said, "Yeah, I know, but it'll have to do, since the restaurant's closed. Ridiculous hour to stop serving. Let me have your cell phone, will you?"

I pulled it from my bag and handed it over,

glancing around to see if anyone at the near-by tables had noticed. One of the things that irritates the hell out of me is users of cellular units ostentatiously making or receiving calls in places like restaurants, shops, and the aisles of grocery stores. My own had rung just the week before while I was trying to pick out a ripe avocado at Safeway, and in my embarrassment I'd almost dived behind a bin full of squash.

Nobody paid any attention as Hy dialed the San Francisco office of Renshaw and Kessell International—the corporate security firm in which he held a one-third interest—and arranged for a guard to be posted at the house in Seacliff. He then called the house and explained the situation to Ricky, who had had plenty of experience with RKI's services the previous summer. As Hy flipped the phone closed and passed it back to me, he asked, "You carrying?"

"Yes." I touched my purse. "Matty sounded so panicked when she called that I brought my thirty-eight along."

"Good. We're going to have to protect her both before and after she flies. This way, I won't have to requisition a weapon from our Sacramento office."

"You really think somebody might go after her up here?"

"Hard to say, when we don't have the foggiest what this is all about."

"So what *do* we have?" I wolfed down a meatball, then began ticking off points on my fingertips. "John Seabrook, a·man whose past only goes back ten years. A man who struggles to make a living off a Christmas-tree farm and can't afford to remodel his kitchen—but who also has access to seventy thousand dollars. A disappearance that he apparently planned for only two days in advance. Plans that included making sure the money would be available to Matty in cash if he didn't return by a certain date. The implication, because the transfer of funds went through, that something went radically wrong with his plans. And his statement that Matty's and Zach's lives are in danger."

"Plus his statement that if he 'survives this' he'll find them."

"Survives *what?*"

"God knows." Hy's mouth turned down grimly.

I ate a limp taquito, then sampled one of the chicken wings. Terrible. The pizza rolls were marginally better.

He seemed disinclined to further analyze the situation, so I looked around the bar while washing down the junk food with wine. It was full of animated, casually dressed people, and I was willing to bet that many were pilots there for the air show.

You can easily recognize pilots when they're discussing flying, because they compulsively and often poetically talk with their hands. As I watched, a woman's slender fingers described a barrel roll; at the next table, a man's stubby hand executed a loop. Because they were in the bar with drinks in front of them, I knew none was a participant in tomorrow's event; in fact, I doubted if most had mastered anything more complex than a spin. But they, like Hy and me, shared with the aerobatic professionals an ingrained love of flight, plus the knowledge that there is no greater thrill than perfectly performing a maneuver while in total control of your aircraft.

I turned back to Hy. He was rolling his glass between his palms and staring into its depths. Thinking of Matty, I supposed. Perhaps remembering whatever had forged the bond between them. For a moment I hesitated, afraid of what I might find out if I interrupted his thoughts. Then I asked, "What?"

He looked up, smiling. "I was thinking about what you said to Matty earlier: *We'll* see that Zach stays safe. We're asking her not to fly until *we* find out what's going on."

"And?"

"Seems like we're working together more and more lately. There was that business down in Baja, and our trek back from the Caribbean, and Ricky's mess last summer. Now there's Matty and Zach."

"I didn't mean to drag you in on my case. Don't feel you have to—"

"I don't mind. Quite the opposite, in fact. We make a damn good team. Besides, I owe Matty."

"I thought she owed *you*. Why else would she have given me all those flying lessons at a cut rate?"

"You ever think they might've been subsidized?"

"By... ? Oh, Ripinsky, you didn't!"

"Sure I did. I wanted you as my copilot."

I was torn between feeling angry and feeling pleased. On the one hand, he'd made me a charity case who'd been singled out by an anonymous benefactor. On the other, he'd cared enough to give me what I so badly wanted. "If I'd known—"

"You'd've refused, and then I'd've had to teach you myself. And that would've been purely hellacious. One way or the other, though, I was bound and determined you'd become a pilot."

"Why?"

He shrugged, suddenly embarrassed. "Oh, I guess I figured if you came to love flying as much as I do, I wouldn't lose you."

He normally revealed so little of his emotions, but when he did...

I put my hand on his forearm and squeezed it. "Well, you wouldn't've lost me—flying lessons or no flying lessons. But now I owe you. All these obligations: you, me, Matty."

"Yeah." His gaze turned melancholy at my mention of her, and he drank off what was left of his beer. "Order us another round, would you? I'll fetch some more of that wretched excuse for hors d'oeuvres."

I signaled the waitress and watched as Hy moved between the crowded tables: tall and lean and handsome in a rugged way that managed to turn a fair number of female heads between our booth and the buffet.

Strange. We owned a home together. We shared a life that, while unconventional, suited us both. He loved me, I loved him—we'd finally gotten that sorted out and put into words. But while I'd thought he'd shared all his secrets with me, I was now finding there were still pockets of his past that remained off-limits.

And it was unsettling to realize that one of those pockets contained memories of my friend Matty Wildress.

Five

The wide plain northwest of Sacramento where the airfield was located lay under a shroud of ground fog. Although the night had been crystal clear when Hy and I flew in, the cold earth had lowered the air's temperature to the dew point, and now mist obscured both the flatlands and the far distant hills. Such fogs can burn off early, though, and at a little before nine I could already glimpse the sun's bright halo.

The airfield was small: a single runway, with one hangar and limited visitor tie-downs—a fact that had prompted us to leave the Citabria at Sacramento Metro and rent a car. Already bleacher seats were being erected and low barriers set up; two men struggled to unroll a red-white-and-blue striped tent, and food concession trucks were arriving. For a while I stood shivering and watching Hy and Matty move around her sleek yellow plane as they did the preflight, checking such things as the hydraulic brake lines, fuel tanks, prop, flaps, and ailerons. Matty was her old self this morning: clear-eyed and confident, long hair tied back with a cheery yellow scarf whose red sunburst pattern matched that on the plane's wings. Hy, on the other hand, had been taciturn and preoccupied since our wake-up call at seven.

By the time he'd opened the engine cowling and their heads were bent over the plane's innards, I decided to go for a walk. Seeing them that way brought back the last time he and I had huddled over an engine in a similar manner; my one and only attempt at emergency aircraft repair had ended in failure that almost claimed him, Habiba, and me.

By now the sun had burned a hole in the fog, and its appearance seemed to cheer the arriving pilots and mechanics. People called and waved to one another, greeted me pleasantly, and studiously avoided comment on the weather. Bad luck to talk about it. Even though fliers claim to understand its vagaries, there are few who don't secretly believe that weather is controlled by a capricious and malevolent deity who is privy to our every utterance.

I walked the length of the field, admiring the planes tied there. Each was beautiful in its own way: Pitts Specials, the tiny biplanes that for many years were the supreme U.S. manufactured aerobatic models; a lean, mean Extra 300S; a Czech-manufactured Zlin monoplane; several homebuilts; a red-and-white Chipmunk Special. I stopped to talk with the owner of a pre–World II Bücker Jungmeister, who claimed his blue biplane was the only type he'd trust for a completely reliable snap roll. He introduced me to a pair of wingwalkers, a husband-and-wife team whose specialty was synchronized movement atop a biplane in flight. In spite of being what I considered quite insane, the couple acted relaxed and normal as they told tales of the early wingwalkers and barnstorming pilots of the 1920s and '30s. After a while I wandered on, admiring from afar a Belgian Stampe, another biplane, whose owner—judging from his scowl as he waxed its wings—was having a bad day.

Finally, though, my thoughts turned to business. I went back to the privacy of the rental car, took out my phone, and called Mick's condo. No answer, only the machine. When I called the office, Ted—who comes in on Saturdays and takes off when Neal's bookshop is closed Monday mornings—informed me that my nephew had come in too.

Mick sounded excessively cheerful for one whose woman friend was seeing someone else. Maybe Keim's date had gone badly last night and she'd stopped by his condo to reassure him as to what a prize he was. But more likely his good spirits had to do with some triumph he'd scored with the computer.

I asked, "So do you have anything for me?"

"Some pretty strange stuff. I'll give you the full rundown. I started with the Social Security numbers you gave me for Seabrook and his kid. They're valid—or at least they don't contain any of the obvious errors you see in fake ones, like a leading number nine or four zeros at the end. Next I checked to see what state they were issued in; three-eight-four and three-eight-six are for Michigan, which agrees with the birth certificates."

"What about the certificates? Are they valid, too?"

He hesitated portentously—a sure sign he was on to something. "Well, vital stats offices aren't open on the weekend, and the same goes for hospital records. But what I did was search

70

Detroit area Information for phone numbers for the attending physicians. Nothing on the doc who delivered Seabrook—he's probably dead—but there was a residence number for the guy who delivered Zach. When I called him, he told me he's retired."

"Good work, Mick! Did he remember the Seabrooks?"

"Very well. They were friends of his son. And he also remembers the blessed event."

Now the tone of his voice told me a surprise was in the offing. "And?" I asked impatiently. I hated it when Mick drew out the report of his findings this way—which was exactly why he did so.

"And," he said, "little Zachary was black."

"What!"

"So were both his parents."

"Huh." I was silent for a moment. "Well, I guess you know what we've got here."

"A case of faked identities."

"You say the doctor's son was a friend of the Seabrooks. Does he know if they're still in touch?"

"They're not. The Seabrooks left the area when Zach was around five months old. The son never heard from them again, and no other doctor ever requested the wife's medical records."

"I'll give you ten-to-one odds that the real Seabrooks are dead and have been for over ten years. And that the man claiming to be John Seabrook requested those certificates and built identities for himself and his son around them."

"Wait a minute," Mick said. "Do birth certificates show what race you are?"

I closed my eyes, trying to picture the Seabrooks', but I couldn't. "I don't know, but even if they do, that can be altered."

"What about the Social Security numbers?"

"The bogus John Seabrook probably applied for them after he got hold of the birth certificates."

"I'd sure like to get a look at his record of payments."

"They wouldn't tell you anything; they'd only go back to when he moved to Los Alegres."

"Still..."

"No, Mick. *No*. The Social Security Administration guards its records more closely than any other federal agency. Even the FBI can't get a look without a court order."

"There's got to be a way."

"Mick, I said no!"

He heaved the martyred sigh of a true hacker. Months before he came to work for me, Mick had broken into the Pacific Palisades Board of Education's computer and used certain information to line his own pockets—an act that had caused his parents to banish him from southern California and place him in my somewhat dubious protective custody. "Okay," he said, "but you don't mind if I make some other searches?"

As recently as a year ago I would have demanded to know the exact nature of those searches, but now I simply gave him the go-ahead and said good-bye.

Maybe, I thought, I'd given in because I knew I couldn't stop Mick once he set his mind to something. Or maybe I'd been dealing with outfits like Renshaw and Kessell—who frequently strayed outside the boundaries of the law—too long to maintain my scruples. More likely, though, they were just plain eroding under constant battering from a world in which nobody really gave a damn.

I didn't want to tell Matty what Mick had turned up—at least not till she was done flying, and that wouldn't be for another five hours. And I didn't want to wait around anymore while she and Hy performed their extensive preflight—not when everything seemed secure here and there were leads to be worked elsewhere.

Back on the field, I interrupted Hy's scrutiny of the plane's ignition system to ask for the key to the Citabria. He looked puzzled, told Matty he'd be right back, and walked with me to the parking lot. "Where're you going?"

"Los Alegres." I took my .38 from my bag and handed it to him. "Here, in case you need it."

"But why Los Alegres?"

"Something's come up—nothing major, but it tells me I should get a move on questioning the people there. I can be back here in plenty of time to watch Matty fly."

He nodded and dug the key from his pocket.

"How's her plane?" I asked.

"Clean, so far. And to make sure it stays that way, I've asked our Sacramento office to send a man over to help Matty's mechanic babysit it till show time."

"How reliable does the mechanic seem?"

"From the way he acts, I'd say he'd lay down his life for her."

"Let's hope that won't be necessary."

After yesterday's departure in the Cessna, flying into Los Alegres in the Citabria was like coming home in a Porsche after leaving in a VW. I was running low on fuel, so I pulled over to the pumps, where I was greeted with a startled blink from Bob Cuda, one of the linemen. I shut it down, put the keys on the dash, and hopped out.

"You've come a long way, baby," Bob said as he attached the grounding wire to the exhaust pipe on the fuselage.

"It's borrowed."

"Somebody must like you a lot, to loan you this beauty." He ran his hand over the high white wing, squinted up at the blue silhouette of an airborne gull on the tail section—the symbol for an environmental organization Hy had once headed and on whose board he still sat.

I fetched the stepladder for Bob while he ran out the fuel line. When he climbed up and began filling the right tank, the strong crosswind— which I'd had to fight like hell on landing— blew the hood of his parka up over his longish gray hair.

"Say, Bob, I've got a question for you. You still spend a lot of time over in the hangars with your mechanic buddies?"

"Fair amount. Why?"

"Matty's noticed some stuff missing from her plane. Nothing valuable, but she asked me to look into it."

He pushed back the hood and frowned at

me. "Why... ? Oh, right, I forgot what line of work you're in."

"You seen any strangers hanging around lately?"

He removed the nozzle and replaced the tank cap, looking thoughtful. "Well, I don't know everybody who flies in and out of here. Strangers're always pulling up to the pumps."

"Any of them stay around, maybe visit Hangar B?"

"Not that I recall. That hangar, a stranger would stand out; for sure somebody'd ask him what he was doing there." He handed me the nozzle, climbed down, and dragged the ladder over to the left wing. I followed and returned the nozzle to him.

"D'you know Matty's boyfriend?" I asked.

"John? Yeah, to say hello to."

"He spend much time out here?"

"You see him around."

"Doing what?"

"Waiting for Matty."

"He talk with anybody?"

"Mostly he sits in the diner, nurses a beer, chats with whoever comes in. But a few weeks ago I did see him having a conversation with Gray Selby."

Now, that interested me. Gray Selby was one of the flight instructors, and no fan of Matty's. A former fighter pilot from the Vietnam era, he had little use for women in the cockpit and even less for women who did aerobatics. While some other male instructors might be skeptical and adopt a wait-and-see attitude toward female students, Selby held to a hard sexist line and refused to teach them. While the others were the first to give credit where credit was due, Selby withheld it, no matter what a woman pilot's accomplishments. Matty had always stood her ground with him, returning his caustic comments with humorous barbs. My way of dealing with Selby was to ignore him.

Bob asked, "What's this got to do with the stuff Matty's missing?"

"Nothing, really. I'm just curious about John; I haven't met him yet."

That seemed to satisfy the lineman. He handed down the nozzle again, and I replaced it and the grounding wire while he wrote up my credit-card slip. After I'd signed it he followed me back to the Citabria and once more ran his hand over its wing, looking wistful.

"One of these days," I told him, "I'll fly her up here and we'll go for a ride."

"Thanks, I'd like that."

It would never happen. Bob was fifty-seven, had spent most of his adult life around the airport, loved aircraft more than anything on earth—and was deathly afraid to fly. He would have been mortified had he realized that everybody saw through his carefully concocted excuses for not accepting rides or taking lessons, so a tacit conspiracy of silence surrounded him. But just as caution makes for a good pilot, a fear of flying can make for a good lineman. Nobody who knew Bob felt compelled to check after fueling to make sure he'd properly tightened the tank caps.

I left the Citabria in the visitors' parking and walked over to the shop adjacent to the flight school and rental office, hoping to question the mechanics, but found it closed. The office was open and doing its usual brisk Saturday business, so I went inside and checked with the woman on the desk to see if Gray Selby was working today. The schedule showed he was due back from a lesson within the hour, at noon.

While I waited, I sat in an easy chair near the door, chatting with old acquaintances as they passed through and slipping in an occasional question about John Seabrook and any strangers who might have visited Hangar B. Nobody could add anything to what Bob Cuda had already told me. Soon the room emptied as people headed for home, the diner, or the sky. By ten after twelve, Gray Selby still wasn't back, so I picked up an issue of *Flight Training* magazine and tried to interest myself in an article on carburetor icing, a subject a pilot can't know too much about, but I wasn't able to focus and found myself going over paragraphs two and three times. Finally I set it aside.

The comfortable room had scale models of aircraft hanging from its ceiling, and its walls were covered with Polaroid pictures of students, taken on the days they'd soloed. I got up and hunted for mine, found a younger version of myself hugging the strut of the old Cessna, long hair windblown, a smile as big as the world on my glowing face.

They say soloing is the greatest high you can experience. And it is.

Half past noon, by the clock behind the counter. I'd give Selby ten minutes more, then grab a burger and head back to Sacramento—

I spotted him through the window: a short, compact man with closely clipped white hair, wearing his old regulation leather jacket, attire that during his term of service—and now—set the elite naval aviators apart from the ranks. Behind him trailed a student of no more than twenty, shoulders slumped, face drawn and weary. Selby took the steps two at a time, breezed through the door, and caught it just before it swung back at the younger man. Over his shoulder he said, "You're not gonna cut it, kid, unless you break those bad habits. And pulling back on the yoke when you're scared is the worst bonehead habit you can get into. Boneyard habit—it'll kill you."

The student didn't say anything, just took the rental log up to the counter to pay. I watched, sympathy for him quickly translating to anger at Selby.

Not that the instructor was wrong in principle; what the student had been doing could cause a fatal accident. When you're a novice flier and you get scared, you're usually scared because you think the plane is going down. So if the plane's going down, your instinctive reaction is to pull back, raise the nose, make it go up. Logical and natural, if you look at it from a layman's point of view. However, pulling back too much can also stall the wing, and if that lift goes out from under it at a low altitude—such as on takeoff or landing—you're heading for the ground too fast to correct for the error.

Once a flight instructor observes such a

habit forming, he or she should point it out calmly, rationally, and nonabusively. The way Matty pointed it out to me. And with no references to "bone*yard* habits."

Selby started for the desk, either to heap more abuse on his student or to check the schedule sheet. I stood up and stepped into his path. For a moment he didn't recognize me; then his eyes narrowed and his mouth turned down sourly. "Ms. McCone," he said, "I hear from Cuda that you've got one very handsome Citabria over in the tie-downs."

"Yes, I do, Mr. Selby." I extended my hand.

The instructor looked at it as if I were offering him my garbage. Then he noticed his student heading for the door. "Hey," he called, "did you schedule for next week?"

"...I don't know if I can make it. I'll call you."

The young man was around us and at the door before Selby added, "Hey, I haven't signed your logbook!"

"Looks like you just lost a student," I said.

He glared at me, deeply ingrained lines of displeasure distorting his otherwise regular features. He would, I thought, have been attractive had he not projected such malcontent—malcontent that had been honed to a fine edge since I'd last seen him. With some surprise I realized that Selby's testiness and unreasoning gender bias were merely the froth on a cauldron of steadily simmering rage.

He said, "You here to rag on me, McCone?"

I shook my head.

"What, then? You won't find your friend, Ms. Wildress, on the premises. She's up in

79

Sacramento at an air show, playing the famous aviatrix."

I decided to meet his thinly concealed anger head on. "Does that bother you?"

A tic rippled the skin below his right eye, and he pushed his lips out, making a flatulent sound. "Why should it?"

"Well, for somebody who's not bothered, you sure do sound pissed off."

"What bothers me—or in your unladylike jargon, what *pisses* me off—is people like you cluttering up this waiting room. If you're not here to meet Wildress or rent one of our aircraft, why don't you clear out—"

"And why don't you and I declare a truce?"

He had been leaning aggressively toward me, about to get in my face. Now he drew back. "Huh?"

"A truce, Mr. Selby. You've never done anything to me; I've never done anything to you. Well, I admit my language was rough, and my remark about your student was tactless. And I apologize."

Selby was used to Matty's barbs, and since he associated me with her, he'd expected more of the same. My apology further threw him off stride, and when I added, "Do you have some free time?" he became completely confused.

"Uh..." He consulted his watch. "Uh, my next lesson isn't till two."

"I'll buy you lunch, then."

"Why?"

"I'd like to pick your brains."

"About what?"

"John Seabrook."

An odd flicker appeared in his blue eyes. "Seabrook, huh? And you're a private cop. She finally wise up and decide to get the goods on him?"

I smiled.

"About time the broad caught on."

"Mr. Selby, you're just the man I want to talk with."

"What makes you think he's hiding something?" I asked in response to Selby's initial series of nonspecific pronouncements about John Seabrook.

He crushed a cellophane-wrapped packet of saltines, opened it, and dumped the crumbs into his chili. Then he added Tabasco, ketchup, and black pepper, tasted it, and nodded his approval. "Okay," he said, his mouth full, "let's see what you think of this. Over there on Hartmann Road"—he motioned to the north end of the field—"there's a paved turn-around. Was supposed to be the entrance to a housing development that never got off the ground."

"I know where you mean."

"About a year and a half ago, in July, I started seeing this truck parked there. Once or twice a week. Was a guy in it—Seabrook."

"Doing what?"

"Watching the planes take off and land. He'd sit there for maybe an hour or two. Just watching."

"You're sure it was Seabrook?"

"Sure I'm sure. I got to pass by there on my way home, so I made it my business to check the guy out."

"Why?"

"He looked suspicious."

"Suspicious, because he was watching the planes? A lot of people do that." As if to prove my point, a Mooney Ranger took off just then; reflexively, my eyes were drawn to it.

Selby was looking at it too. "Well, you can't be too careful." He speared a french fry from the side dish he'd ordered, dipped it in the chili, and popped it into his mouth. "It was Seabrook, all right, and he kept it up all summer and into the fall. The next thing I know, he's seeing Matty. Now he's got an excuse to watch the planes from the diner."

"Mr. Selby, that's what people *do* here."

"Yeah, my point exactly. They drive over here, have lunch, and watch. They don't lurk across the road in their truck; they don't need to take up with some woman pilot as an excuse to come in here, sit down, order, and watch."

"I really doubt Seabrook started seeing Matty as an excuse to have a Seven Niner burger."

"Then why didn't he ever come in before?"

"Maybe he's shy. Maybe he was on a diet."

"McCone, if you're not gonna take me seriously—"

"Sorry. Go on."

"Okay. After a while I start wondering about the guy. Matty tells everybody she doesn't like to fly, won't go up with her. But what kind of guy will sit watching the planes for hours every week, when he doesn't like to fly?"

"Bob Cuda."

Selby snorted and waved his hand in dismissal. "Cuda's a case of arrested development.

I'm talking normal guy."

Who's normal? I thought. You? Me? But he did have a point. "I take it you decided to investigate."

"You bet I did. You can't be too careful."

"Why? Surely you weren't looking out for Matty's sake."

"Hell, no. That broad can take care of herself. I was looking out for airport security."

"What, you thought Seabrook was maybe preparing to launch a terrorist attack on Los Alegres Municipal Airport?"

He scowled. "Okay, McCone, you're from the big city, fly in and out of SFO or Oakland now, you think we're small potatoes. But you look around here, this is an affluent community. Stick your nose into the hangars, check out the tie-downs, and you'll see millions of bucks' worth of aircraft. That plane of Matty's alone cost over a quarter of a mil, and that classic collection in Hangar C—well, I don't even want to guesstimate what that would go for."

"You're right; I wasn't thinking."

Somewhat mollified, Selby looked at my plate. "You going to eat that pickle?"

"Take it."

"There're other considerations besides the safety of the aircraft," he went on, brandishing the dill spear at me and then crunching. "We've seen a number of modified twin-engines through here in the past few years—modified to carry cargo. Makes you wonder what they're transporting."

"Drugs or other contraband?"

"Could be. And a guy who's watching them land and take off, a guy who doesn't look like the law… well, it makes you wonder some more."

"So you kept an eye on Seabrook, and… ?"

"Well, I didn't want to get too close to him, maybe tip him off. It would've looked funny, seeing as Matty and I haven't ever been on the best of terms. So I just watched and listened. McCone, do you know the difference between a wet oil sump and a dry oil sump?"

"No."

"Not many people besides mechanics do. It's not really important, now that they've solved the problem of wet sumps icing up. Basically, it's just an engine design feature. But Seabrook knew that Continental engines have wet sumps. I heard him talking about it with Steve, the head mechanic."

"So he knows engines. Is that a crime?"

Selby ignored the question. "When you're taking off behind a larger plane, where should you start your roll in order to avoid wake turbulence?"

"From the same point or before it did."

"And rotate it?"

"Before the larger plane's takeoff point."

"How many hours did you have before you learned that?"

"Ten? Twelve? I don't know."

"Well, Seabrook knew that with zip hours."

"You heard him talking with… ?"

"Mark Casazza, about an iffy takeoff one of Mark's students made behind a Citation."

"Huh."

"There was other stuff, all of it pretty damn revealing."

"I see what you're getting at. So you eavesdropped"—Selby frowned, and I corrected myself—"you listened for how long?"

"About six months all told, every chance I got. Kept notes, too. Then about three weeks ago I decided old John and I should have a conversation."

"About?"

"You going to eat the other half of that burger?"

I'd planned to, but in the interest of sustaining our fragile rapport, I passed my plate to him. "About what?" I repeated.

"The weather."

"The *weather?*"

"Best subject I could think of that wouldn't put him on his guard. He was already wary of me—Matty must've told him she hates my guts. So I bitched to him about having to cancel my lessons the day before on account of the low ceiling, said I hoped I'd get through all of them that day before it came down again. And Seabrook said I'd probably manage if I planned to stay in the pattern, since there was still four hundred feet of leeway, and the ceiling seemed pretty static."

"So what did you take that to mean?"

"Let me refresh your memory about the landing pattern here. The clouds were right at the top of the hills—"

"Two thousand feet."

"And the pattern altitude is—"

"Eleven hundred."

"Two thousand minus eleven hundred is nine hundred."

"Minus the legal five hundred below the cloud cover equals four hundred."

Selby smiled triumphantly. "The guy not only knew the FAA requirements for VFR, he knew the height of those hills and our pattern altitude."

I considered. "Couldn't he have remembered that from talking with Matty?"

"He isn't a flier, doesn't like to fly. Why would it've come up? And even if it did, why would he have remembered it? Or been able to compute it that easily?"

"You're right. Why? Unless—"

"There's more. From there I steered our discussion to that crash over on Sonoma Mountain last month. You read about that?"

"Uh-huh." The longer I fly, the more I find myself reading newspaper accounts of crashes—not to scare myself, but for assurance that they were caused by some pilot error that I myself hopefully never would make.

"Well," Selby went on, "I worked the ELT into that, and damned if Seabrook didn't know that it transmitted on 121.5."

"How'd you find that out?"

"He corrected me when I said it was 121.7. I covered by saying I'd mixed it up with our unicom here—122.7."

I stirred the cubes in my iced tea with the straw, thinking that one over. Very few people who don't fly know about the ELT—emergency locator transmitter—a radio device that the FAA requires on aircraft, and that is triggered by impact to send distress signals on both civilian and military frequencies.

I said, "It transmits on a universal emergency frequency; he could've known about that if, say, he'd worked around ships."

"Maybe, but given the other things I picked up on..."

"So you're telling me John Seabrook is a pilot."

Selby nodded. "The way I figure it, for some reason our boy doesn't want Matty or anybody else to know. But he is, and he loves flying. Why else would he sit across the road watching the planes week after week, month after month? Then he takes up with Matty, and he can hang around here all he wants, absorbing—what is it you city folks call it?—the ambience. But hanging around an airport—hell, living with a pilot— he gets careless. He lets things slip that give him away to anybody who's really listening. He lets a *lot* of things slip."

A lot of slips—or maybe just one too many.

Six

McCone! Over here!"

I turned at the sound of Hy's voice but couldn't pinpoint where it was coming from. The day had turned clear and surprisingly warm, bringing out a huge crowd for the air show. People were still streaming through the gate from the parking area, many of them lugging coolers, blankets, and folding chairs. Others lined up at the food stands, over-flowed the bleacher seats, pushed up against the low metal barriers around the field. Still others milled around in the striped tent, where a pilot shop was hawking its wares, or admired a display of homebuilts put on by the local experimental aircraft association.

Sweat beaded my forehead, and I felt trapped inside my overly heavy sweater; I ran the back of my arm over my face, then used it as a visor as I searched for Hy. The smell of Mexican food from a nearby catering truck combined with the heat to make my stomach queasy; I wished I hadn't let Gray Selby eat most of my lunch. Hy called my name again. I pivoted, and a small girl ran into me, dribbling ice cream on my foot.

A roar rose from the spectators. Cokes and hot dogs momentarily forgotten, they tilted their heads back and shaded their eyes as they watched the blue Bücker Jungmeister whose owner I'd talked with earlier sketch lines of smoke against the sky. The red chevron design on its top wings was easy to see because it was flying upside down.

"And there he goes, folks," the announcer said over the loudspeaker, "a perfect Cuban eight!"

Finally I spotted Hy shouldering his way around a film crew from KXTV News. He grabbed my hand and led me toward the barricade, asking, "What the hell took you so long?"

"Traffic—both at Sacramento Metro and on I-Five. When's Matty flying?"

"She's next up."

When we got to the front row of spectators, a Spandex-clad young woman moved aside and allowed us to squeeze in next to her. Hy said, "Thanks for saving our place."

I leaned forward, my hands braced on the top rail of the barricade, and peered at the taxiway. Matty's clean-limbed monoplane waited at the hold line, ready to turn onto the runway once the biplane finished its routine and landed.

I said, "I wanted to get back in time to wish her luck."

"And she wanted to see you. Here—she left you this." He took the yellow-and-red scarf she'd worn earlier from his pocket. "You're to wave it, so she'll know you arrived safely."

"That's Matty—always concerned about the other guy." I took the scarf and put my foot on the middle horizontal of the barricade; Hy boosted me up and I waved it vigorously. Matty's hand extended through the plane's open canopy, waggling two fingers in a victory sign. Then it disappeared and the canopy closed.

Hy eased me down, and I tied the scarf around my neck. "How's she doing?"

"She's been flying high on her own for hours. I tell you, McCone, the adrenaline level around here is infectious."

I could feel it in his hands and body; feel it rising within me, too.

The announcer said, "And now—the hammerhead."

I looked up at the biplane; its pilot was ruddering over at the top of a hammerhead turn, going into a steep accelerating dive, white smoke trailing. My stomach lurched as if I were in the cockpit with him.

Hy squeezed my shoulders. I leaned back against him, watching the pilot begin his recovery, only hundreds of feet above the runway. Hy asked, "Did you find out anything in Los Alegres?"

"Yes—and Matty's not going to like it." My eyes still tracking the blue plane, I related my conversations with Mick, Bob Cuda, and Gray Selby.

"What a guy, that Seabrook," Hy said when I finished. "The bastard lied to her. Deserted her and his own kid. Left them in an indefensible position. McCone, we've got to help them."

"We will."

"You sound so confident."

I shrugged. "It's the first step toward being confident."

"Watch this, folks!"

The crowd noise intensified as the blue plane began a fast lateral roll at the top of a loop. "Jesus," I said to Hy, "what's he doing?"

"It's called an avalanche."

"Sounds ominous."

"Can be."

The biplane blended the snap roll into a smooth descent down the back of the loop.

"Let's give Joe a big hand, folks!"

Beside me, the young woman who had saved our place said to her much older male companion, "Why would anybody *want* to do that?"

"Because it's fun, darlin'."

I tipped my head back and looked up at Hy. His eyes met mine. Yes and no, they said. I nodded.

Aerobatics is about a lot of things, and fun is only one of them. It's also about discipline and self-sacrifice, long hours spent practicing, and endless self-evaluation. It's about control and power: making your aircraft do exactly what you want it to do. It's about sheer defiance of nature: that's gravity and human frailty you're thumbing your nose at. It's about overcoming fear and feeling alive and pushing your limits.

And finally, on the professional level, it's about showmanship. The pilots who fly aerobatically for money and glory are aviation's rock-and-rollers. But instead of seeing their names in neon lights, they write their accomplishments in smoke against the sky.

The biplane shot upward in a vertical climb, dived straight back down, and recovered with split-second timing. As the crowd cheered, it climbed out and sedately entered the landing pattern. But on final, the pilot waggled its wings—waving exuberantly at the spectators. They greeted its touchdown with roars of approval.

I peered across the field at Matty's yellow plane; it looked small and vulnerable as it waited at the hold line. The loudspeaker system screeched and groaned.

"...Matty Wildress, who captured second place last September in the U.S. Aerobatic Championship. Matty's flying a customized Stirling Silver Star—three hundred and sixty horsepower, with a roll rate of three hundred degrees per second. This Arkansas-manufactured monoplane is all metal..."

I tuned out the commentator's voice as Matty turned onto the runway. Full power, fast ground run, and back on the stick for a smooth climb-out.

She began her routine with a basic loop; she was known for playing games with her audience by starting out with deceptively simple maneuvers and then surprising them. In my mind I followed her movements: back on the stick; full throttle as the Star pulled up through the vertical; pressure on the stick relaxed as she went upside down over the top; reduced throttle on the back side of the loop. Return to straight and level.

Easy to imagine, but I'd performed clumsy loops at sixty-five hundred feet, and she performed an elegant one at only a few hundred.

"Kind of a pedestrian beginning," the man next to us commented.

Again Hy and I exchanged glances: *Watch this.*

The Star shot upward, smoke spewing from beneath its fuselage. Spun up and up—a ballet dancer performing a pirouette. Then down in a vertical dive. Recovery, perhaps a hundred feet off the runway. The announcer exclaimed, the crowd cheered.

A high spiral next, leaving a corkscrew smoke trail. Then a slow horizontal roll, more difficult to maintain than a fast one. A high loop, followed by a series of joyous turns that wore S's against the sky.

"God, she's good!" I exclaimed.

She was soaring upside down now. The red sunburst pattern on the wings sparkled in the afternoon light. The Star reached mid-field, then tumbled forward, tail over nose. Tumbled again and again.

"Wonderful!" the man next to us said. The crowd evidently thought so too.

I grabbed Hy's arm. "What's that?"

"*Lomcevak.* Czech word meaning 'imbalance,'

most often applied to overimbibers of slivovitz. There're infinite variations on it; it's never done exactly the same way twice. High negative G's, and she handled them beautifully."

"There it is, folks—the ultimate aerobatic maneuver! Give Matty a big hand. You're looking at the next U.S. champion. A couple more years, and she'll hold the world title."

Again Matty put the Star into a loop, higher up this time.

I asked Hy, "What d'you suppose she'll do for a finale?"

"Can't imagine. She—What the hell... !"

The Star was on the back side of a low loop now—diving much too fast.

"Christ," Hy exclaimed, "she's not easing off on the throttle!"

I grabbed the top rail of the barricade. Pulled back with my right hand, as if I could control the throttle for her. Hy's fingers did the same, gripping my shoulder.

An eerie hush fell over the airfield; all motion, save that of the Star, seemed suspended. Seconds stretched and stretched as it plummeted straight down—

"Matty! No!" Hy's voice, my own echoing it.

The Star smashed into the runway, metal ripping and shearing. Screams erupted from the spectators, but the sound of the explosion drowned them out. I rocked back against Hy as a fireball ballooned upward. His fingers went slack on my shoulders and he moaned.

I pushed away from him and started scrambling over the barricade.

"McCone, stop!"

I swung my feet to the other side, jumped down, and ran toward the billowing smoke and flames.

"Stop!"

The heat was intense, the fumes thick and oily. I paused, gasping for breath.

"What the hell're you *doing!*" Hy's hand grasped my arm above the elbow.

I swung around, saw his wild eyes. Tried to pull away, but his fingers bit into my flesh.

"Ripinsky, we've got to go to her!"

He didn't move. I lashed out at his hand, trying to break his grasp. He tightened it. Then he wrapped both arms around me and pulled me to his chest.

I looked over my shoulder. Black smoke and orange flames, fire truck on the move. People running, panicked. Screams and shouts and that hideous roaring as the fire consumed—

Oh, Jesus, Matty... !

Hy dragged me back to the barricade, pushed it aside, and began moving me toward the parking area, arms rigid. I stumbled on something. When he righted me, I looked down and saw Matty's brilliant yellow-and-red scarf hanging limply from my neck.

Hy kept moving me along. We were going against the flow of the crowd, toward the gate. I stumbled again. Again he righted me. Resistance spent, I leaned on him. My face was wet. I touched my fingertips to it, heard myself sob. How long had I been crying?

I looked up at Hy. No tears. Just eyes that seemed to be all black dilated pupils looking out of a deathly pale mask—and a grim purpose in the set of his mouth.

We were in among the parked cars and trucks and vans before he spoke. "Where'd you leave the rental car?"

"...I don't know."

"*Where?*"

"I don't *know!* Ripinsky, we can't leave. Matty—"

He pushed me back against the side of a van—hard. Held me by the shoulders and looked into my eyes.

I stared at him through my tear-clogged lashes. What I saw brought to mind something Anne-Marie Altman had said of him on the day he and I first met.

He's still dangerous.

"Matty's dead," he said flatly. "There's nothing we can do here."

I tried to reply, but my larynx wouldn't work.

"The NTSB will investigate," he went on, "and they won't come up with anything conclusive; there's not enough left of the plane. But you and I know what happened: the Star was tampered with. *After* Matty and I preflighted it."

Was that right? Or was he trying to reassure himself that he'd been in no way responsible for what happened? No, he always took on the blame if blame was due. But perhaps he'd overlooked something. No, he'd spent his whole life around aircraft. He wouldn't have missed a detail, not when it came to the safety of someone he cared about.

"It could've been pilot error," I said. "She was so stressed—"

"McCone, that last loop was a piece of cake for Matty. She wasn't stressed enough to make that kind of mistake—look at how she performed the rest of her routine."

"Then what... ?"

"Something happened in the cockpit. Something that threw her off just long enough."

I sucked in my breath, images flashing through my mind of what it must have been like for her. They were more than I could handle—now or ever. I shook my head, trying to drive them away.

"McCone?"

I looked up at Hy. Angry fires burned in the depths of his eyes. Beneath my insulating layer of shock I felt the same fires ignite inside me.

"Ripinsky, we'd better talk with the NTSB investigators—"

"No, we talk with no one." He scanned my face, searching for—what? I didn't know, but after a moment he apparently found it. "We talk with no one," he repeated softly, "because I don't want officials getting in my way. Because I am going to find out who did this to Matty. And when I do, I am going to kill the bastard."

He would. I knew he would. He'd killed before.

I closed my eyes in an effort to cut through my swirling emotions. Narrowed my focus to the days and years behind us, to the days and years ahead.

Then, for reasons of my own that had nothing to do with Matty and everything to do with Hy, I said, "I'm with you."

Three Years Ago

"So what's your altitude, McCone?"

"...Nine hundred feet."

"And your airspeed?"

"Out of control."

"And what should it be?"

"Sixty-five."

"And at this point on final, what should your altitude be?"

"A hell of a lot lower."

"So what're you gonna do?"

"Full throttle, and go around."

"All right!"

"You like that, huh?"

"I'd like it a hell of a lot better if you'd get off the carburetor heat and raise those flaps."

"Oops! I knew I was forgetting something."

"That's okay. You worry about cleaning up the plane after you put that power in. Now—you know what just happened?"

"...I'm not sure what you're getting at."

"When you opted to go around, you exhibited good judgment. With some prompting from me, of course."

"Jesus, Matty, I make judgment calls every day of my life—and most of them are pretty good."

"But you aren't making them in the left seat of a plane on final. That was a first. Now, why don't you try to put this thing on the ground again?"

"Right. Los Alegres traffic, Cessna three-two-Sierra, turning base."

"You know, McCone, what flying is all about—the absolute essence of it—is good judgment. You make the best call you know how under the circumstances, and then you move on it—no hesitating. And if that call involves aborting a takeoff or a landing, you don't worry about what the folks sitting around outside the diner are going to think of you. You just do it, and don't let your pride get in your way."

"Are we talking flying here? Or are we talking life?"

"What do you think? Hey, look at that—a perfect glide path. You've got the airport made."

PART TWO

November 23–27

Exercises 3–7

Seven

'll try to get the key to Matty's room," I said to Hy.

He nodded and went to stand in the doorway of the bar. I crossed the deserted motel lobby to the desk. My shock-induced insulation was intact again; I felt calm and purposeful, as if this were an ordinary afternoon, as if this were an ordinary act in the course of a routine investigation. The clerk was reading *People* magazine; he barely looked up when I said I'd misplaced my key to room 211, just reached for the rack where the duplicates hung. I took the one he held out and hurried back to Hy.

He stood rigid, staring at the big-screen TV that was playing to a nearly empty room. My eyes were drawn to the lurid images of a special news report: billowing smoke and twisted wreckage and firefighters dousing the flames. Then the horrifying scene was replaced by a publicity still of Matty. I moaned and turned away. Hy, his face set, put his arm around my shoulders as we went outside.

"Do you suppose the Bay Area affiliate is carrying that?" I asked.

"Most likely. Have you ever known the TV news to pass up a really good disaster story?"

"God, what if Zach sees it? He shouldn't find this out that way!"

"Better call, warn Rae or Ricky."

101

I fished out my phone and punched in their number as we skirted the pool in the courtyard. Rae answered, sounding shaky. When I started to explain why I'd called, she said, "Too late. The kids were channel-surfing, and they just saw the news spot."

"Damn! How's Zach dealing?"

"Badly. He ran out onto the lower deck and is just standing at the rail, staring at the water. Ricky's giving him a minute, and then he'll try to comfort him."

"Poor kid! Listen, we'll be leaving here pretty soon. I'll come straight to the house, see if there's anything I can do to help."

"Okay, we'll look for you. Shar, what's going to happen to Zach now?"

Good question. Logically, since John Seabrook had no relatives that anyone knew of, Zach should be turned over to the juvenile authorities until his father could be located. But I wasn't about to inflict that kind of abandonment on a sensitive and grieving boy—especially now that I had full reason to believe his life was in danger. "I know this is a lot to ask—"

"No, it's not. He's welcome here as long as he needs a place to stay. You know, you might bring Hank or Anne-Marie in on this; Zach should probably have legal counsel, somebody to look out for his best interests, in case his father doesn't turn up."

"Good point. We'll talk more about that when Hy and I get there." I broke the connection as we reached the door to 211. Matty had kept her room, planning to clean up and rest before flying back to Los Alegres. As I inserted the key I asked Hy, "Exactly what are we looking for?"

"Seabrook's letter. Matty took the lamb in the plane with her, but I suspect she left the letter here. It didn't sit at all well with her, and she'd've considered it bad luck to fly with it aboard."

"Was she really that superstitious?"

He shrugged, stepping into the room. "No more than you or I."

"I'm not superstitious."

"No? Then why do you always keep that piece of coral Hank brought you from Hawaii in your purse? Why do you automatically transfer it when you change purses?"

"…I don't know. Habit?"

"Would you fly without it?"

"I wouldn't cross the street without it."

"I rest my case."

The room was afternoon-warm and stuffy. Housekeeping had been in, but there still was a half cup of coffee on the small table; a T-shirt printed with the likeness of Beryl Markham and the legend "Women Fly" was draped over one of the chairs. Quickly I looked away.

Hy went straight to the duffel bag that sat on the low bureau, pawed around inside it, and came up with Seabrook's letter. He handed it to me and continued searching.

"We've got the letter, Ripinsky. Let's head back and see to Zach."

"Hold on a minute. Here it is." He held up a black leather notebook. "Matty's appointments calendar."

I took it and thumbed through the past couple of weeks. "Listen to this. Three o'clock on Wednesday: 'Dr. Sandler, re John.' "

"What kind of doctor?"

"Doesn't say."

"And why did she consult with him about Seabrook?"

I shook my head and slipped the notebook and the letter into my bag. "Are we out of here?"

"Yeah, but I want to stop by the desk a minute, ask what time Matty's mechanic checked out." Hy leaned against the wall by the door, his face haggard and sad. "I bet they'll tell me he checked out this morning, rather than this afternoon."

"I don't understand."

"When Matty and I got back to the field after lunch, the mechanic, Ed Cutter, was gone. He told us this morning that he planned to stay on tonight, party with some friends, but he left a note for Matty saying he'd been called away on a family emergency. She took it at face value; I shouldn't have."

"You think Cutter was the one who tampered with the plane?"

"Had to be. Our man was on the job before we finished the preflight, and I gave him orders not to let anybody but Cutter near it. When Matty and I got back to the field, he said that Cutter had been fiddling around in the cockpit, but nobody else had touched it."

"What do you think Cutter did in there?"

"Planted some kind of device—a smoke bomb, whatever. Probably remote-controlled. Cutter knew Matty's routine, would've known at what altitude and attitude she'd be unable to recover if distracted."

"So he claimed to be called away—"

"And was somewhere in the crowd, pushing the button. Dammit, McCone, I read him completely wrong, and I'll never forgive myself for it."

Two hours later we arrived at the house in Seacliff. Rae opened the door, took one look at my face, and put her arms around me. Ricky appeared, clasped Hy's hand, said, "I'm sorry, man."

Hy acknowledged the sympathy with a remote nod. He'd been silent on our flight back from Sacramento, as silent as Zach on yesterday's flight from Los Alegres. When Rae released me I asked, "How's Zach?"

"Still on the deck and not talking at all. Both Ricky and Habiba tried to get through to him—and failed."

"Let me try." I escaped to the powder room, where I washed and composed my face. Then I went downstairs.

The lower floor of the house opened onto a cantilevered deck high above China Beach. In the gathering twilight I spotted Zach's thin frame standing erect and very still at its rail. The strong sea wind stirred his curls and made his too flimsy cotton shirt snap like a flag. I started across the room that Rae and Ricky had furnished as an entertainment area for the kids, then stopped when I saw Habiba at the sliding glass door.

She stood as still as Zach, watchful, one hand clutching the edge of the brightly patterned drapery. Her knuckles strained white, and when I came up beside her, I saw a tear snake down her cheek. I touched my fingers to it and brushed it away.

Without looking at me she said, "He's been like that ever since we saw it on TV."

"Rae says you tried to talk with him."

"He told me to go away."

"He's hurting, Habiba."

"I know that. But I thought I could help him; I was hurt the same way."

"You *can* help. Just give him some time."

After a moment she sighed and let go of the drapery. "Sharon, why does stuff like this have to happen?"

"It doesn't *have* to. It just... does." The inadequacy of my reply left me feeling small and powerless.

Not so with Habiba. She turned on me, dark eyes flashing. "Well, it shouldn't!"

"No."

"Are you going to get Zach's father back?"

"I'm going to try." Finding John Seabrook now served a dual purpose: only he could tell me who had reason to kill Matty.

"You better," Habiba said. "He needs his father... like I needed mine!"

Surprised by the accusatory note in her voice, I looked closely at her. Yes, her anger was directed at me. With a stab of pain, I realized that at some point since the previous spring, Habiba had found out that I was present and helpless when her father was killed. I reached toward her, but she whirled and ran for the stairs.

For a moment I pressed my fingers to my eyes, fighting back fresh tears. Then I went outside to Zach.

He didn't look around when I approached, even though I took care to make noise. When I came up beside him I saw his unblinking eyes were fixed on the Marin headlands. I put my hand on his shoulder; in spite of the chill, he wasn't shivering. "Zach," I said, "I'm sorry."

No response.

"We need to talk."

He shrugged my hand off.

"I loved Matty too."

Silence.

"When you're hurting, it helps to talk to somebody who's hurting for the same reason."

He leaned forward, arms on the railing, staring down at the beach now. Darkness had fallen, and only the waves' white spume was visible; the fog was rolling in, and the horns began their mournful chorus. Zach shuddered at the sound. I took off my leather jacket and draped it around his shoulders, then leaned on the rail beside him and waited.

"Sharon?"

A single hesitant word, but at least he'd taken the first step. "Yes?"

"Did you... see it?"

"Yes."

"Was it awful?"

"It was over very fast."

"Do you think Matty was scared?"

"I don't think she had time to be."

"But you can't say for sure."

"Well, no. But I've been in situations where I came close to dying, and I was too busy trying to prevent it to be afraid."

"But you didn't die. Matty did."

I had no reply for that. God, I wasn't any good at this kind of thing!

We leaned on the rail in silence for a moment. Then Zach said, "I don't think Matty ever got scared."

"I don't think so, either." It was a lie, but I wanted him to be able to convince himself. He'd have enough to deal with without the horrifying images I'd already entertained—would never fully exorcise, no matter how long I lived.

Another protracted silence. Then he asked, "What's going to happen to me now?"

"Rae and Ricky would like you to stay here till we locate your dad. Is that okay with you?"

"I don't care. Whatever. I just don't want to go home or to Uncle Wes's. Or back to school."

"I understand. Do you want to go inside now? It's pretty cold out here."

"In a minute."

"Shall I go on ahead?"

"...No, stay."

"All right." I waited for him to speak again, listening to the foghorns' plaint.

"Matty really *didn't* get scared," he finally said. "This one time? She was flying me around in that old Cessna so I could take pictures for a school project, and its engine cut out. She had to land in this field, and the whole time she explained everything she was doing, so I wouldn't panic."

"She was good in an emergency."

"My dad's like that too. I've only seen him scared once."

"When was that?"

"When my mom died."

I frowned. Matty had told me John came to Los Alegres when Zach was a baby; I'd assumed he'd never known his mother. "How old were you then?"

"Around two."

Come to think of it, he did look older than eleven. "You can remember that far back?"

"Uh-huh. Dad always says I must've imagined it, that nothing like that ever happened. But it did. Why else would he refuse to talk about her?"

"I don't understand."

"Well, because of the way she... it was. Bad, really bad. Like Matty."

I waited.

"Somebody shot her. She was coming out of the grocery store. Dad and I were waiting for her in the car. We saw it happen."

"The memory isn't extensive," I said. "Just his mother waving at them right before she was shot, and his father dumping him and his car seat on the floor of the backseat."

"But those details." Rae shook her head. "They're really vivid. Her pink dress, the blood, the close-up of his father's wedding ring as he grabbed for him, the sand on the carpet in the backseat."

"What was it he called the grocery?" Ricky asked me.

"The good-bye store."

"Symbolic, maybe, of saying good-bye to his mom there."

He, Rae, Hy, and I were gathered around the fire in the living room, draperies drawn against the thick fog. Zach and Habiba, their fledgling friendship mended, were talking quietly in the kitchen, and my unusually subdued nieces had gone downstairs to watch TV. Initially I'd been concerned about what effect the newscast might have had on them, but Ricky had talked with them and assured me they were okay. During a trip to the zoo earlier that day, they'd gotten on well with Zach; it was his distress, rather than the violent video-taped scene at the airfield, that had upset them. Having been raised on too much TV, they were, I supposed, inured to disaster—fictional or real-life—on the small screen.

"Seabrook's reaction interests me," I said. "His wife's coming out of the store and she's shot, but instead of going to her, he moves to protect his son."

Ricky frowned. "What father wouldn't, with a sniper on the loose?"

"But Zach remembers he and his dad were parked in the shade of some trees far across the lot from the store. At that distance, why would Seabrook assume Zach would be the next target? And why, eleven or twelve years later, did he think that both Matty and Zach were at risk?"

On the couch beside me, Hy tensed. I took his hand and moved closer to him. He squeezed mine, but absently.

I said, "I wish I could gauge how accurate Zach's recollection is. Can kids remember things from when they were two or younger?"

From where she was curled up in the corner of the other couch, Rae stretched out one leg and nudged Ricky's thigh with her stocking foot. "We've got somebody here who claims to be a kid expert—although you could've fooled me last night."

He caught her foot and held it. "Okay, so I had a temporary lapse. Who doesn't? But to answer your question, I'd say Zach's memory is pretty damn accurate. Those details, they're the kind of things that get lodged in kids' minds under traumatic conditions." He smiled painfully. "You remember your aunt Clarisse's bedtime stories?"

Aunt Clarisse was a disturbed woman who pretended to dote on kids while secretly despising them; I suspected her pathology included a sadistic streak that would have put the marquis himself to shame. She expressed it in the form of nasty, terrifying bedtime tales guaranteed to cause late-night shrieks and screams, and by the time she died, she was well on her way to warping the young psyches of two generations of our family.

"How could I forget them?"

"My point exactly. Your sister and I finally cut old Clarisse off from story hours when Brian was a little under two. God knows why we waited that long. But Brian can still recite word for word the tale about the wolf ripping the little bad boy's heart out. And I wouldn't be at all surprised if he doesn't also have the occasional nightmare."

"Jesus!" Rae exclaimed.

"Yeah, Red, she was one mean old lady. Now, here's another example; it doesn't put Charly or me in a particularly favorable light, but the present company's got no illusions, anyway. When Charly told me she'd 'accidentally' gotten pregnant with Lisa, we had one hell of a knock-down-drag-out. As I recall, it involved an awful lot of broken dishes, lamps, and glassware. I couldn't tell you exactly what or how much, but Molly—who was two—can easily give you a full inventory."

"I get the picture."

Hy said, "So Zach's memory is probably the genuine article. Which tells me that John Seabrook did something back then that put his family in jeopardy."

I nodded. "And after his wife was killed, he created new identities for himself and Zach and went into hiding in Los Alegres."

"Hiding—just like he told Matty to do. Dammit, McCone, we should've encouraged her to follow his instructions. Or at least lie low until we could figure out what was going on."

"Hindsight's no good, you know that."

"I don't know anything, except that Ed Cutter's gonna pay for her death. He's gonna pay big-time."

Eight

The headlights of Hy's old Morgan swept the interior of Pier 241/2 as we drove in; their probing beams made shadows move eerily and distorted the shapes of familiar objects. We got out and climbed the iron stairway, our clanging footsteps a counterpoint to the rumble of bridge traffic. A shaft of light lay across the catwalk; Mick was already in his office. My nephew had been willing and even eager to come in at ten on a Saturday night—a sure sign that his relationship with Charlotte Keim had ended.

But maybe not. As we neared the door I heard Keim's deep-throated, bawdy laugh, followed by the words, "Way to *go!*" The Texas accent she'd labored to lose after moving to San Francisco always surfaced when she was excited, and now it rang loud and clear. Mick said, "We're not there yet, Sweet Charlotte. Hold on." Keim laughed again.

Anyone who didn't know the players might have assumed they were engaged in some sex game, and had they been anywhere other than the office, I wouldn't have ruled out the possibility. But here their computers were the center of their universe; when I stepped through the door I wasn't surprised to find Mick hunched over his PowerBook, Keim leaning over his shoulder so her long brunette curls brushed his cheek.

"Got it!" he exclaimed.

I asked, "Got what?"

He swiveled abruptly, knocking Keim off-balance and grabbing her by the waist to steady her. "God, Shar, don't do that!"

"Sorry." The overhead noise had the property of masking sounds within the pier itself—something that often made me wary when working alone late at night. "So what've you got?"

"The address you asked me to track down.

Ed Cutter lives on Airport Road in an unincorporated part of Sonoma County northeast of Healdsburg. Information wasn't easy to come by because—"

I cut off his self-congratulatory explanation by turning to Hy. "Do you know where that is?"

"I might. Maybe six months ago I was fueling at Willits and the lineman introduced me to a guy name of Matthews, flies a Twin Comanche. Lineman mentioned I'd flown for K-Air in Southeast Asia, and it turned out Matthews was a pilot for one of the other big outfits there. A few years ago he bought an abandoned airport in the Healdsburg area, runs charters out of it, and he asked if I was interested in picking up some work. Of course I turned him down. But he did say I should stop and see him sometime and that there's a good independent mechanic who rents a place on the property. Could be Cutter. I've got a sectional in the car; let me fetch it."

When I turned back to Mick, he was looking put out because I'd interrupted him. Keim sat on the edge of the desk, trying to jolly him out of it by rubbing her foot against his calf. I was in no mood to indulge him, so I quickly outlined the additional searches I wanted him to make.

By the time I finished, he was sufficiently intrigued to get over his mood. "I don't know, Shar. A shooting in a grocery-store parking lot ten to twelve years ago. Sand on the floor of the backseat. Not much to go on."

"There's another detail, remember? The good-bye store."

"Like Dad suggested, probably a symbol—"

"Or an actual name—Good B-u-y."

"Ah. That'd help a lot. Anything else you need?"

"To locate a Dr. Sandler, probably in the Los Alegres area."

Keim said, "Simple. I'll take care of it."

I shook my head. "I can't use you on this; your caseload's already too heavy."

"Just let me pick up the slack for Mick tonight."

"Well, okay—but only tonight. Now, I've got some bad news." I explained about the plane crash.

"Shar, I'm sorry," Mick said. "I know you really cared for Matty. But if we don't have a client—"

"Matty gave me a retainer; we'll work on her case till it runs out."

Hy came back just then, an open sectional in his hands. He spread it out on the desk and pointed to an area on a triangular course between the circles for the airports at Healdsburg and Cloverdale. "There it is."

I leaned closer, studying the location of the magenta circle containing the letter *R*, which indicated a private or restricted airfield.

He added, "We can be there within the hour if we hurry."

"Tonight?"

He nodded and folded the sectional.

Somehow I'd thought it would take longer to track down the man who'd sabotaged Matty's plane. I'd thought I'd have time to decide on a course of action....

115

Seeing my hesitation, Hy said, "Let's take a walk while we talk this over."

The fog hung motionless and murky, hazing the security spots and muting the streetlights along the Embarcadero. A thick, warmish blanket that could possibly extend inland from the coast, creating poor visibility. No problem for Hy, of course; he had over two decades of instrument flying under his belt and would be sure to get a weather briefing and file an IFR flight plan, if necessary. Or maybe if IFR conditions prevailed, he'd decide against going. I could point out that filing IFR would constitute evidence he'd been to Cutter's and that not filing was a violation of regulations—

But when had Hy ever felt bound by the regulations?

He took my arm and guided me to the walkway alongside the pier. "You having second thoughts about being with me in this, McCone?"

"The weather's got me spooked. And that airport looks to be in the hills; landing there in the fog could be risky—even for you."

"If we wait till tomorrow, we might never catch up with Cutter. He's probably making plans to leave the area before anybody figures out what he did."

We reached the end of the pier. He let go of my arm and leaned on the rail in a manner reminiscent of Zach leaning on the deck rail. Another grieving figure, looking down into black water.

I asked, "So what're you going to do if and when you come face-to-face with Cutter?"

He didn't reply.

"What are you going to do?" I asked again. "I need to know."

"You know what I want to do."

"Yes."

"But I won't. Cutter's not the one."

"What?"

"Oh, he sabotaged the plane, I'm sure of that. But he did it for money. He's not the one who planned it, but he sure as hell can finger the person who did."

"And after he does? What then?"

"You mean, what am I going to do to Cutter? Nothing."

My silence must have told him I didn't believe that. He raised his head and looked at me, his eyes glittering in the light from the security spots. "I may be crazy, McCone, but I'm not totally insane. And it would be insane to fly to an airport where I'm known and kill a man. I'll save my revenge for the person who ordered the hit."

I nodded and joined him at the rail, looking out over the water. A Saturday-night harbor cruise was churning past, its wake sloshing high among the pilings. Mist wrapped it, muting the light in its windows, obscuring the carefree partygoers.

Saturday night...

At Lake Tahoe, after a good dinner and some low-stakes gambling at one of the casinos, Anne-Marie and Hank were probably returning to the cabin he'd inherited from his father. Here in the city on nearby Tel Hill, Ted and Neal would be serving brandy to cap off one of their elegant dinner parties—this time a Chinese feast, their latest culinary enthusiasm. Across town, Rae and Ricky were by now ensconced in the hot tub, without benefit of swimsuits. And in southern California, my sister would be back in the arms of her new husband—and giving heartfelt thanks for the defection of at least two of her children. Hell, even Mick and Charlotte were having a good evening, on their romantic journey through cyberspace.

And Hy and I? We were about to fly off under marginal weather conditions to a remote airport. About to embark on a reckless path that might lead us anywhere. I'd never believed in vendettas, and neither had he. Could Matty's death have changed us so much that we'd actually carry through with one?

"Sometimes you've got to break the rules, McCone."

I knew that, because I had—over and over again.

"Are you still with me?"

"I'm still with you."

The airport's beacon light flashed ahead of us—green, white, green again.

"Some of the runway lighting systems at these private fields are radio-controlled. Let's see about this one." Hy keyed the Citabria's microphone.

Within a few seconds lights came on below: the blue of the taxiway, the white of the runway. The fog hadn't spread inland after all, and now the field lay in clear outline. I could make out a dark building to its right.

"We'll fly over, check it out." Hy cut back on power, flew slowly, scanning the ground. I pressed my nose to the backseat window, identified a house trailer and a few tethered planes.

"There's Matthews's Comanche," he said. "Surprised he hasn't come outside to see who activated his lights." He turned, flew downwind, and squared off for our final approach.

"I think I spotted another trailer down that access road," I told him. "At least I saw some lights."

"Could be Cutter's place."

"How do you plan to handle this?"

"I'll tell Matthews the engine's giving me some trouble and I want the mechanic to take a look at it. If it is Cutter, we'll say we could use a walk and wander on down there."

"What if Matthews insists on calling Cutter first?"

"We'll have to discourage that however we can. I don't want Cutter forewarned—or Matthews overhearing our conversation with him."

He turned his attention to landing, forward-slipping to lose altitude quickly. We touched down in a perfect three-point and soon were rolling past the building I'd spotted from the air—a hangar, buttoned up for the night. There were no lights on in Matthews's house trailer, although a Jeep stood next to it.

Hy said, "He's probably out someplace—Saturday night, you know. With any luck, we won't have to deal with him." He stopped the plane at a set of tie-downs near the Comanche and shut it down. By the time I climbed out, he was securing the last chain. "Let's go."

We walked along the runway toward the access road, the field plunging into darkness as the lights turned off automatically. Gently curved hills rose around us, and above them the sky was moon- and starshot, although high wisps of fog drifted from the west. The air was crisp and so cold I could see our breath. I smelled pines and felt a stab of sorrow as I pictured the Christmas-tree farm and the home Matty would never return to.

Hy's voice rescued me from the image. "You still carrying?"

"Yes."

"Better be ready. No telling what Cutter might do when he sees us."

I reached into my bag for the .38, tucked it into my waistband.

We came to the road and started walking along it toward the lights I'd glimpsed earlier. Except for the crunch of our footsteps, the night was very still. I moved off the gravel so that the vegetation would muffle our approach; Hy followed. Now I could see the outlines of the house trailer, perhaps twenty yards ahead. Light blazed in all its windows, and a white pickup was parked near the steps on the side nearest us.

"It's Cutter's place, all right," Hy whispered. "That's the truck he was driving this morning." He started to walk faster, but I held back. "What?" he asked impatiently.

I shook my head, looking around. A feeling of wrongness, small but insistent.

"Come on, McCone."

Half the distance and I stopped again. "Listen."

He cocked his head. "A TV. Jesus Christ, after what he did, he's watching TV."

We cut across the road, closing in. I glanced at the truck, saw its rear tires were flat. And lying over the tailgate was a—

"Ripinsky, look!"

"What... ? Ah, Jesus."

It was a dog. Indeterminate breed, long pale fur matted and bloody. Bent and broken, lying in a way that looked as if it had lunged over the tailgate at its attacker.

I grabbed Hy's arm and whispered, "Let's move in from the rear."

The land around the trailer was cleared, but a windbreak of pines protected it on the side where we stood. We slipped over and took shelter behind them, walked along quickly. About twenty feet of open ground lay between the trees and the trailer's rear wall. I turned to Hy, raising an eyebrow, and he nodded: *I'll go first; you cover.* I pulled out my .38, held it in both hands and looked around; nothing moved near the clearing, and the only sounds were the wind in the pine branches and the mutter of the TV. I nodded back at him: *Go ahead, I'm ready.*

In a crouch he ran across the open space and flattened himself against the flimsy wall; it gave a rumble like simulated thunder on a stage set. I tensed, gun ready, but there was no reaction from inside. After a minute I followed him, taking care not to touch the wall when I stopped next to it.

The trailer's entrance was midway down the side wall. I looked around the corner, saw a thin stripe of light spilling over the four steps from the partly open door. The sound of the TV was clearer now—the mindless giggle and shriek of a sitcom. Good God, I thought, commit murder by day, watch reruns of *The Brady Bunch* by night. Hy nudged me, and I started around the corner; edged along and moved up the steps with my gun ready. The Bradys' laugh track roared, but no one in the trailer joined in.

I looked back at Hy, jerking my chin toward the door: *I'm going in.* He nodded and began moving up the steps behind me. I straightened, raising the gun, then kicked the door all the way open and was through it before it could smack into the wall. I swept the room with both the .38 and my eyes and found it empty.

A combination living room and kitchen, with the TV playing to an empty recliner chair. Somebody had been there recently: a half full beer bottle and a full ashtray sat on a table, and fresh cigarette smoke overlaid the odors of stale tobacco and wet dog. A short hallway opened to my left. I slipped down it and checked out the single bedroom and bath. No one, but in the bedroom the window was open, its screen removed and, from the looks of it, hastily tossed aside.

When I went back to the living room, Hy had silenced the Bradys. The night was still again— so still that drips falling into the kitchen sink sounded loud as a drumroll. I touched the beer bottle with the back of my hand. Lukewarm. "Looks like Cutter went out the bedroom window," I said.

"So what the hell happened here?"

I shook my head.

"I'm gonna take a look at the dog."

A task I wouldn't have volunteered for. As he went out, I tucked the .38 into my bag, pulled on my gloves, and began sorting through a jumble of mail on the breakfast bar. Mostly junk, a few overdue bills, and travel brochures for various destinations, all of them in warm climates. Early winter dreaming, or had the mechanic been planning a trip—perhaps a permanent one?

Hy came back, his lips white, eyes dark with anger. "Truck's rear tires're slashed, and the poor bugger was shot at close range, damn near ripped apart. Looks like the shooter used wadcutters."

Hollow-tipped bullets that fragment and cause extensive damage. Overkill for a dog, overkill for humans, too. And a top choice of pro killers. "So the shooter arrives..."

"And the dog starts barking. He whacks it, then slashes the tires."

"I don't buy that. Why wouldn't he let the dog bark, wait for Cutter to come out to see what was happening?"

"Maybe he did, but Cutter stayed inside, so he shot the dog to shut it up. Then he goes into the trailer, but Cutter's already out the window."

"And then, instead of chasing him, he takes the time to slash the tires?"

"Well, there aren't a hell of a lot of places here to go on foot. Odds are Cutter was heading for the airport, Matthews's trailer. The shooter probably guessed that, so he slashed the tires to make sure Cutter couldn't double back to the truck and drive away."

"But if Cutter got to the field and alerted Matthews—"

Hy's eyes met mine and he nodded. "McCone, we'd better check it out."

We found Matthews behind his Jeep, a short-barreled rifle beside him. He'd never had the chance to fire. Cutter's body was wedged between the hangar and a waste-disposal bin—the last place left to hide. Both men had been repeatedly shot.

In the garish light of the flash Hy had fetched from his plane, the men's mangled and torn remains were easily the worst I'd ever seen. I stayed only long enough to make sure there was nothing we could do for them, then went behind a clump of scrub oak and was violently sick. Hy maintained a tight control, but I could tell he was sickened too.

When I came back to the Citabria, we huddled in the cockpit for warmth. He said, "What do you think—a vicious pro, or personal?"

"I'd say a pro who enjoys his work entirely too much. Cutter was the target; Matthews just got in the way."

"Jesus, what was John Seabrook into?"

I hugged my elbows, seized by an attack of shivers that had little to do with the cold. After a moment I asked, "Who has jurisdiction here? Sonoma County sheriff, I guess."

"McCone, we can't report it."

"Why not?"

"For the same reason we can't talk with the NTSB investigators."

"We can't just leave those men here like this!"

He reached over the seatback and cupped his hand under my chin, turning my face up so he could look into my eyes. "It isn't going to matter to either of them. You know that."

I grabbed his wrist, held it tight. He was right, but something in me shrank from leaving the bodies to become further victimized by night-crawling predators. Besides, failure to report a double homicide could put my investigator's license in jeopardy.

"Okay, I know how you feel," Hy said after a moment. "We'll get out of here and report it anonymously."

"I could call now, on my cell phone."

"No. Nine-eleven has caller I.D. They wouldn't be able to tell where you are, but I think the number might still come up on the screen, and it's listed to you. We'll fly into Santa Rosa and use a pay phone. I'll make the call, and if somehow they identify me, you weren't along for the ride."

"You shouldn't have to take all the responsibility—"

"You've got something to lose. I don't."

I hesitated, trying to think clearly. "Okay, then we'll have to make sure you aren't identified. I'm not comfortable with calling from Santa Rosa; we've flown in there late at night before, and there were people around."

"Right. Someplace that's bound to be deserted. Sea Ranch or maybe Ocean Ridge."

125

"Why along the coast?"

"Because you and I need to be at Touchstone. It's the one place we might find some peace."

Two hours later we lay in our own bed in our stone cottage by the sea. We'd tried to make love immediately upon arriving—a clothes-shedding, fever-pitch frenzy that hadn't been good for either of us. Too many demons for one heated act to banish, too little tenderness and emotional connection. Finally we gave it up as a bad idea and linked hands, resting side by side in the darkness. And that simple touch eased some of the pain, erased some of the horror.

Long after Hy drifted into restless sleep, I remained awake, thinking of Matty, Cutter, Matthews. For them it would always be night. No matter what lay ahead, Hy and I would at least see the morning.

Nine

Fog's hovering on the horizon like a goddamn turkey vulture. I'd just as soon head back to the Bay Area after we have our coffee."

I turned away from the refrigerator as Hy came into the main room of the cottage. "That's just as well—coffee's all we're getting. The bread we left here in September isn't fit for anything other than manufacturing penicillin."

He went to the window, opened the draperies, and stared glumly out to sea. "McCone, I've been thinking. Maybe we should ease off on

126

this crazy crusade before we're in too deep."

Maybe *I* should ease off on it was what he meant. As he'd said the night before, I had something to lose. He didn't.

"We're already in too deep," I told him. "Last night—"

"Jesus, I don't ever want to witness anything like that again. I had my fill of atrocities when I was ferrying rich refugees and drug lords out of war zones."

"I know." I poured coffee into yellow Fiesta ware cups and took one to him. He thanked me and sipped absently, his eyes still on the horizon. "Revenge aside," I added, "you're forgetting a couple of things: Matty hired me to find John, and now there's Zach to consider. He needs his father."

"Does he? His father's into something heavy that makes him dangerous to be around."

No disputing that. I took my coffee to the couch and curled up there, tucking my bare feet under the hem of my long robe. "Still," I said, "something's got to be done about the kid, and the first step to that is resolving the situation with his father."

"Can you afford a maybe lengthy investigation, on the amount Matty gave you as a retainer?"

"No, but I have an idea—" The phone rang. "Who the hell could've figured out we're here?" I said as I picked up.

"There you are!" Mick exclaimed. "I kept getting the machine at your house and the office, and your cell phone's dead."

"Oh, I must've forgotten to turn it back on when we landed last night."

"I suppose you also forgot about Ralph and Alice."

My cats. They'd surely make me answer for my long absence when I got home. "I may forget, but I don't neglect. I cut a deal with the kid next door to feed them if she doesn't see my car or lights."

"No wonder they looked so smug right before they chowed down on the can of Friskies I gave them."

"You went over there?"

"That's where I'm calling from. I got worried about you and wanted to make sure you hadn't been strangled in the shower."

"Nice lurid imagination you've got there."

"Runs in the family. Anyway, after I fed them it struck me that the airstrip you were talking about flying to last night is closer to the cottage than it is to the city, so I gave it a try."

"About that airstrip..." I glanced at Hy. "You and Keim haven't mentioned it to anybody, have you?"

"We know better than to talk about our investigations to outsiders. What's the matter, did something happen there?"

"I can't discuss it, but you'll probably see something about it on the TV news or in tomorrow's paper. That'll be the first time you've heard of the place."

"...Right."

"So why'd you call?"

"Well, for openers, Lottie located that Dr. Sandler, first name Robert. He's got a family practice in Los Alegres. She called his office and left a message on the machine for him to contact you, but here's the interesting thing: part of the recording said, 'If you're calling to schedule an FAA medical examination, we perform them on Tuesdays and Thursdays.'"

"That *is* interesting." Only certain doctors are authorized by the FAA to issue pilot medical certificates. Why would Matty have consulted one regarding John? Of course, Robert Sandler could also be the Seabrook family doctor....

"It's not nearly as interesting as what *I've* come up with," Mick said. "You were right about the Good Buy store; it's a small chain on the west coast of Florida. I accessed the Library of Congress for old indexes to newspapers in that area and found a few articles about a shooting in the parking lot of their Gulf Haven branch in March, ten years and eight months ago."

"That was fast! What're the details?"

"Well, the local paper there is too small to have full-text online, and of course their offices are closed for the weekend. So I downloaded a story from the Saint Petersburg Times. I'll read it to you."

I grabbed a pad and pencil and made notes while he read. When he finished, I asked, "Will you do me a favor? Make me a reservation on any flight after"—I glanced at my watch—"three this afternoon to anyplace within driving distance of Gulf Haven. Reserve a rental car, too."

"I don't care where I stay," Zach said. "Leave me here, stick me someplace else, it doesn't matter. Except I don't want to go back to Los Alegres." Sunk into an oversized armchair

129

in Rae and Ricky's living room, he appeared quite small in spite of his height.

Hank Zahn took off his horn-rimmed glasses and held them up to the light, looking for smudges. It was a delaying tactic I'd seen him use in the courtroom. "You must have some preference."

Zach shrugged.

Hank put on the glasses and transferred his gaze to me. "May I see you in the kitchen for a minute?"

I nodded and we went out there. The house was Sunday-evening quiet; Ricky had taken Molly and Lisa to the airport, and Rae was working in her home office—probably on the manuscript of a novel, which she'd so far refused to discuss with any of us.

Hank leaned against the butcher-block island, his arms folded across his blue ski sweater. "I know Zach's depressed and confused, but he isn't making it easy for me to decide what should be done for him."

"No."

"My recommendation has to be in the best interests of the child. With a boy of Zach's age, I like to take his wishes into consideration."

"Well, if it'll help any, I can definitely say that it's in the best interests of his safety to remain here with the RKI guard in place."

"In your opinion how significant is the threat to his life?"

"Very significant."

He ran his fingers through his wiry gray-brown hair. "Let me ask you a few questions. This client of yours who was killed—what was her relationship to the father?"

"Significant other, of close to a year's standing."

"And he left the boy in her care?"

"Yes. I have a letter from him to my client stating that was his intention."

"And she, in turn, left him in your care?"

"To ensure his safety."

"This was an oral agreement?"

"Yes."

"Any witnesses to it?"

"Only Zach."

He considered. "Now, the father—he's been missing how long?"

"Over a week."

"And there are no other living relatives?"

"If there are, I wouldn't know how to go about contacting them."

"And you're actively trying to locate the father?"

"Yes."

"How optimistic are you about your chances?"

I hesitated, wanting to pour out the whole story to Hank. I could trust him; he'd been a close friend since the days when we were housemates at U.C. Berkeley, and I often confided in him things I would tell few others. But even though he was my personal attorney, I wasn't sure whether the details of this conversation were protected by attorney-client privilege. Given how far over the line Hy and I had already strayed, I didn't want to place Hank in a position where he could be forced to testify against either of us.

He saw the conflict on my face. "Okay, I have every confidence in your abilities, so I'll assume your answer to my question is in the affirmative. And it's my opinion that Zach's best interests will be served by his remaining here until you can either locate the father or determine he's not locatable, or dead."

"It's a good call, Hank."

"I hope so; the legal situation is clouded at best. Did you say you're going to Florida tonight?"

"Yes, red-eye." It was the only flight on which I'd been able to get a reservation.

"May I ask who's financing the investigation now that your client's dead?"

I'd worked out the details of my plan on the way back from Touchstone; now was a good time to run them by Hank. "Tell me what you think of this: I didn't have a contract form with me when Matty—the client—hired me, but she did give me a check, which I cashed at her bank, and she wrote on it that it was a retainer. That constitutes an implied contract, right?"

He nodded.

"So I can assume that it's binding on me to carry out the terms of that contract—locate John Seabrook—so long as the retainer lasts. And it's possible that I could bill her estate for any excess fees."

"If there is an estate, yes."

"There is, in a way. The account that she drew the check on contains a sizable amount deposited there by John Seabrook by wire transfer the day Matty hired me. There's documentation in the letter I mentioned to prove the money was for the purpose of her taking care of and protecting Zach."

"Then any claim you make on a portion of

it would probably be valid and recognized as such."

"Okay, my fee and expenses are covered. But let's take it a step further: Suppose Zach retains you as his attorney? Kids can do that, as I recall from Habiba's situation last spring. Then, acting in his best interests, *you* could hire me to locate Seabrook."

"Shar, what's the difference? I'm glad to advise Zach free of charge."

"But if you hired me to investigate, your attorney-client privilege would extend to me. And I couldn't be forced to answer questions about the investigation."

Hank's eyes grew concerned, and he regarded me silently. The seconds stretched out till I turned away and began fiddling with a snapshot of Rae and Ricky that hung crooked from a magnet on the fridge. "So say something!" I finally exclaimed.

"Are you in trouble?"

"...No."

"Are you anticipating being in trouble?"

"Maybe."

"My advice to you is to stay out of it. But when have you ever taken my advice?"

"Uh, last year, when you told me to get my downspouts and gutters cleaned?"

"You see? A chance comment during a dinner party on a rainy night you paid attention to. The costly legal advice I've been giving you, you ignore."

"Hank—"

"I know—don't start. Okay, I'll need to see that letter about the money and Seabrook's reason for depositing it."

"Can't you just take my word that it exists?"

"No, I can't. Is there something in the letter that you don't want me to see?"

I was silent, trying to remember its exact wording.

"Oh, for God's sake, just make me a copy and black out whatever it is!"

I smiled and nodded.

"And now, before you drive me completely crazy, I suggest we go ask Zach if he even *wants* me as his attorney."

"He will. Rae tells me Habiba's been singing your praises all weekend."

Ten

Monday morning: Gulf Haven, Florida

"Normally I'd tell you to get the hell out of my office and my jurisdiction," Lieutenant Mack Gifford of the Gulf Haven PD said. "I don't like private operators, and your California license doesn't mean squat here."

Framing a reply, I watched the lieutenant shake a cigarette out of a pack on his desk and fumble in his shirt pocket for a Bic. He was lean and wiry, with a narrow face and a thin-lipped mouth bracketed with deep lines of discontent. His soft southern accent—from one of the border states, perhaps?—blunted the impact of his words but not the force of what I took to be controlled anger in his dark eyes.

"You say 'normally.'"

"Yeah." He exhaled a stream of smoke toward the ceiling of his small office. "But you say you're interested in the Marie Fuller case, and that gives us something in common. Let me see if I've got this straight: you're looking for a man who you think is Ron Fuller, who's been living in your state under an assumed name. Routine skip trace."

"Right."

"He must've skipped owing a lot, for you to come all this way."

"My client's a well-financed attorney, and I've got to admit that I became intrigued when I turned up this former identity. Particularly since the man's wife was murdered."

Gifford's expression was noncommittal; I couldn't tell if he had bought my story or not. When he didn't speak, I prompted him. "You were the investigating officer..."

"My bad luck to catch the call. Case has been a thorn in my side for over ten years now— enough of a pain to make me break my rules and talk with you." He pushed away from the desk and swiveled slightly, looking at a No Smoking sign posted on the wall. "Of course," he added with a wry twist of his lips, "I break my rules a lot."

I smiled faintly, waiting.

"We got a lot of rules, laws, whatever around here," Gifford went on. "Most don't need too much enforcing. We got the usual problems with drugs and disappointment, but on the whole, that's about it."

"Drugs I understand; they're everywhere. But what's this about disappointment?"

"Ms. McCone, what d'you know about our community?"

"Only what I observed driving in."

135

"Then maybe this'll help you put the Fuller business in perspective. Gulf Haven is one of those places nobody's from; it barely existed thirty years ago. Wasn't much here to recommend the area; it's not even on the Gulf, just the river. But then a developer came along, bought the land cheap, dredged the canals, put houses with private docks along them. Folks sick of the winters up north snapped them up: retirees, of course, but young people and families as well.

"The retirees, they come here and find that everyday Florida life ain't like it was on their vacations, sipping fancy rum drinks around the hotel pools in Miami or Lauderdale. Instead, it's heat and boredom and waiting around for the monthly visit from the cockroach exterminator. A lot of them take to hanging out at the air-conditioned mall; others die out of sheer discouragement, and a fair number kill themselves one way or another. The younger ones, they find the job market's bad in this part of the state; they've got to take low-end positions they wouldn't've even considered up north. The smart ones cut their losses, pack up, go home. The dumb ones—it's drink and drugs and domestic violence, all of which lead to too many homicides."

"More than in other places?"

"Eight, nine percent higher than the average. Suicide pacts. Wives killing husbands. Husbands killing wives. Parents killing their kids. Drunken shootings at parties." He paused, looking squarely at me. "What we do *not* have, however, is shootings that look like contract hits."

"You mean the Marie Fuller homicide?"

"Yes, ma'am. One bullet, a twenty-two, placed right in the heart. A clean, cold kill. Nobody saw the shooter; he was methodical and cool, disappeared into a panicky crowd. By the time I got to the scene, he was probably clear of the area. I knew we'd never make a collar, but I started going through the motions. And then Ron Fuller and his son turned up missing."

"How soon after the murder?"

"Immediately. I never got to question him. Didn't even know he was on the scene till one of my men interviewed a neighbor of the Fullers who'd talked with Marie in the store. Mrs. Fuller said she was in a hurry because it was hot and her husband and son were waiting outside in a car with a busted air conditioner."

"Fuller just drove away and left his wife lying there?"

"Apparently. Pretty callous, wouldn't you say?"

On the surface, yes, but he'd probably known there was nothing he could do for his wife and had opted to save his son and himself. "Did Fuller go home or leave town straight from the store?"

"Don't know. None of their neighbors saw him. Doesn't prove anything one way or the other."

"What happened to their house and possessions?"

"House was a rental. After my team went through the personal effects, I told the landlord to store them. Guess by now they've been disposed of."

"You find anything significant?"

"No. Their stuff was cheap and relatively new. There weren't any personal papers, keepsakes, letters—nothing. The Fullers were people without much of a present or a past."

"And you say you canvassed the neighbors?"

"Yeah. Nobody knew anything about the family. They didn't socialize, didn't have any more contact than the usual polite greetings and talk about the weather."

"What did Fuller do for a living?"

"He claimed to be a freelance writer."

"Claimed?"

"Have you ever heard of a writer who doesn't own a computer or a typewriter?"

"He paid his bills, though?"

"On time, on an account at a local bank. Except for the house rental; his brother rented the place before the family moved here and continued to send a check the first of each month."

So Seabrook had a brother. "You recall his name?"

"Sure—Dave Fuller. But when we tried to locate him, it turned out he'd never lived at the address printed on the checks. The credit report the landlord pulled on him belonged to somebody else." Gifford laughed humorlessly. "That Dave Fuller worked for the U.S. Marshals Service and was not amused at somebody else benefiting from his good record."

Another dead end. "And you never came up with a suspect?"

"No, and I never will. It's my opinion that Ron Fuller ordered the hit on his wife—had

138

been planning it for some time, whatever his reasons. Now that you tell me he's been living in California under an assumed name, it makes me wonder: has any other woman died because of him?"

I stepped out of the police station into a glaring noon sun and reached for my dark glasses. The day was balmy, in the mid-seventies—a far cry from the weather during my last visit to Florida. Then it had been hot and muggy, adding to my irritation as I tried to get out of the state while eluding another private investigator who was bound and determined to stick close to me.

Why was it, I thought, that Floridians conspired to annoy me? For the past thirty minutes Mack Gifford had peppered me with questions about my investigation. I'd sidestepped them, claiming an extension of attorney-client privilege, and that had prompted him to issue an ultimatum: tell him everything I knew about Ron Fuller's present whereabouts or leave his jurisdiction immediately. I replied—quite truthfully—that I hadn't the faintest idea where Fuller was. Gifford chose not to believe me and showed me out.

As I pulled out of the station parking lot in my rented Ford, a squad car started up and followed. Apparently I was being escorted out of town. I drove a few blocks, watching it in the rearview mirror, then made a series of turns that took me to the highway leading to the airport at Fort Myers. A sleek white bridge rose over the river; when I reached its crest I saw the squad car pull onto the shoulder and make a U-turn. Gifford might not have taken my statements at face value, but my actions had satisfied his officer. I continued across the bridge, found a place to make a turn of my own, and headed back to Gulf Haven.

The main street resembled a strip mall rather than a town. Its buildings were low concrete rectangles painted in pastel colors, none more than three stories high except for a bank that towered above the rest and looked out of place. Sandy vacant lots indicated a lack of planning or perhaps cash-flow difficulties on the part of the developer, and the spindly palm trees on the sidewalks were yellow- and dry-leafed, as though they had a disease. On the drive in from the airport the flatness of the terrain and the sparseness of the vegetation had depressed me; now the town made my spirits plunge lower. Keeping an eye out for police cars, I pulled into a parking space and consulted the map the rental-car company had provided; then I set out for the Fullers' former neighborhood.

The residents of Gulf Breeze Drive appeared to be losing a battle against browning lawns and sickly plants. The one-story pastel homes backed up on a narrow canal, and sail- and powerboats were moored at many of their docks. The Fullers' former house—number 318—had an entryway flanked by orange trees; most of the fruit lay rotting on the ground, a cloying odor rising from it. I rang the bell, but nobody answered.

At the house to its right a young woman responded to my knock on her screen door.

No, she told me, she hadn't known the Fullers; she and her husband had moved down from Brooklyn only the year before. "You could try Mr. Simmons," she added. "Number three-sixteen. He's retired and has been here for-ever."

Mr. Simmons didn't look old enough to be retired, much less to have lived anyplace "forever." Trim and tanned, wearing only shorts and boat shoes, he wasn't a day over fifty. When I showed him John Seabrook's photo-graph, he said he remembered the Fullers well and invited me into an airy green-and-white living room where, in spite of the day's coolness, a ceiling fan turned briskly. Outside the patio door a swimming pool sparkled in the sunlight, and in the canal beyond it a cabin cruiser rode on the wake generated by a passing speedboat.

Simmons said, "I was about to have a beer. Will you join me?"

"Yes, thanks." I followed him into the adjoining kitchen and watched him open cans and pour into pilsner glasses. A pot of some-thing that smelled like marinara sauce simmered on the stove; a portable radio was playing classical music. Simmons motioned for me to be seated at the white rattan dinette table and set a glass in front of me.

"So why are you looking for Ron and Billy?" he asked.

His tone had been warm when he said he remembered them; the skip-trace story would destroy our rapport. I gave him an abbrevi-ated version of the truth: Fuller had disappeared, abandoning his son, and I'd been hired to locate him. "Very often," I added, "the key to a person's present lies in his past. What can you tell me about the family?"

"Well, you know how Marie died?"

Of course that was what he'd remember most clearly. "Yes."

"Terrible tragedy. She was such a nice woman. When they moved in next door, I was in the middle of a very bad period; my wife had left me, and I was taking it hard—going a little crazy, actually. Marie Fuller went out of her way to do things for me: a casserole when she noticed I wasn't eating properly, the occasional dinner invitation. Ron helped me repair my dock when a storm damaged it. And the little boy was a delight; they adored him. I can't imagine Ron abandoning Billy."

"He may not have done it voluntarily. Did the Fullers socialize with any of the other neighbors?"

"No, I was the only one they made an exception for. I suppose they felt safe with me. On the whole, I'm a pretty innocuous fellow, and they sensed I was wounded too."

"What do you mean, wounded? In their case, that is."

"I never did find out the details, but there was something in their past that made them extremely fearful. They stuck close to the house, except to run the necessary errands. The blinds were always closed; the doors, too. They even put up shades on their screened porch. Frankly, I was surprised when Ron offered to help me with the dock, and I noticed that he kept glancing at the boats that passed, as if he was afraid someone on board might harm him."

"Did he ever discuss his fears with you?"

"No. I'd finally made up my mind to broach the subject when Marie was killed and Ron and Billy disappeared."

"Did you see Ron after the shooting? Speak with him?"

"I tried. That afternoon I was watching an old movie on TV when they broke in with a news bulletin. Naturally I went over to Ron's house to see if there was anything I could do. A man came to the door; he said he was Ron's brother and that he had the situation in hand."

"Odd way of phrasing it. Can you describe him?"

"About my age now—forty-nine. Short blond hair, cleanshaven, wearing a tan business suit. There wasn't anything particularly memorable about his appearance or speech, but he made me uneasy. Ron had never mentioned having a brother in the area, and the man didn't look enough like him to be closely related."

"So you didn't even get inside the house?"

"No, I didn't. There was a gray Buick, this county's plates, in the driveway. I came home and watched. A few minutes later the blond and a dark-haired man came out with suitcases and loaded them into the Buick. Then Ron and the boy drove away in it with the blond. They didn't seem to be under duress, but still, I wondered. The dark-haired man went back inside; fifteen minutes later he hauled some cartons out to Ron's car and drove away in it. And that was the last I saw or heard of the Fullers."

I thought over the scenario he'd described. "Mr. Simmons, did the police come around to question you about the Fullers?"

"Yes, within fifteen minutes of the time the second man left the house."

"Did you tell them any of this?"

"...No."

"Why not?"

"I suppose I felt protective of Ron and the boy. The officer who interviewed me hinted that Ron might've been involved in Marie's death in some way, and I knew that couldn't be true. As one who had suffered through a marriage where the love was one-sided, I'd come to recognize genuine mutual caring. Ron loved Marie very much."

I thought of Fuller's wedding band, still preserved among his treasures, and nodded. "Do you know who the Fullers' landlord was?"

"A local real-estate broker named Suzie Kurth. She has her own firm, Kurth Associates, on the boulevard."

I thanked Simmons for his time, and he showed me to the door, but once I was outside, he seemed reluctant to let me go. "You know," he said, "Marie's death was a wake-up call for me. Before that, I was an insurance broker, always hustling to make the Million Dollar Roundtable. But when she was killed so randomly, I saw that none of it mattered and took my retirement. I've never regretted the decision."

Maybe Matty's death should have been a wake-up call for me, but instead it had spurred me on to my own brand of hustling. I wasn't sure that was good, but it was the only kind of response that I knew.

"Yes, Mack Gifford inventoried the contents of the house, but I didn't store the Fullers' things." Suzie Kurth shook her curly blond head and glanced impatiently at her watch. Time was a precious commodity; there were commissions to be earned, and I wasn't a prospect.

"What happened to them?"

"Suzie," the receptionist said, "the title company's on line one."

"Take a message. I've got an appointment at that Harborside property in fifteen minutes." She started for the door, motioning for me to follow. "Now, what did you ask me?"

"The Fullers' things—what happened to them?"

"Oh, right." She held the door open for me, and we stepped out onto the sidewalk. The sky had clouded over, and there was a hint of rain on the air. Kurth sniffed it and muttered, "Should have brought my umbrella."

"The Fullers... ?"

"Let me think." She closed her eyes, jingling a set of keys. "That's it—the brother. He came with a U-Haul, took everything away."

"Ron Fuller's brother?"

"Right. First name Larry."

"Do you recall what he looked like?"

"A hunk, if you like guys with button-down collars."

"Age? Hair color?"

"Early thirties. Brown hair, dark. Blue eyes. But not my type at all."

145

Different brother—more likely no relation. "Had Gifford given you permission to release the things?"

"No, but he'd been through them, so I figured it was okay to let a relative have them. And Gifford never asked after them again." She glanced at her watch once more. "Is that all you need? I've got to be going."

"I'd like to see the Fullers' lease, if it's still on file."

"Sorry, I don't keep paperwork that long. Frankly, that house has been a pain in the ass; all my tenants keep getting divorced or dying."

"A bad-luck place, I guess."

Kurth regarded me sternly. "Ms. McCone, there are no bad-luck houses, only bad-luck people."

I pulled into the parking lot of the Good Buy store and stopped next to the line of scraggly pines at its perimeter. Ten years and eight months had passed since John Seabrook—a.k.a. Ron Fuller—had watched from this spot as his wife was gunned down. Over ten years, and what did I expect to gain from a visit here besides the morbid feelings that nightmares thrive on?

All the same, I sat there watching the shoppers enter and leave. Imagined a faceless woman in a pink dress waving to her husband and son across the lot. Heard the sound of gunfire, the screams of the crowd. After a moment I shut my eyes and the sounds intermingled with an explosion and the screams of the spectators at the air show. The images became confused: Matty, waggling her fingers in a victory sign at me...

the woman in the pink dress, waving… my panicky run toward the flaming wreckage… John Seabrook's panicky move to save his son…

The stuff my worst nightmares were made of, on a balmy Florida afternoon with the sun peeking through the gravid clouds and a rainbow forming.

I opened my eyes and forced the bad feelings down, kept them at bay as I turned my attention to what my next move should be. No use in questioning the people at the grocery store; ten years was a long time as memories went, a long time as job tenure went, too.

Think, McCone. Think about what happened that day.

"One bullet, a twenty-two, placed right in the heart. A clean, cold kill."

A clean kill, and later a clean disappearance of Marie Fuller's family. Husband and son spirited away by two strangers claiming to be relatives, leaving most of their possessions behind. Most of their possessions and Marie Fuller's body. How could the man Matty had known as John Seabrook leave his wife unclaimed in the morgue, when he'd preserved his wedding band in its velvet box for over ten years after her death?

He'd had no choice about leaving.

I sat still for a few more minutes, an idea forming. Then I took out my phone, deciding to run the idea by the person whose judgment I trusted most. But Hy wasn't at my house or at RKI's San Francisco offices. I checked my office, then Rae and Ricky's house on the off chance he'd paid Zach a visit. No one had seen him. But when I called the terminal at Oakland

Airport's north field and spoke with a friend of ours who worked in the office, I found he'd flown out early that morning.

"VFR?" I asked.

"VFR, and quite evasive about his destination. All he'd tell anybody was 'Up and around.'"

Now I was concerned. Quickly I phoned Touchstone. No answer. The same at his ranch near Tufa Lake. Hy was on the move and being secretive—always a bad sign.

Well, there was nothing I could do about that now. I ran down a mental checklist, then called my friend Adah Joslyn at SFPD Homicide.

"McCone! How the hell are you? You must be out of shape in a major way; I haven't seen you at the health club in weeks."

"I've been swamped with work. Listen, are you still in contact with Craig Morland?" Morland was an FBI agent based in Washington, D.C., who had been on temporary assignment in San Francisco earlier that year. He'd been supportive of Joslyn when she got herself into some serious trouble, and I suspected only distance had prevented the relationship from becoming a romantic one.

Testily she said, "How are you, Adah? Oh, I'm fine, McCone. Sorry I haven't been in touch, Adah. Oh, that's all right."

"I *am* sorry—okay? But I'm calling on my cell phone at seventy-five cents a minute, plus long distance from Florida, and this is important."

"And there I was, thinking you'd phoned me up to ask me about my love life."

I pictured her: slumped low in her swivel chair, long legs stretched out and crossed at the ankles, wearing one of her elegant outfits and a playful smile on her honey-tan face.

"So you are still in touch with Craig. I really need to talk with him—today."

"I'll give you his number at the Bureau."

"No, that won't do. He can't talk about what I need to ask him on a Justice Department line, and he won't want to answer my questions, anyway. You're the only person I know who can persuade him to."

"Well, I'm a good little persuader where Craig's concerned. You said this is important?"

"Yes."

"I'll call him, see what I can do, and get back to you."

"Thanks, Adah."

"You know, McCone, sometimes I wonder if it was worth it."

"If what was worth it?"

"You saving my goddamn life. I'd always heard that when you save a person's life you're responsible for them, have to look out for them from then on. But ever since you saved mine, *I've* been looking out for *you*."

After I flipped the phone closed, I remained in the parking lot, watching the ebb and flow of customers at the Good Buy store.

Other people come to Florida for the sun and the beach, I told myself, but not you. *You* come to stare obsessively at the spot where a woman you never knew died violently over ten years ago. This kind of morbid focus is dangerous.

But I couldn't bring myself to start the car and drive away.

A trio of young mothers came out of the store, laughing, their offspring belted securely into the carrier seats of their heavily laden carts. Two teenage boys skimmed along on skateboards, calling to each other. An older couple went over their list before they entered, sharing both the weekly chore and an easy closeness that comes of happy years together. A bag boy accurately sailed a cart toward a long linked chain of carts he was preparing to return to the store, and in reward received a smile from a pretty blonde.

Everybody going about the many small acts that weave the fabric of our daily lives—and none realizing how quickly that fabric can be torn by an event such as a single gunshot.

Suddenly I felt an isolation so severe that hollow pain spread under my breastbone. I looked at my watch. There was a flight to Miami in fifty minutes. I could catch it, connect with the afternoon nonstop for San Francisco. Go home, tell Hank it was impossible to locate John Seabrook, let him deal with the problem of Zach. Tell Hy we had to abandon our vengeful and potentially disastrous course. Take up a normal, connected life.

Sure. And cats can fly from nine stories high.

A normal, connected life was an illusion, at least for me. Perhaps there had been some semblance of one when I was a fresh-faced high school cheerleader. But even then my bouncy coordination and flashing smile and perky mannerisms had concealed private demons.

150

And in the end the effort had been too much for me; my facade had crumbled the day I turned my last cartwheel.

"Craig took a lot of persuading," Joslyn said, "and the only way he'll talk with you is in person."

"Where and when?"

"Eight o'clock tonight, at Raffles Bar in Georgetown." She gave me the address, near DuPont Circle. "Can you make it?"

"I'm sure there's an available flight from Miami to D.C. within that time frame."

"I'll confirm it with him, then. Call me if you have a problem." She hesitated. "McCone, something's going on with Craig. I can't get a handle on it, but we talk on the phone a couple of times a week, and he's... different."

"How so?"

"Just different. See if you can pick up on it, and try to figure it out. Tell you the truth, I'm kind of afraid for him."

Eleven

Monday evening: Washington, D.C.

Adah was right: Craig Morland had changed.

When I stepped through the door of the small dark bar in Georgetown, I at first thought the FBI agent had failed to keep our appointment. But then I saw a slender man in sweats and running shoes get up from one of the stools and come toward me. I'd never known Morland to wear anything other than a suit and tie, even when he wasn't working, and I'd certainly never seen him sporting a mustache, with his dusty brown hair grown longish. Outer manifestations of what was going on inside, perhaps, but an improvement on the staid and rather colorless man I'd known last spring. So why was Adah concerned?

But then I clasped his outstretched hand and looked into his eyes. Saw there what she'd undoubtedly sensed, but could put no more name to it than she had.

Morland ordered me a glass of wine and himself another Scotch, and we took our drinks to a banquette toward the rear. As he sat down, he glanced around at the other patrons as if to reassure himself that we were well out of their earshot. Then he leaned across the table toward me and said in a low voice, "So what are these questions you told Adah I won't want to answer?"

"Actually, I've got a scenario I want to run by you first."

In detail I outlined the Marie Fuller homicide and the disappearance of her husband and son. "What does that sound like to you?"

He shrugged. "It could be one of many things. Why're you asking me?"

"Because I think the two men at the Fuller house were from the Justice Department. More specifically, the U.S. Marshals Service."

"Why? Because the man whose credit rating was used to rent the house was with the marshals?"

"That's part of my reasoning, but there's more. The Fullers acted as though they were afraid of retaliation for something they'd done. Mack Gifford says Marie's killing was a contract hit, and it does sound that way; even the newspaper accounts picked up on it. The Fullers' neighbor claims they had no friends and never mentioned a relative in the area, but Ron was able to summon the men who got him and his son out of town immediately after the shooting."

Morland nodded, eyes narrowed thoughtfully.

I went on, "The neighbor went over to Fuller's house after the shooting; he didn't believe the man who came to the door was Ron's brother, but he also said he didn't sense that Fuller and his son were under duress when they left. To me, it sounds the way things would go if the family was in the federal Witness Protection Program."

"I've always suspected you had an overactive imagination." But Craig's smile didn't reach his eyes.

"*Is* that the way it would go?"

"It might be. Or it might not."

"Did they teach you to duck questions like that at the FBI Academy?"

"Actually, it's a self-acquired skill." He signaled for another round of drinks—stalling for time.

I asked, "Will you refresh my memory about the program?"

"No reason I shouldn't; we make no secret of it."

"I've heard it called both the Witness Protection Program and the Witness Security Program. Which is it?"

He shrugged. "Either, I suppose. I've heard

people refer to it as Sec Sec, meaning Security Section. But they also call it the Protection Program, so take your pick."

Only in the federal bureaucracy could the individuals responsible for a program be unable to agree upon its name.

Craig went on, "It began in the early seventies as a joint operation of the Bureau, Justice's Criminal Division, and the Marshals Service. The marshals run it."

"And it's mainly designed for people who testify against organized crime figures?"

"Originally that was its purpose, yes. But protected witnesses have also testified against non-mob-affiliated drug dealers, gunrunners—you name it. In addition, we established the Short Term Protection Program in the early nineties, for witnesses who don't require permanent relocation. And various other jurisdictions—New York, for example—have their own programs. It used to be that witness intimidation was something associated with the higher levels of organized crime, but now it extends all the way down to your lowest street criminal. Nobody hesitates at taking out a witness anymore. So you see, when I say your scenario might or might not be how it would go with the program, I'm not really ducking the question. The Fullers could've been under the protection of any number of jurisdictions—or none at all."

"How likely do you think it is that they were in some program?"

"I'd say it's a good possibility."

"And if the threat to them was of a serious, long-term nature, wouldn't it be logical that Justice was the department involved?"

He remained silent while the waiter delivered our drinks, watched him walk away before replying. "Why do you assume it was serious and long-term?"

"Because Ron Fuller, under another identity, is still running scared over ten years later."

Morland raised an eyebrow.

"That's all I can tell you. Client confidentiality—I was hired by an attorney."

"There's been some debate on the legality of that premise."

"Okay, maybe I could be ordered to testify before a grand jury, but I don't have to volunteer information to you or any other law-enforcement officer."

"Unless you're obstructing an active investigation."

"To my knowledge, there isn't any."

He smiled skeptically.

"Okay," I said, anxious to get off that tack, "witnesses who enter the federal program are relocated, given new jobs, new documentation, new names?"

"In legal closed-court proceedings. The identity changes are strictly legitimate; we can't have our administrators perpetrating fraud."

I hadn't known that, and it argued against John and Zach Seabrook being new identities created for the Fullers by the government. The birth certificates that I'd found in John's files had most certainly been acquired by a widely used illegitimate method—so widely used that by now most departments of vital statistics had instituted safeguards against it.

Ignoring that hitch for the moment, I continued, "Say I've testified against someone and received threats. How do I go about getting into the program?"

"You request it through the party at Justice who's handling the case. If you're accepted, you go to the nearest U.S. Marshals office and read a document called an MOU—Memorandum of Understanding. It outlines the conditions of the program. If you can live with them, you initial the MOU page by page, sign it, surrender all your old I.D., and you're in. A deputy marshal is assigned to protect you, arrange for your new identity, relocate you. Afterward, if you have problems or an emergency arises, you can call on him."

"Do people ever turn the program down?"

"Some do. Its conditions are pretty stringent."

"Such as?"

"Most important is that you never go back to what we call the danger zone—the location where the threat is most severe. That's usually the person's home, where all his or her family and friends are. You also can't go places where you know anyone, so that rules out the rest of your relatives and friends. Nobody from your past life can phone you; you can call them, but the marshals prefer you don't. Any mail you receive from people in your past has to go through a post-office box held by the Marshals Service, and packages—like Christmas or birthday presents—are forbidden."

"That's got to be tough."

"On a normal person, it is. Say you have aging parents: You tell them good-bye, knowing you'll never see them again unless they're on their deathbed or in their coffin. When they do die, you're not allowed to attend the funeral; a private viewing in the presence of a deputy marshal is all the closure you'll have."

"I see what you mean."

"Oh, there's more. You can't practice your former profession, and any job you're likely to get will be low-level because you don't have a verifiable résumé. You can't go back to college or retrain because you don't have access to your transcripts. You can't enjoy your former hobbies. You become afraid to make new friends because you might let something slip, might call your spouse or kids by their real names. If you're unmarried, you can't develop any truly intimate relationships because one of the conditions of the program is that you tell no one about your past. And while you have genuine documentation—Social Security card, driver's license, birth certificate—you don't have a credit rating or personal health records. Everything about you, everything you worked your whole life for, is erased."

As he spoke, Morland's normally soft voice had become louder and emotional. He must have heard himself, because he glanced around and lowered it. "I guess you can tell this subject really gets me going. The program does the most for the least deserving people, like low-level mob figures looking to get a fresh start. The innocent bystanders who just happen to witness a crime and the good citizens who think they're doing the right thing by coming forward—they're the ones who suffer."

"You sound as though you've had some experience with people in the program."

"A number of my informants have entered it; some could hack it, some couldn't. A few got to the point where they felt safe, went back to their old habits and haunts; they were recognized and killed.

"I'll give you one example: nice middle-aged woman, unmarried, an accountant with close family connections and an active social and volunteer life. She uncovered massive money laundering at a firm where she was temporarily employed and came to us with the information. The threats started before the trials, and afterward she requested permanent protection. The marshals relocated her from Virginia to New Mexico. The only job they bothered to find for her was as a clerk at a pizza chain. They rented her a crappy apartment and told her she was on her own. She went to work, holed up in the evenings and on the weekends, made no friends, did nothing.

"After a while the isolation and dislocation got to her. The deputy marshal assigned to her was indifferent. That happens sometimes. He told her to adapt or leave the program. Finally she called me, asking if I could persuade the marshals to move her someplace else or at least arrange for a better job. I couldn't, and she must've interpreted my failure to mean I was indifferent, too, because she stopped calling. Six weeks later she broke the rules and made a secret visit to her family in Virginia—the danger zone. The marshals found out and terminated her from the program. She returned home and within the month was shot to death while crossing the street to go to a job interview."

"That's horrible!"

"Yeah. And she's not an isolated case. What's even worse is that the scum out there—some of whom you'll find in the very best of company—think nothing of blowing people like her away. And what's the absolute worst is that there's nothing Justice can, or sometimes will, do about it."

"What do you mean—nothing they *will* do about it?"

He looked down into his drink and after a moment muttered, "God, why am I doing this?"

I waited.

He made eye contact again, and now I identified what I'd earlier seen: edginess and anger, and an emptiness.

"Sharon, you're the last person I should be telling what I'm about to—but maybe that's the reason I will. Try to remember that this conversation never took place."

I nodded.

"Every year, the Justice Department receives referrals of close to a hundred thousand criminal matters from various federal investigatory agencies. The U.S. attorneys review and dispose of them—either by deciding to charge or by deciding not to make a case. What percentage of that hundred thousand do you think is disposed of without charges being filed?"

"I couldn't begin to guess."

"Over sixty percent. Granted, many are without merit, or there're serious problems with the evidence or witnesses. But others—"

A couple had taken the booth opposite us. Morland glanced at them, then slid around the banquette until he was close beside me.

Putting his hand on mine and speaking low, as if we were having a lovers' tryst, he went on. "Let's take a hypothetical case. Say our San Francisco office has been investigating a businessman who happens to have been a major contributor to the president's campaign fund. The identity of the hypothetical president can vary according to your party affiliation. Anyway, we turn up solid evidence against the businessman of fronting money for drug deals. The matter goes to the U.S. attorney out there, and after review, he decides not to make a perfectly good case. Now, why do you suppose that happens?"

I shook my head.

"It happens because the businessman has called his senator, whose campaign fund he also contributed to. The senator has placed a friendly call to the Oval Office. In turn, the Oval Office has called the attorney general, who is appointed by and responsible to the president. Next thing you know, the U.S. attorney in San Francisco is told to let the matter drop or start looking for another job."

"It really happens that way?"

"Damn right it happens." Morland's fingers were rigid on my hand, his eyes now hard and angry.

I said, "You sound more than disillusioned with the system."

"Way more. It's been a gradual process. When I joined the Bureau I was pretty green; I couldn't believe that that kind of deal could be cut, much less that Justice could be party to it. Later on, I tried to rationalize: political stability is essential to the national good; we can't allow the reputations of our high elected officials to be dirtied. Well, after a while I decided that was a crock, but still I told myself, This is the way our system works; it sucks, but it works."

"And now?"

"Now you know why I let Adah talk me into meeting with you tonight. I just don't give a shit anymore. I've turned into a loose cannon, and I'm setting myself up to take a fall."

"Why?"

He looked away from me, lips tightening. "A combination of things. The specifics aren't important."

"Is one of them all the nonsense that went down around the Diplo-bomber investigation last spring?"

"Yeah, one of them." His eyes met mine again. "That's enough about me. What else do you need?"

"If the Fullers actually were in the Witness Protection Program, is there any way I could get the details?"

"Sure. Our ADPT—automatic data processing and telecommunications equipment and services—isn't as secure as it should be. About half a million insiders have access to it, and there's always someone who'll misuse information for fun or profit. Or for the sake of old times. Of course, you and this insider would be committing a crime."

He was teetering on the same invisible line I'd crossed so many times. Some of those crossings I regretted, and I couldn't make myself give him the shove he was asking for.

"There's no legal way?"

"...Well, you could work it from the other end."

"How?"

"You know when Marie Fuller was killed. You know the husband's still running scared. That indicates he was the primary target, the witness. If the threat was that serious, that long-term, there should be publicly available documentation of the circumstances that produced it."

"I hear what you're saying."

"And I understand why you're refusing my offer. It'll still be open if the legal way doesn't work. But go ahead and try it from the other end first. You know how to do it."

I didn't, not exactly—but Mick would.

Twelve

Tuesday morning: San Francisco

Alice, my calico cat, ran ahead of me up the front steps of my house and pawed frantically at the door. I juggled my purse and travel bag while trying to fit the key into the lock.

"Don't panic," I told her. "I'm here, all's well."

Neither Allie nor her orange tabby brother, Ralph, was a night creature; in fact, they hated to be left out after dark. I was sure they'd been inside on Sunday night, and I'd given the Curley kid next door explicit instructions to confine them to the house in my absence, but it seemed that at least one of the wily beasts had slipped out—and now heartily regretted it.

Gray light filtered through the windows of

my parlor and guest room, dissipating the gloom in the hall. I reset the security system as Allie streaked toward the kitchen—intent, no doubt, on her food bowl. Yawning widely, I dragged the bag that I hadn't opened the whole time I'd been away toward my bedroom at the rear of the house.

I'd caught a series of red-eye flights across the country—preferring motion over a hotel room or long hours at the D.C. airport—and now felt justifiably rumpled and cranky. While I'd slept heavily on the planes, I'd more or less navigated SFO, the shuttle to the parking lot, and the drive home on autopilot. I badly needed coffee and a shower. In my haste I didn't bother to turn on the lights in the sitting room, miscalculated where an end table was, and banged the bag against it. The lamp toppled onto the couch, and someone moaned in protest. Startled, I fumbled for the switch and put on the overhead.

Hy squinted up at me over the edge of a brightly patterned cotton throw. His dark blond curls resembled a clown's wig, his eyes were red, and he wore two days' worth of stubble on his chin. "Jesus, McCone, are you trying to wake the dead?"

My surprise turned to relief, followed swiftly by annoyance. I'd been calling everywhere for him between flights, and he'd been here the whole time. "Why did you let my calls go on the machine?"

"What'd you find out in Florida?"

"Where were you all of yesterday?"

"What the hell time is it, anyway?"

"Where's Ralph? Are you the one who let Allie out?"

He grinned and sat up, running his fingers through his tangled hair. "This isn't getting us anyplace. Ralph was asleep in the guest room the last I saw him. Allie might've sneaked out, I guess. I only got here a couple of hours ago, and the phone hasn't rung. And as far as the more complicated stuff goes, you're up first. What'd you find out?"

"Why don't you put some coffee on before we talk. I need to shower."

"Deal."

By the time I wrapped myself in my long white terry-cloth robe and went to the kitchen, the coffee had brewed. Hy paused in pouring it, looked at me, and said, "What is it about you in that robe that turns me on?"

"I can't imagine. It hides virtually every inch of my body."

"Maybe that's it—the mystery factor. Come here and give me a kiss."

I went to him, pleasure sharpening as he wrapped me in his arms. Even the rasp of his stubble against my face didn't dull the odd combination of excitement and safety that I always felt on coming home to him. After a moment he stepped back and held me at arm's length, saying, "I think I'll buy you one of these robes in every color, just in case they stop making them."

"Do that. In the meantime..."

"Coffee."

We took our mugs to the sitting room, pushing aside the throw and cushion he'd had bunched up under his head. "You know, I do own such a convenience as a bed," I told him. "You didn't have to await my return on the couch."

"I planned to go to bed, believe me, but I lay down here to rest my eyes, and next thing I knew, a lamp was falling on me. So how was the trip?"

"Fruitful. I ended up in Washington, D.C." As I filled him in on the past twenty-four hours, I could see him becoming quietly excited.

"McCone, that's good stuff. Now let me tell you what I've been doing, and we'll see how all this fits together. Yesterday morning I got to thinking about that mechanic, Ed Cutter. It occurred to me that if somebody wanted to approach him about planting a device in Matty's plane, they couldn't just go in cold, now, could they?"

"Not very likely. Cutter, as you said, appeared devoted to Matty; anybody who knew that would've been hesitant to approach him."

"Right. So it figures that whoever put Cutter up to it—and later killed him—knew something about him that we didn't."

I nodded. "Something that would lead him or her to believe he was the man for the job. Maybe something the person could use as leverage to get Cutter to take the job."

"My exact reasoning. So here's what I did: Since early yesterday morning Two-eight-niner and I have flown all over northern California. I've fueled up enough times to put a serious balance on my credit card, spoken to God knows how many linemen, mechanics, pilots, and fixed-base operators. I've drunk about eighty-seven cups of coffee,

165

eaten six cheeseburgers, and collected dozens of rentals and repairs price lists from the FBOs—all of this so I could ask questions without seeming too obvious.

"I'd land, chat up whoever was around, and then I'd say, 'Hey, you hear about those murders at the strip over near Healdsburg Saturday night?' Of course everybody had. Then I'd say, 'You know either of those guys?' A fair number of people had. And the upshot of all that chatting—to say nothing of probably ruining my stomach lining—is that Ed Cutter was dirty. Matthews, too."

"In what way?"

"That's the interesting part. Nobody could—or would—pin it down for me. But there's this widespread perception that the word was out: you want something done, see Cutter or Matthews." He laughed, shaking his head. "I should've known something was wrong at that strip. Now that I think back on my conversation with Matthews at Willits, I realize he was very interested in the fact that I'd worked for K-Air. He'd been in Southeast Asia himself, and their rep wasn't any too clean. I'll bet when he asked me if I wanted to pick up some work, he was feeling me out about doing some flying below radar level."

"Transporting contraband."

"Right."

I thought about that as I sipped coffee. "Okay, what was Cutter's role in this?"

"Probably making undocumented modifications to aircraft—things that, if they were noted in the logs, would've tipped the FAA off to the fact that the planes were being used for illegal purposes. Removing seats to make space for additional cargo; installing extra fuel tanks or special radar equipment."

"Interesting. In your travels, did you stop at Los Alegres?"

"No. The folks there know I was Matty's friend; they'd've seen through me in a heart-beat."

"Well, they know I was Matty's friend, too, but I didn't hide the fact I was working for her. Maybe I'll drive up there this afternoon, ask some more questions. And I'll find out if there's going to be a memorial service for her."

"Why drive? Take Two-eight-niner."

"No. I also want to visit Seabrook's former partner at the tree farm, so I'll need my car."

Hy nodded, his eyes moving away from mine, focusing on the cold fireplace. After a moment he said, "You know, McCone, it was damned lucky Cutter was dead when we got there Saturday night. I know I told you I was-n't going to harm him, but now I'm not so sure I wouldn't've killed him with my bare hands if I'd faced him down and he'd admitted what he did."

"And I'm not sure I wouldn't have helped you."

"Jesus, we're really out of control, aren't we?"

"Seems so. I keep waiting for some sort of... settling, whatever. For some sense of wanting justice rather than revenge."

"Isn't happening."

"No."

"Trouble is, now it seems like Matty's dying was a small part of a very big picture. Maybe we'll never get the satisfaction of taking down the one who's responsible."

"Maybe what we're after is more important than taking down a single individual."

I spent part of the morning in the office catching up on paperwork and getting Mick started on his latest assignment. As I'd expected, my nephew welcomed the challenge of backtracking the Fuller family's movements and quickly shifted into high gear; when I left him he was talking to the PowerBook as he might to a woman: "You and I are going to have one hot time today, baby!"

Since Seacliff was only a slight detour from the direct route to the Golden Gate Bridge, I decided at the last minute to drop in at Rae and Ricky's to check on Zach. The semicircular driveway of the redwood-and-glass house was clogged with vehicles, and after my I.D. passed scrutiny of the RKI guard, Ricky's keyboards player, Pete Sherman, answered the door. Tuesdays and Wednesdays, I belatedly remembered, were reserved for rehearsals, with two band members flying up from southern California and two others driving in from their Bay Area locations.

Pete kept me in the entryway for a few minutes while he showed me a fresh batch of photos of his baby daughter, then pointed me toward the kitchen. There I found Ricky eating a bagel with cream cheese while his drummer, red-haired Jerry Jackson, rummaged in the fridge. When he heard my voice, Jerry turned, winked at me, and handed me a jar of mayonnaise. "Set that on the counter, would you?"

I put the jar next to an astonishing assortment of deli food and went over to Ricky. "Good trip?" he asked.

"Productive. I stopped by to see Zach."

"He's not here. Red had to go to Monterey—something about a deposition in a case she worked for All Souls down there last year. She decided Zach needed a change of scene, so she took him along and promised they'd do the aquarium this afternoon."

"Nice of her. She didn't drive all that way in the Ramblin' Wreck, did she?" Rae's ancient Rambler American was aptly named.

Ricky grinned, triumph showing in his eyes. "No, she took my Porsche. I think I've finally convinced her that the Wreck is a menace to life itself. She's even agreed to go look at cars with me later on this week."

"What do you think she'll get?"

"Well, I know what she wants—one of those sexy Japanese sports models. Whether she'll accept it from me is another story." He spread his hands helplessly. "The woman's positively prickly about me spending money on her; it's a wonder she doesn't insist on paying rent."

"At least you know it's you she loves and not your money."

"She's left me no doubt on that score. But I swear... I had to marry your sister because I got her pregnant with Mick; now I may have to marry Red in order to get her to share the wealth."

"You're seriously considering marriage?"

"Sister Sharon, I'm the marryin' kind." He watched my face, smiling at what he saw there. "Yeah, I know—you're thinking that I'm also the cheatin' kind. Well, no more. Those days're over."

I believed him—almost. Time would tell.

"To get back to Zach," I said, "how's he doing?"

"Fair to middling. He's still awfully quiet, and you can tell he's grieving. Last night when we went up to bed, we heard him crying. But he's opened up enough to talk to both of us about missing Matty and his dad, and we're taking care of him the best we know how."

"I'm really grateful to the two of you. Listen, I'm driving up to Los Alegres after I leave here; maybe I can pick up some of his clothes and other stuff. Is there anything you think he might want?"

"He did mention that he wishes he'd brought his portable CD player. And there was something about a book he was reading and forgot to pack. Science fiction? Probably. See if you can locate it."

"I will, if I can get access to the house."

Behind me, Jerry Jackson exclaimed, "Voilà!"

I turned and saw the drummer admiring the granddaddy of all Dagwood sandwiches. It must have contained half the contents of the fridge.

"Thank God it's tax deductible," Ricky said.

The flag flew at half-mast at Los Alegres Airport.

I parked my MG by the terminal building and walked out onto the field to the gas pumps, where Bob Cuda was fueling a Bonanza. After the plane pulled away, I went over to the lineman. His shoulders were slumped, and he greeted me listlessly. "Nice tribute to Matty," I said, motioning at the flagpole.

"It's the least we can do. Better for her than some goddamn politician. What brings you up here? You're not still working on finding out who took the stuff from her plane, are you?"

"No. John's son is staying with friends of mine in the city, and I came up to get more clothes for him."

"So John's still out of town. Does he even know about Matty?"

I'd been watching the wind snap the flag around, but now I turned back to Bob, unable to keep the surprise out of my voice. "You know where he is?"

"Uh-uh. He didn't go into details, just said he'd be away and unreachable for a while."

He'd told the lineman, but not the woman he lived with—the woman he'd placed in extreme danger. "When did he tell you that?"

"The day before he went. He wanted Matty to know he was thinking of her before the air show, so he asked me to put her good-luck lamb in the plane on Friday afternoon. I think it had some kind of message from him inside." Bob frowned. "That lamb—was it one of the things she thought was stolen?"

I nodded absently. At least the question of who returned the lamb to the plane was answered. "Did you mention to Matty that you knew John was out of town?"

"No. The lamb was supposed to be a surprise, and I was afraid I'd give it away if I said anything. Do you know if she got the message, or whatever it was?"

"She did."

"Well, at least she had that."

"Yes." I looked out across the field. In spite of ideal weather conditions, there was a marked lack of activity today; Matty's death seemed to have paralyzed the small airport. "Bob, did you hear about Matty's mechanic, Ed Cutter?"

"Getting shot to death? Yeah. It's no surprise."

"Because he was into illegal activities?"

"That was the rumor. Matthews, the other guy who was killed, too. Weird that it happened the same day Matty died."

"Did she know about Cutter?"

"She couldn't have; Matty went strictly by the book, and she'd've turned him in if she'd known. Cutter was a new mechanic, had only worked for her a couple of months. I tried to warn her, hinted around, but I don't think I got through to her."

"If you tried, then other people must've, too. Not like her to ignore what her friends were saying—or not to pick up on rumors."

Cuda sighed. "Not like the old Matty, no. But she was different this past year. She was in love and didn't spend much time here, except for lessons and to practice. You know how she always used to call us her airport family? Well, she'd left us for a real family."

"Speaking of family, have any of her relatives planned a memorial service?"

Bob's lips tightened. "You know her sister, the one in Red Bluff?"

"Never met her." Hadn't known she existed.

"Well, Mark Casazza met her when she

172

was down last summer and remembered her name, so he called to ask what she had planned. She said she'd been in touch with the NTSB and the Sacramento County coroner's office and would be down here later in the month to collect Matty's things."

"That's it?"

"That's it. If you ask me, the sister is one cold fish."

Unsentimental, that was for sure. Matty had mentioned a dysfunctional family; apparently they were even more so than mine. At least the McCones honored their dead. Of course, there was my paternal grandfather, whose ashes still resided in a closet at my father's house. Grandpa had hated cemeteries, and so far nobody had been able to get it together to figure out what to do with his remains.

"There will be a service, though," Bob added. "Sunday afternoon. A bunch of us are going to fly to a favorite spot of Matty's, say some words, swap some stories. You're welcome, if you want to come—your boyfriend, too."

"*You're* flying?" The words were out before I could stop them.

To my surprise, Bob smiled. "So you're on to me too. Turns out I haven't been fooling anybody all these years. Yeah, I'm flying—with Mark. He promised not to do anything to scare me any more than I already am. Funny: all my life I wanted to fly but couldn't get myself up into the air. But for Matty, I can do it."

His life was changing. Matty had made a difference to so many people; even in death she had that effect.

I asked, "Where's the special place?"

"Out at the coast—Bodega Head. There's a private airstrip not far away. Owner was a friend of Matty's; he's letting us use it."

I should have known. A couple of years before, Hy and I had come up to Los Alegres and flown out that way with Matty in the FBO's Cessna 172. When we reached the headland overlooking the sea at the mouth of Bodega Bay, she'd asked me to take over the controls and had sat quietly in the left seat, looking down, her face serene and joyful. While Bodega Head was beautiful, it was no more so than many places along the coastline, and I wondered what had made it special for her.

Now, with a stab of regret, I realized I never would know.

Thirteen

The woman behind the desk at the flight school was on the phone, so I went around and checked the schedule myself; only Gray Selby was instructing that day.

"Doesn't it just figure?" I muttered, running my finger down the column and noting the time he was due back from his last lesson. Selby wouldn't let a little thing like a death in the airport family disrupt his routine. Hell, he was probably out hustling Matty's students!

Back outside, I looked up at the hills and saw dark-bellied clouds piling above them; the wind had shifted, the air cooled. November weather, swiftly changing and hazardous to fliers. I remembered Matty sweeping the late-autumn sky with practiced eyes and saying to me, "When I see conditions like this, I know something's coming in."

She spoke so authoritatively that I was sure the mystery of weather was about to be unraveled, and I eagerly asked, "What?"

Shrugging, she replied, "Something."

The memory did not make me smile as it once would have. Instead I felt a fresh onslaught of grief and rage toward the person who'd had her killed.

The rain started as I drove into the parking lot of Seabrook's Christmas Tree Farm—big, splatting drops that kept me confined to the MG for a few minutes until it let up some. The red-and-green building was decked out in a garland tied with gold and silver ribbons, sodden now. Wood sculptures of reindeer cavorted on the narrow strip of lawn. A dirty white pickup was parked to one side, and I knocked on the double doors, hoping to find Wes Payne.

After a few seconds a bolt was thrown and one door swung open. Payne peered out at me. No jolly Santa Claus look-alike today, his face was pale, eyes reddened, mouth dour. He blinked in surprise when he recognized me.

"You didn't have to drive all the way up here just because I called."

"You called me? When?" I stepped inside, wiping my muddy feet on a mat.

"Couple of hours ago. I wasn't sure I should, but the wife said it was the right thing to do."

"What's happened?"

"Zach's missing. The wife and I spent the weekend down at our daughter's in Danville; when we heard about Matty we tried to call the folks that the boy was supposed to be staying with, but didn't get any answer. Late last night we finally reached them, and it turns out he didn't go there after all, because their boy came down sick—so sick that they spent most of the last three days with him at Santa Rosa Kaiser."

"Oh, God, I should've let you know! Zach flew down to the city with me on Friday. He's staying with friends of mine." Stupid of me not to realize the Paynes would worry!

"Well, that's a relief. How's he doing?"

"Fair. The people he's with are good with kids, and they've taken a liking to him, so he's in good hands."

"He's welcome to stay with us, you know."

Of course Payne couldn't be expected to realize that Zach was in danger, and I didn't want to waste time explaining. "I know, but he didn't want to come back to Los Alegres; being in a place that doesn't hold any memories may be helping him deal with what's happened."

Payne nodded somberly. "Maybe that's for the best, given what I found at their house. I went over there yesterday, on the off chance Zach might be holed up. The place's been trashed. That's another reason I called you."

"Vandalism?"

Payne shrugged, avoiding my eyes.

"Did you call the police?"

"No. It shames me to admit it, but I thought

Zach might've wrecked the house when he heard about Matty."

"It's a perfectly natural assumption," I said, although I couldn't imagine the quiet, well-mannered boy doing such a thing. "What about here at the sales office? Was anything disturbed?"

"Now that you ask, somebody went through the files and desk drawers. I didn't pay attention to it at first, because I thought you and Matty might've left it that way the other day. But later I remembered you'd put it back the way it was."

"I gather you have a key to the house."

"Uh-huh. John and I had a good-neighbor checkup arrangement."

"May I borrow it? I want to pick up some things for Zach, and I can look over the damage at the same time."

Payne took a set of keys from his pocket and handed them to me. "The one marked with nail polish is for the front door—the wife's system."

"Thanks. I'll bring them back, and then we'll talk some more."

When I opened the door of the farmhouse, its hinges squeaked in protest, as if trying to tell me I had no right to be there. The hallway was chilly, and rain blew in after me and onto the polished floor. I shut the door and flicked on the old-fashioned overhead lights, deliberately averting my eyes from the photographs on the wall.

To my left was a parlor dominated by an entertainment center. A shabby brown corduroy

177

couch and an aging leather recliner faced it; the cushions on both had been slashed, their stuffing pulled out. A CD tower had been emptied, the discs opened and tossed on the floor, and videotapes had been similarly mistreated. Even the ashes in the fireplace had been sifted; streaks from them lay across the carpet.

Not vandalism. A search. But no way of telling what the person or persons had been looking for.

Across the hall was what seemed to be a multipurpose room containing an oak desk, a treadmill, a bookcase, and a big cluttered table. The desk drawers had been emptied onto the floor. I went through their scattered contents, noting the usual canceled checks and bank statements and bills, both paid and unpaid, and all in Matty's name. FAA notices and publications mingled with a few postcards and letters from people whose names were unfamiliar to me: "Kauai is beautiful and deserted this time of year. Next trip, you and John come too!" "Your aunt Martha is recovering nicely from her surgery. She sure wishes you could visit." "Hey, old fishin' buddy, how's that handsome man you hooked?"

The books on the shelves—mostly standard aviation references—had been disturbed but left there. No one had bothered with a stack of sectionals or Matty's flight computer. When I looked over the table I saw her plotter lying next to a stack of holiday mail-order catalogs and felt a pang; she'd never again use the instrument to demonstrate to a student how to map out a cross-country course. For a moment I considered appropriating it as a keepsake, but then thought better of it. Zach liked to fly; maybe one day he'd have a use for both it and the flight computer.

Back in the hallway I had to step over a pile of clothing that had been dragged from a closet under the stairway. I spotted a down jacket in Zach's size and picked it up; the vest he'd worn to the city on Friday wasn't nearly warm enough. In the kitchen I found broken dishes and utensils heaved this way and that; the door to the fridge stood open, milk and butter and vegetables spoiled.

I shook my head, shut the door, and retraced my steps to the stairway. Matty and John's bedroom had received a thorough going-over—bedclothes pulled off, pillows and mattress slashed, closet emptied. The sight of the upended dresser drawers gave me pause; I checked the things scattered around them until I located the velvet box containing John's wedding ring, picked it up, and put it in my bag. He—or Zach, in the event his father never returned—would want it cared for.

Zach's room had received a more cursory search. Anxious to be out of there, I found his portable CD player, grabbed a handful of discs, and went to the closet. There was a large duffel on the shelf; I pulled it down and packed it full of clothing. A paperback book with a cover illustration of a garish moonscape lay broken-spined on the nightstand—probably the one he'd been reading and forgotten to bring along. I slipped it into the duffel and went downstairs.

When I closed the front door, it gave another weak sound of protest—the house trying to tell me that even my intrusive presence was preferable to standing violated and abandoned.

When I got back to the tree farm, Wes Payne was behind the sales desk, marking prices on tags with a purple grease pencil, his thoughts obviously elsewhere. When he heard me come in, he looked blank for an instant. Then he asked, "You get what Zach needs?"

"Yes. The house is pretty badly torn up."

"Doesn't look like the work of vandals, though."

"I'd say somebody was trying to find out where John went. It's impossible to tell if they learned anything or not." I went up to the counter and leaned against it. "Do you mind if I keep the keys, in case Zach needs something else?"

"Go ahead. I've got another set at home."

"Thanks. You feel up to answering some questions?"

"Why not? Talking keeps me from brooding. You still working on locating John?"

"Yes—for Zach's sake now. Do you know if a doctor named Robert Sandler is the Seabrook family physician?"

"Yeah. Originally he was Matty's doc, but John and Zach took to seeing him too."

"Why would Matty have made an appointment to consult him about John?"

"Did she?"

"It was noted in her appointments book for three o'clock last Wednesday, the day before she called me. Could she have thought John might be ill?"

"I suppose so, but it's not likely he was."

180

"Why not?"

"Oh, hell—no sense in hiding it now. It was supposed to be a Christmas surprise for Matty. John went to Dr. Sandler for a student pilot's medical exam; he's been taking flying lessons over at Petaluma Airport. Matty must've suspected and gone to Sandler to find out for sure."

"I thought John hated to fly."

"He did, but he said he'd get over it once he started his lessons. He wanted to be able to share flying with Matty and Zach."

"How long ago did he start?"

"No more than six weeks. He's been going at it pretty intensely, would be over there for a few hours three or four times a week, so he had to let me in on the secret because he needed me to tend the nursery while he was gone."

Interesting. John Seabrook, who displayed the knowledge of an experienced pilot, had been taking flying lessons. To me it said that his license had been under his real name; he couldn't simply get current again but had had to start from square one. "Do you know the instructor's name?"

"It was an odd name. John made a joke about it once—said it wasn't a good advertisement for somebody you were entrusting your life to." Payne thought. "Yeah, that's it: Grimly. Don't know his first name."

Not a good advertisement was understating it. But the name would make the instructor easy to locate.

I wanted to talk some more with Gray Selby, so I drove back across town, hoping that in spite

181

of the rain he'd still be at the airport, perhaps giving ground instruction to his last student.

I found them at the big table at the flight school, going over a sectional; Selby was explaining the meaning of the various symbols with more patience than I would have given him credit for. He tried to glower when I came in, but it was a weak effort, and finally he held up five fingers and pointed to his watch. I nodded and sat down beside the phone extension reserved for customers' use and called the offices of Dr. Robert Sandler. When the physician came on the line he sounded rushed.

"Sorry I didn't get back to you, Ms. McCone. I have your message on my desk."

"I won't take much of your time. I understand Matty Wildress was one of your patients."

"...Are you a family member?"

"A former student and a friend as well as a private investigator she employed to locate John Seabrook."

"I see. As you must be aware, I can't discuss—"

"I'm not interested in confidential information. I know John went to you for his student pilot's medical, and I also know that Matty made an appointment with you last week, to ask why John had seen you. All I need to know is if she kept the appointment and if you answered her questions."

"She did, and I told her that I couldn't discuss why John had seen me."

"She mentioned that he was missing?"

"Yes. I strongly advised her to file a report with the police."

"But you still wouldn't tell her why—"

"I couldn't imagine what relevance his taking flying lessons had to his disappearance." Now the doctor sounded defensive. "I did tell her not to worry about his health."

At least he'd eased her mind on that score. I thanked the doctor and broke the connection.

Selby's student was folding the sectional and gathering his things. The instructor turned to me, hands on hips, striving for his usual swaggering pose. The effort fell short, and he gave up on it. "Still on the case, McCone?"

"Yes. You done for the day?"

"I'm done."

"Let me buy you a beer."

He hesitated. "A beer I could use, but not at the diner. Too damn depressing around here. You know Mario's, downtown?"

"Uh-huh."

"I'll meet you there in fifteen minutes."

Mario's was on Main Street—one of those wonderful period pieces with neon martinis glowing in the windows and an abundance of glass block and Naugahyde and chrome. I'd used the intervening time to check with my office, so Selby was already seated in a booth when I stepped in from the rain; as I sat across from him, two frosty mugs of beer were delivered.

He raised his in a little salute and drank. "Nice to have somebody to commiserate with."

"Commiserate about what?"

"Wildress, of course. What a goddamn waste."

I raised an eyebrow, surprised.

"Yeah, I know. You think my stand about women in the cockpit doesn't let me feel for a woman who dies that way. Well, let me tell you—in death we're all equal. Christ, what a way to go. Somebody like me, I've been flying damn near all my life. I went through a *war*, for God's sake, saw buddies buy the farm left and right. Even now that I'm stuck in this backwater town at that... benign little airport, I still lose a friend now and then. Happens, when everybody you know flies; we're a small community. But none of it compares to that woman executing beautiful maneuvers one minute, and the next, she's just... toast."

"No, nothing does. I was there when it happened."

"It getting to you?"

"...Some."

"If you got any guts at all, you won't let that happen." He set down his mug, eyes focused on the distance. "I flew F-4s—Phantom fighters—in 'Nam, off a carrier. You'd lose guys, sure, and every time you took off from the flight deck you knew your number could come up next. But I didn't let it get to me, and every time I came home to that carrier and felt the tail hook catch the wire—well, McCone, it was the experience of a lifetime."

During the Vietnam War, the fighter squadrons had trained at NAS Miramar, not far from my parents' home in San Diego. I remembered watching the Phantom jets slice through the sky, swift and graceful and lethal.

I said, "After flying one of those, anything else must be—"

184

"You got it. And now you're wondering why, with that kind of experience, I'm stuck in this burg, instructing."

"Something like that."

"In two words, family responsibilities. Sick and aging parents, handicapped kid brother. So home I came, and home I've remained. I'll tell you, it was a hell of a note, realizing my life was over at twenty-eight and then having to put up with the attitude in this country."

"You mean the attitude toward people who fought in the war?"

He nodded.

"You guys got a bad deal."

"How the hell would you know? You were—what? Just a kid at the time. That's good; at least you weren't one of the people spitting on us." He grasped his mug and drank deeply. Set it down—hard.

I waited a moment before I said, "I wasn't so much of a kid that I didn't know what was going on. My father was career navy, enlisted, and he got spit on a few times himself."

Selby looked me in the eyes, the rage in his gradually cooling. With a sigh he said, "Oh, hell, McCone, I've been mad for such a long time. So long that I'm sick of it. Can we talk about something else now? Like why you're still looking for John Seabrook? Wildress is dead, don't make no never mind to her anymore."

"John has a son—Zach. Maybe you've seen him around the airport?"

"Oh, right. Nice kid. You working on this for his sake?"

"Yes."

"That's good. Boy needs friends to look

out for him; boy needs a father. So what d'you want from me?"

"You'd been keeping a close watch on Seabrook, so I thought you might've noticed something that happened two weeks ago today. Matty told me she was supposed to have lunch with John at the diner when she got back from her morning lesson, but he met her, acting upset, and canceled. You remember anything about that?"

"Two weeks... Was that the day—yeah! The guys in the Stirling Silver Ranger."

"What guys?"

"Okay, here's what happened: I was hanging around on the deck outside the terminal, and this Silver Ranger—very new, very pricey private jet manufactured by Stirling Aviation—lands. The passenger gets out, comes over to the terminal while the pilot ties. Then he spots the diner and starts across the parking lot. Seabrook's just pulled in and is getting out of his truck to open the gate so he can drive out onto the field; they see each other, and even at a distance I can tell there's big surprise on both sides. They talk for a minute, and then the guy goes on to the diner and Seabrook gets back into his truck and drives to the FBO's tie-downs, where Wildress and a student have just taxied in."

"Could you tell how Seabrook and the guy related? Did they appear friendly?"

"Cordial, anyway. But the pilot's another story. Seabrook gets out of his truck at the tie-downs and hugs Matty, but then he spots the pilot walking away from the Ranger and

186

freezes. This guy he doesn't like. The pilot changes course, veers toward him; Seabrook says something to Matty, then jumps back in the truck and races off the field."

"And the Ranger's pilot?"

"Stops and watches him go. By this time I'm curious, so I head his way, ask him if he needs help with anything. He says he wants to talk to the head mechanic, so I tell him his name and point him toward the shop."

"You get the pilot's name?"

"Uh-uh."

"Can you describe him?"

"Sure. About six-two, real thin. Black hair—too uniform, looked dyed—slicked back from a whatchamacallit... widow's peak. Angular features, high cheekbones, dark eyes. Could've had some Indian blood, like you. Clean-shaven, spoke with a southern accent."

"You make a good witness. What about the passenger?"

"About five-ten, stocky. Silver-gray hair—kind of matched the plane—and plenty of it. Big nose with a bump that looked like it'd been broken—the kind of guy women think is handsome in a rugged way. No facial hair, small U-shaped scar on his chin. I didn't catch his eye color; he was wearing shades."

"What about the plane's number? I don't suppose you recall that."

"Sure I do." He tapped his right temple. "I've got a good memory, and it's near photographic when it comes to numbers. Three-three-one-seven-Juliett."

I scribbled it down on a scrap of paper that

was floating loose in my purse. "One more thing—what's the head mechanic's name?"

"Steve Buchanan."

"You know his phone number?"

"Uh-uh, but he's local and listed."

"Thanks, Gray. I owe you."

"Yeah, you do. How's about you spring for another beer? I feel like sitting here and hoisting a few to Wildress tonight."

"Yeah, I remember him," Steve Buchanan's voice said. "Name was Calder Franklin. The guy with him was called Winthrop Reade. They were on their way to a business meeting in Seattle and had a small problem with that Silver Ranger—nothing I couldn't fix, and believe me, it was a pleasure to take a look inside one of those beauties."

I shifted the phone to my right hand and cranked down the MG's window a couple of inches. The defroster had never worked properly, and the windshield was so fogged I could barely see the driving rain, much less through it.

"You talk with either of them while you were working?" I asked.

"A little. Reade didn't say much; the two of them didn't seem to be getting along. But Franklin, he was more friendly."

"And you talked about... ?"

"Well, the plane, of course. But mainly he was interested in Matty. He'd seen her outside and thought she was a real fox. When I told him she flew competitively in a Silver Star, he was really impressed, asked if she was single. Looked disappointed when I said she was living with somebody."

"He ask who?"

"Yeah. All I told him was a guy who owned a Christmas-tree farm west of town."

And that was when John Seabrook started running again.

Fourteen

The FBO at Petaluma Airport's closed, so I can't get hold of Grimly, the flight instructor. And Mick's having trouble coming up with a method of researching the Fullers' background. And my mind is boggling— Just what does that mean, anyway? To boggle?"

Hy patted the couch cushion beside him. "Take it easy, McCone."

I continued to pace back and forth in front of the sitting room fireplace. "I can understand why John wanted to fly again, living with Matty. What I don't understand is why he risked it."

"Flying's a passion, you know that. And it had been over ten years; he felt safe in his new identity."

I thought of what Craig Morland had said of his informants who had gone into the Witness Protection Program: "A few got to a point where they felt safe, went back to their old habits and haunts; they were recognized and killed." John had been recognized simply because he was at an airport—an old haunt.

"Give it a rest," Hy said.

"Oh, sure, you're a fine one to advise me! You, who flew all over northern California yesterday–"

"Sit!"

"Now you're talking to me as if I were a dog!"

189

"You're acting like one worrying at a bone."

I collapsed on the couch, but folded my arms across my breasts and made sure there was a good-sized space between us. Hy dragged me across it and began to nuzzle my ear. I pushed at him, but then he started to kiss my neck. Neck-kissing will do it for me every time.

After a moment I said, "I still don't understand why Mick's having trouble—"

"I'm starving. Should I order a pizza?"

"He's a computer genius, for God's sake! It should be simple for him."

"Italian sausage, anchovies, mushrooms, pepperoni?"

"Maybe he's so entranced with Keim that his brain's going. Maybe it was a mistake to hire her. Olives and extra cheese, too."

"Large or extra large?"

"Extra. We can have cold pizza for breakfast."

"I'll call. Your job is to set the table and open the wine."

Grimly was a woman—first name Sara.

We met at a coffee shop in downtown Petaluma at nine the next morning. The rain had stopped, the sky was clear, and she was looking forward to a full day's worth of instructing, having called all her students and warned them to schedule while weather permitted. Perhaps twenty-five, she was petite and dark-haired and very enthusiastic. Her eyes glowed when she talked about flying, and she admitted she was teaching in order to build up enough hours to get on with an airline.

"Instructing's okay, but you have to fly all the time to make ends meet. I want to buy my own plane someday, and the only way I'm going to be able to do that is if I have a really good job or marry well—and right now I don't even have time to look for a boyfriend."

"So tell me about John Seabrook. What kind of a student was he?"

Her small face grew serious and she took her time removing the teabag from her cup. "Refresh my memory. You said on the phone that John's missing."

"For the past two weeks."

"And his kid's staying with friends?"

"Right."

"What about the girlfriend?"

"That's... over."

"Then the kid needs him. I'll tell you about John, even though it's my policy never to talk about my students—although how that can help you find him, I don't know. John was an unusual student. I soloed him at six hours and probably could've gotten out of the plane sooner. He completed his hours within a month, flying several times a week, studied for the written on his own. He passed it with high marks, and the FAA check ride on the first try."

"He must have quite a talent for flying."

"It's not called talent."

"What, then?"

"Experience."

"You're saying he already knew how to fly."

"He'd already been the whole nine yards."

"You didn't call him on that?"

She shrugged. "I figured he had his reasons—and that they were none of my business."

"Weren't you concerned that you might be abetting him in perpetrating fraud?"

"What's fraudulent about fulfilling the legal requirements for certification? The man had valid I.D. and a student medical. He wrote checks and they cleared."

Straightforward and pragmatic, and she'd needed the money. "Did John ever talk about his life? His son, his girlfriend, perhaps his past?"

"I knew the son and girlfriend existed, that's all. He was very intense about the lessons, as if he didn't have time to waste on conversation."

"After he got his license, did you hear from him again?"

"Once. He came down here, asked if I'd check him out in a tail-dragger."

"When was this?"

"Exactly two weeks ago. Must've been the day before he disappeared. We went up in a Super Cub—his choice. He checked out like he'd been flying it his whole life."

The invitation lying on my desk looked festive and elegant, with clusters of autumn leaves framing its gold calligraphy. Thanksgiving dinner was to be served at Ted and Neal's tomorrow afternoon, and although we'd been asked weeks ago, Hy and I were now formally and cordially invited. I'd completely forgotten about the holiday.

"Cozy domesticity!" I snorted, tossing the invitation aside.

"What's wrong with that?" Rae asked. She lounged in one of my clients' chairs, her feet propped up on the other.

"Nothing, except that everybody seems to

be into it these days. Look at you: making lasagna, including the pasta. Next thing you'll be keeping a recipe file and passing out cute little cards that say 'From the Kitchen of.'"

"You're just mad because you had to leave before the lasagna was ready to be served."

"No, I'm mad because there are more important things in life than table linens that coordinate with your china and silver—and nobody seems to realize that!"

Rae frowned, realizing the criticism was directed at her. Neither she nor Ricky had brought much in the way of household furnishings to their new home, and for months now they'd been blissfully shopping. I'd run into them at Union Square one Saturday and accompanied them to Gump's, where I watched with fascination while they earnestly discussed flatware and china and crystal. By the time I got bored and left, they were still undecided, and the salespeople were scurrying around like an army of ants, carrying crumbs of merchandise to the celebrity customers. The change in Ricky—who, during his marriage to my sister, had seldom been home even when physically present—alternately annoyed and amazed me.

Finally Rae said, "You of all people ought to know that things like table linens, china, and silver are how we keep the big bad world at bay."

It was a return shot; when Hy and I first took possession of the cottage, I'd plunged into an acquisitive spree that had nearly bankrupted me—a disgraceful period that I didn't care to be reminded of.

"Hell of a lot of good linens and china and silver did for Matty Wildress!" I snapped.

Rae flushed and compressed her lips, not chastened as she once would have been—angry. For a moment she contemplated me sternly.

"Shar, I know you've lost a friend and are hurting, but that's no excuse to take it out on the rest of us. Don't spoil Ted and Neal's pleasure by putting down their invitation. It's their first Thanksgiving together, and it means a lot to them to have their friends gathered around their table. Just like it means a lot to Ricky and me to have you guys there on our first Christmas Eve."

Ouch. She'd cut to the core of my behavior and scooped out the rotten part.

"I hate it when you're right," I said.

"Indulge me—I so seldom am." She grinned, her nose crinkling.

"So how was your trip to the Monterey Bay Aquarium?"

"You mean how was Zach? So-so. The sea otters made him laugh, but sea otters could cheer anybody up. Thanks for dropping that stuff off for him; a touch of home was what he needed."

I pictured the wreckage of that home. Even if I found John Seabrook and reunited him with his son, would they ever be able to live happily there?

"Well," I said after a moment, "thank you for being so kind to him."

Her gaze turned inward. "I remember what it's like to all of a sudden have nobody. Right now Zach feels as unsafe and unloved as can be."

Rae's parents had died in a drunken car crash when she was a little girl, and the grandmother who raised her took pains to let her know she was a burden. I suspected that in spite of an early marriage and a great number of superficial and short-term relationships, she'd never felt either safe or loved until Ricky came into her life.

She looked at her watch and stood, stretching. "Guess I'd better do some work. Are you and Hy going to be at Ted and Neal's tomorrow?"

"I don't know, but I'll tell Ted we'll try."

She hesitated as though she wanted to say something more, then nodded and left my office.

There were times when I wished I were more like Rae—less driven, more committed to the personal side of my life. But where did the professional stop and the personal begin? The line between the two had blurred when Matty died.

"Maybe I can help you," I told Mick.

The belligerent expression that settled on my nephew's face reminded me of a day when he was five and I was baby-sitting him, Chris, and Jamie. Giving me that very same look, he'd refused to pick up his toys, and I'd said calmly, "If those aren't in the toy box in two minutes, I will kill you." Never before or since had I seen him move so fast. And in spite of Charlene's fear that my brand of behavioral control had scarred her eldest for life, he exhibited no signs of deviancy; if anything, he was tidier than the average male.

"What're you grinning at?" he asked grumpily.

"Nothing in particular. Look, why don't we talk about the problems you're having with this

195

search? Exactly what is it that's hanging you up?"

"I'll show you what's hanging me up— that!" He motioned at one of two computer-generated color-coded maps of the United States that were taped to the wall above his desk. "This country's too damn big!"

"Explain, please." I sat down on a packing crate that contained my old files. Even though we'd been in residence at the pier since last summer, Ted hadn't yet gotten around to ordering cabinets to house them.

"Okay, you told me that in the Witness Protection Program they try to relocate people at a significant distance from the... what d'you call it?"

"Danger zone."

"Right. So on the map, Florida's red. Originally I coded blocks of other states from hot to cool colors, depending on how far they are from Florida. Then I logged on to DIALOG—"

"To what?"

"Shar, it's a major commercial vendor I use— Oh, Christ, why am I even explaining? You probably think the information highway is somewhere in Ohio!"

"All right, I remember what DIALOG is. Go on."

"I've gotta back up a step. The assumption I was working on is that whatever Ron Fuller was involved in had to be heavy-duty and high-profile. He must've testified about something major, in order for somebody to have his wife killed. That indicated a periodicals search was in order. There're a hundred and thirty-two U.S.

newspapers available full-text online, and DIALOG carries fifty-six of them. I started with the *Detroit Free Press*, thinking that Fuller might've had some connection to Michigan, since the Seabrook birth certificates were issued there. My initial search was two years to either side of the date Marie Fuller was shot, in categories such as drugs and arms trafficking and organized crime."

"Sounds like solid methodology to me."

"Except that I came up with zip. Next I moved to Illinois. Same result. I was heading for Indiana when it finally hit me: those're all cold-climate states."

"So?"

"Where do people living in places like that go for their winter vacations?"

"The Caribbean? Oh, right—Florida. The Justice Department would never relocate somebody there who came from one of those states. Too much chance he'd run into vacationers he'd known in his past life."

"That's what I figured, so I scrapped that block, as well as the East Coast, and went west. People out here tend to take their winter vacations in Hawaii or Mexico. It would make more sense—"

"There's a flaw in that logic."

"Tell me about it! As John Seabrook, Fuller ended up here. They wouldn't have relocated him in California if the danger zone was anyplace nearby. Unfortunately, I didn't catch on to that until I'd run up a mondo bill with DIALOG. By then it was ten o'clock, and I had a headache, so I packed it in."

"And this morning?"

"This morning at about four o'clock I sat straight up in bed and said 'Shit!' The assumption I'd based doing a periodicals search on was also faulty. What if the case *wasn't* high-profile? What if for some reason it didn't melt the media's chocolate bar? I should've been going at it from the federal-courts angle." He motioned at the second map. "Those other color-coded blocks represent the eleven federal districts."

"How far have you gotten with them?"

"Far enough to know I can provide you with a wealth of info on appellate cases, bankruptcy court, and civil actions. But so far I can't locate a resource for information about federal criminal actions. And I'm certain it was a criminal action, because of the contract hit on Fuller's wife."

"Well, there's got to be a resource someplace. Those cases are matters of public record."

"Oh, there is, and eventually I'll find it. But right now my brain's going into meltdown. And you know what? About five minutes before you came in here I had another horrific thought: What if the case never went to trial? What if I'm wrong in assuming only people involved in criminal actions order contract hits?" Mick's shoulders slumped. "I could be a white-haired old man drooling and mumbling over an obsolete PowerBook before I come up with something."

"I think you're on the right track," I said with more confidence than I felt.

"Yeah?"

"Sure. Just keep at it and... tell you what: when you come up with the answer, I'll treat you and Keim to dinner at the restaurant of your choice."

He sat up straighter. "Here, or anyplace?"

"Let's confine it to the city limits."

"Too bad. I was thinking of this restaurant in Paris that Dad told me about. But that new place they reviewed in the pink section last Sunday might do; it had four stars after the dollar sign." He swiveled back to his desk and commenced tapping the keyboard.

As a motivator, I'd come a long way from the day I threatened to kill him.

When I dropped by Ted's office to tell him that we'd try to make Thanksgiving dinner, he held out the phone receiver to me. "Adah Joslyn."

"Hey, there," I said to her. "Thanks for setting things up with Craig."

"How'd you find him?"

"Different. I think he's experiencing major disillusionment with the Bureau. He exhibits all the signs of a midlife crisis."

"Huh. I thought those went out in the eighties. How bad is it, do you think?"

"Bad. He offered to access classified information for me—pushing the envelope, I'd say."

"Jesus, McCone! You didn't take him up on it?"

"Not yet."

"Don't—"

"I won't if I can help it. But you know what? I think he was disappointed that I didn't. He wants out—badly."

"Why can't he just quit, like a normal person?"

"God knows. Maybe he has a flair for the dramatic. I think you should talk to him—persuade him to take a vacation."

"I might. Thanks for the suggestion."

Mick's questioning of his basic assumptions had made me question mine. I went back to my office, intent on dictating some letters on tape, but instead began brooding. By the time Keim appeared in the doorway, I was on the verge of making myself crazy.

"I know you told me you couldn't use me on this Seabrook thing," she said, "but I had some extra time and I couldn't resist. That money he had transferred into Matty Wildress's account came from a bank in the Cayman Islands."

"How'd you find out?"

"You don't want to know." Without another word she turned and walked away.

No, I didn't want to know, but a head-in-the-sand attitude on my part could spell disaster for my agency. Sometime soon I'd have to sit down with my employees for a little talk about professional ethics, as defined by the state department of consumer affairs. The pressures of learning how to run a growing business were no excuse for straying far across the somewhat meandering line I'd set for myself in that area; I was the one ultimately responsible for the actions of those who worked for me, and they'd have to be curbed—

Enough beating up on yourself, McCone. It's lunchtime.

I walked along the Embarcadero as far as Miranda's, my favorite waterfront diner, and ordered a burger to go. Carried it back to the pier and ate at my desk while catching up on paperwork. Two prospective clients came in during the afternoon; one I assigned to Keim, whose computer expertise makes her a natural for going under cover in offices; the other, what my detective friend Wolf calls a worried-mother job, went to Rae. All the time my mind was half on the Ron Fuller problem; my ears strained to hear Mick coming along the catwalk to announce he had the solution. And underlying it all was the nagging notion that I'd somehow dropped the ball on this, ignored an important piece of information.

It was four-thirty before I realized I'd definitely fumbled. I was sitting in the armchair under my schefflera plant, staring aimlessly out the window; a Cessna turned out toward Treasure Island, as low as it could legally fly, monitoring traffic. I peered at it, trying to make out the identification number; a friend flew a similar plane for Metro Traffic Control, the big outfit that supplies reportage to Bay Area radio and TV stations, and I wondered—

"Dammit, McCone!" I exclaimed, snapping my fingers. "How could you not follow up on something like that?"

Somewhere in my purse were the notes I'd made while talking with Gray Selby at Mario's yesterday afternoon. I rummaged around and found them tucked into my wallet with the change I'd gotten at the tollbooth on the Golden Gate. Some fine degree of organization there! I scanned the scribbled page until I found the number 3317J, then sat down at the desk and drummed my fingers on its edge. How to go about this...?

Hy could tell me, of course, but he was in La Jolla and unavailable today, attending to RKI business at their world headquarters. The FAA could tell me, but they were a bureaucracy and unlikely to respond this late on the day before Thanksgiving. Still, there had to be a way....

Then I remembered the bad-gas incident that had happened when I was a student pilot. Contaminated fuel had been delivered by Chevron to numerous Bay Area airports, including Los Alegres; when the problem became apparent, it fell to the managers of the facilities to notify those who had received it. I remembered Matty helping Art Field, the airport manager, with the time-consuming task of going through his microfiches of U.S. aircraft identification numbers so that Chevron could repair or replace their customers' damaged engines.

I called Information, got the airport number, and dialed. Art was there, and sounding as low as I'd ever heard him. Small wonder: he and Matty had been flying buddies for years. When I explained what I needed, he readily agreed to look up the name and address of the registered owner of the Stirling Silver Ranger that had briefly stopped there two weeks before.

I stepped through the door of Mick's office and said, "Try Arkansas."

He swiveled around, frowning.

I added, "Specifically, anything to do with Stirling Aviation, in Alda."

Ironically, the Silver Ranger was not only

made by but registered to the aircraft company that had manufactured Matty's plane.

Mick's eyes widened and he shook his head. "Here I've been slaving away all day, and you come up with a lead like that without even using a computer. I'm not going to ask you how you did it."

Just as well. I didn't want to tell him that the information that would have put an end to his slaving had been in my possession since the previous afternoon. "You having any luck with the federal criminal-proceedings records?"

"As a matter of fact, I was about to buzz you. Cornell University has a database of millions of federal district court cases going back over the past sixteen years. It's limited to cases that were fully tried, but it may be useful."

"What about newspapers? Are any in Arkansas online full-text?"

"I'll check." He turned to the desk and thumbed through a sheaf of printout. I perched on the packing crate. After a moment he said, "Only one—the *Arkansas Democrat Gazette.* It's probably got a statewide circulation."

"Give both it and the Cornell index a try."

"It'll take some time, Shar."

"That's okay."

He surveyed me, looking uncomfortable.

"What, have you got something going for tonight?"

"No."

"So?"

"I can't concentrate with you hovering over me."

"Hovering? I'm just sitting here."

"I know, but your... presence is filling up the room."

"What d'you mean, presence?"

He sighed. "Didn't anybody ever tell you that when you're on the scent of something your personality is bigger than usual?"

"No. How big is it usually?"

"Pretty substantial."

I frowned, unsure whether I liked that assessment.

"Go home, Shar. When I find out something I'll page you."

"I never thought I'd see the day you'd order me around—and get away with it."

He grinned and turned back to the PowerBook. "It's been a long time coming, and in a way it's better than sex."

Mick paged me several times that evening. At around nine I called Craig Morland, waking him up, and asked him to check Justice Department files so he could confirm or deny a set of assumptions I'd made; he promised to get back to me first thing in the morning. At midnight Mick appeared, carrying a thick file; by two a.m. I'd read it twice and exhaustively compared the grainy newspaper photographs of a young blond-haired, mustached man to the one of John Seabrook. Craig called at six-thirty on Thanksgiving morning with the confirmation I'd expected, and at eleven I caught a flight to Dallas–Fort Worth. There I'd make a connection for Fayetteville, Arkansas, only miles from where it had all begun.

Three Years Ago

"Stop trying to crawl on my lap, McCone. Sit straight in your seat and ride it out."

"Sorry. Oh, God..."

"You're not gonna throw up, are you?"

"No, I don't throw up—much. But... oof!"

"Just a little updraft. Nothing you haven't felt before. What's the matter with you today?"

"I'm edgy, that's all, and this turbulence isn't helping any."

"Is that crash last night what's causing the problem?"

"...I guess. One of my so-called friends phoned this morning to tell me about it. She said, 'Maybe now you'll give up on this insanity.'"

"And you said?"

"'Thanks for your concern, but I've got a lesson at noon, and I'm going.'"

"Good girl. What did you learn from that crash?"

"That the pilot must not have bothered to get a weather briefing or else he'd've known those squall lines were coming in and never taken off."

"Or?"

"Or that he did get a briefing but ignored it, thinking he could outrun the thunderstorms."

"Which means?"

"He was stupid or arrogant—or both."

"Are you stupid or arrogant?"

"I hope not!"

"Well, then. You know, McCone, some people have a lot of baggage about flying, and when something *like that crash happens, they're going to try to hand it to you. You can't stop them, but you sure as hell can stop yourself from bringing their baggage on board the plane. Think of the cockpit as a special place where absolutely nobody can get to you."*

"Hey, you're not trying to crawl on my lap any-more."

"Nope."

"This is a pretty strong crosswind. Would you be more comfortable if I was on the controls while you land?"

"No. I've handled crosswinds before; I can handle one now."

"Yeah, you can. And after we land and you go home, what're you going to do?"

"Call up my so-called friend and tell her to get a life."

PART THREE

November 28—December 1

Fifteen

Friday morning: Fayetteville, Arkansas

I got back into my rental car in front of the federal office building on East Mountain Street and glared up at the austere granite-and-glass structure. Last night, while eating a lonely room-service version of Thanksgiving dinner at the Hilton, I'd planned a simple and direct course of action designed to obtain the maximum amount of information in the minimum amount of time. Now, at only nine-thirty in the morning, circumstances were conspiring to defeat it.

The weather was cold but clear, and sunshine brightened the hilly streets of the college town. Fayetteville was an attractive city where old-fashioned clapboard houses mixed with more modern structures, and the redbrick buildings of the University of Arkansas clustered to the north. Near my hotel, a classic old post office—now a restaurant—sat in a square surrounded on four sides by buildings that must have dated from the mid-1800s; most had been converted into shops offering all manner of stylish merchandise. At this early hour on the day after the holiday they were closed and few people appeared on the streets. Even here in the shabbier area near the courthouse, where bail bondsmen's and attorneys' offices abounded, only a handful of pedestrians hunched against

209

the strong wind as they hurried toward the federal building's entrance.

It was through one of those doors that a man named Ashton Walker had stepped over ten years before, and it was there in the office of the U.S. Marshals Service that he and his wife, Andie, had read and initialed each page of the Witness Protection Program's Memorandum of Understanding before forever relinquishing their true identities. Ash Walker, who then had metamorphosed into Ron Fuller and, later, John Seabrook. Ash Walker, former U.S. Air Force flier, test pilot for Stirling Aviation—and man who knew too much.

I hadn't bothered to stop by the Marshals Service. Craig had supplied all the details I needed, and chances were that no one in the office would have talked with me anyway. I did speak to a clerk in the field office of the FBI, who told me that the agents who had conducted a major investigation of the aircraft company had been reassigned; the Bureau, he said, could not reveal their new locations. That left me at a dead end, unless I pursued my secondary course of action.

From my pocket I pulled a scrap of paper on which I'd jotted the phone number of the local bureau of the *Arkansas Democrat Gazette*, where Iona Fowler, the reporter who had chronicled Ash Walker's testimony during a string of federal trials, had worked. I called, asked for Fowler, and found she was no longer with the paper.

"She's living up around Berryville now," the man who'd answered added. "Got a farm or some such. That's about all I can tell you."

I thanked him, broke the connection, and got out my map. Berryville was about ten miles east of the historic Ozark town of Eureka Springs, not far from the Missouri border. An hour's drive—two at most. I called Information, got a listing for Fowler, and called her. She seemed eager to talk to me, and in a gently accented voice gave me directions involving a number of state and county roads, ending in a seven-mile unpaved stretch. I told her I was on my way.

The northbound freeway took me through Alda, where Stirling Aviation was located. On the same sort of impulse that had made me visit the Good Buy store in Florida, I exited and drove along the frontage road until I found their facilities: a large airfield and numerous nondescript concrete buildings and hangars, covering many acres. The entire plant was fenced in chain-link topped by barbed wire, and one of Stirling's early models, the single-engine Silver Explorer, stood on a massive pedestal near the gated entrance. I studied the layout for a few minutes, then drove on, thinking about what had happened there over a decade before.

Stirling Aviation was founded in the late fifties by a former naval aviator, David Stirling. As the firm moved from manufacturing single-engine aircraft to making multiengines and small jets, it became one of the strongest in the state's burgeoning aviation- and aero-space-products industry. But in the early eighties Stirling was disabled—ironically, in

211

an auto accident—while en route to the air-field; unable to resume his duties as CEO, he turned control over to his only child, twenty-six-year-old Duncan.

Duncan Stirling: in the accounts I'd read he'd been variously described as a master criminal and a rich boy dabbling in a dangerous hobby; as a clever manipulator and a naive tool of his associates; as a man in control of himself and those around him and a cokehead whose habit controlled him; as a sociable man who threw lavish parties and a loner who frequently disappeared for weeks at a time. All agreed that he was more interested in guns, cocaine, and living on the edge than in aviation. And being given free rein over his father's company was all it took to push him over that edge.

Within months Dunc, as he was known, formed a cadre of greedy and unscrupulous pilots who flew secret missions for high wages; some were recruited from the ranks of test pilots at Stirling, others through that web of connections spun around any area of enterprise, legal or illegal. The Stirling plant became headquarters for a fleet that exported arms and imported drugs; employees who would jeopardize the organization were let go, and the process of transforming the aircraft company into a multimillion-dollar illicit empire began.

Eventually the Arkansas State Police became interested in the unusual activity at Stirling Field. Planes touching down at night without their headlights aren't all that uncommon; a lot of pilots, myself included, feel landing lights distort their perception by making the

212

runway seem to come up too fast at them. But the fact that most planes arriving after dark at Stirling were without both landing *and* position lights was cause for suspicion, as was the fact that the aircraft never made a blip on the radar screens at the nearby Fayetteville airport. And then there was the heavy truck traffic at the field, as well as employees working around the hangars at late hours.

The state police called in the FBI, and the usual bureaucratic squabbling ensued, about which agency had primary jurisdiction over the investigation. Finally the state agency continued to monitor the airfield and look into tips from disgruntled former employees of Stirling; the federal agency examined the company's bank accounts and tax records, taking note of a gradual decline in production. And Dunc Stirling went about business as usual, ignoring the warnings of his cohorts. Whatever else he might have been, Dunc was arrogant and thought himself untouchable; mere mortals like the law simply didn't trouble him.

Strangely enough, what brought Stirling down was not the main thrust of his operations but a nasty little sideline in murder-for-hire. It began when he asked one of his pilots to "take care of" a former girlfriend who was attempting to barter her silence about the organization for an upgrade in lifestyle. The next victim was a mechanic who wanted out after he heard about the killing. Murder done once may cause shock waves, but repeated incidents make it routine; soon several of Dunc's employees had no hesitation at accepting contracts to take out people who were causing trouble for their boss or his associates. And Dunc Stirling remained oblivious to the growing horror of a pilot named Ash Walker.

When Walker was approached about flying import-export missions, he was twenty-nine, on the verge of bankruptcy due to a failed business venture, and awaiting the birth of his first child. Six weeks later his wife miscarried, and Walker plunged into the illicit work with a vengeance. He'd always kept to the straight and narrow, and in exchange he'd been eased out of a promising military career because of downsizing. The airlines weren't hiring, and his own small fixed-base operation, which he'd financed with funds borrowed against his home and airplane, inexplicably failed. And when he'd finally found a good job and was looking forward to reducing his debts and starting a family, the company was handed over to a criminal. Then anxiety about the situation precipitated his wife's miscarriage.

Maybe, Ash Walker reasoned, it was a sign that he wasn't meant for the straight life.

Later Walker would admit to a great deal of self-doubt during his time at Stirling, but one doubt he never entertained was about his inability to stomach—much less commit— murder. Quietly ingratiating himself with Dunc's inner circle, to the point that Stirling used him as his personal pilot when temporarily incapacitated by a knee injury, Walker began to gather evidence and keep a detailed journal. And three years after Duncan Stirling initiated the destruction of what his father had labored to build, Ash Walker went to the federal building in Fayetteville and turned over the accumulated evidence to the FBI.

The Justice Department moved swiftly, securing a series of indictments against Stirling and his associates, ranging from conspiracy to distribute controlled substances to capital murder. But the day after the indictments were handed down, a federal judge in Fort Smith— who had been appointed by a former governor whose campaign fund had benefited substantially from David Stirling's contributions—decided that Duncan Stirling, in spite of his access to aircraft and large amounts of cash, posed no significant risk of flight. Released on a half-million-dollar bond secured by his father, Dunc vanished within twenty-four hours. Ash Walker made a convincing witness against the other defendants and all were convicted, but the man who had given the orders got away.

So maybe he was above mere mortals.

Six months after the last sentence was pronounced in Fort Smith, Ash Walker's wife, Andie—now known as Marie Fuller—was gunned down in a grocery-store parking lot in Florida. Ash and his young son, Roger, were taken to a Marshals Service safe house in Miami, and sometime during the night they slipped out and disappeared. Disappeared, until a pilot named Winthrop Reade, now CEO of the revitalized Stirling Aviation, spotted Ash at Los Alegres Municipal Airport.

Soon I turned east onto a highway that narrowed to two lanes; traffic gradually grew light as the road climbed into the Ozarks, and the pavement wound sharply, yellow-and-black-striped markers warning of dangerous curves. I sped through a series of switchbacks, and looked down on gently rolling valleys that were gray with bare-limbed trees. The strong wind whipped dried leaves across the road and made the little car shudder.

Tourist cabins and motels told me I was approaching Eureka Springs; at the turnoff for the town's historical district I came up behind a slow-moving tram that reminded me of San Francisco's motorized cable cars. Thanksgiving weekend, and it was packed with sightseers. Their carefree faces brought to mind my call to Ted and Neal's from Dallas–Fort Worth Airport yesterday afternoon: festive noises in the background, including a Texas-accented whoop that had to be Keim's, and Ted on the line saying he was sorry Hy and I couldn't make the party, but he understood.

Hy wasn't there? I asked, surprised.

No, he'd called with his regrets.

Ted put Neal on then, and after we talked, Neal summoned Rae; Rae, in turn, summoned Ricky, who later turned me over to Zach. After I'd spoken with nearly everyone there, I tried to locate Hy, but there was no answer at any of his numbers or my own.

Off somewhere—and doing what? Most likely brooding because he felt ineffectual and powerless. He hadn't been able to save Matty, and now he feared his chances of avenging her death were slipping away. Yesterday morning when I told him this trip to Arkansas was one I had to make alone, I'd seen his frustration. He understood my reasoning: we both had too

216

emotional a stake in my investigation, and under such conditions our feelings tended to feed on each other's, often building to dangerous levels. Still, he hadn't liked being excluded, and I didn't blame him.

By the time my Fayetteville flight was called, I was well into some serious brooding of my own. Over the course of our relationship Hy and I had encountered obstacles that would have finished most couples, but we'd confronted them head on—and together. I didn't lie to him; he didn't lie to me. If we disagreed on a course of action, we aired our differences—often heatedly—and compromised. But since Matty's death we'd begun telling half-truths and going about our business separately. I didn't really know why he'd gone down to RKI's headquarters on Wednesday; he might even be pursuing an investigation that paralleled mine.

With such thoughts on my mind, was it any wonder that I'd drunk a whole bottle of expensive Chardonnay with my lonely room-service Thanksgiving dinner?

After the tram turned off, I put on speed past fast-food outlets and the ubiquitous crafts and antiques shops. At Berryville—a larger town than I'd imagined—the road widened to four lanes and I began looking for my turnoff. Iona Fowler had said it was difficult to spot, but I found it easily. Then I drove straight past the next turnoff, had to double back, missed her dirt road, and ended up in Missouri.

So much for my navigational prowess.

After backtracking, I located the road, marked by a dead end sign. It took me past several frame farmhouses—and through several axle-threatening potholes—and downhill over a creek; pastureland where brown-and-white cattle, huddled against the cold wind, stretched uphill. A graded track bisected the cattle graze and disappeared behind a stand of trees at the top; I followed it and came to a brown frame house with a red barn behind it.

The house was small and attractive, girdled on two sides by a wide deck overlooking the valley. A collie lay at the foot of its steps, and as I pulled in next to a Jeep Cherokee, the dog got up and came to greet me; its cold nose nuzzled my hand when I got out of the car. Together we went up on the deck and I knocked at the door, then turned to take in the view: rolling pastureland falling away to a line of bare-limbed trees through which I made out the silver-gray flash of a river.

The tall, handsome woman who answered my knock had a thick braid of white-blond hair wound around her head like a crown; she looked down her long nose at me in a way that would have seemed haughty had it not been for the lively curiosity in her blue eyes. When I tried to show her my identification, she waved it aside.

"Come inside quick!" Iona Fowler exclaimed. "Colder'n a witch's titty today, but I've got coffee brewed and a fire in the woodstove. No, Jody, not you, you're all muddy from your run through the creek." She blocked the collie with one booted foot, held the door open for me, and shut it emphatically against him.

The room I stepped into was a cozy one, with overstuffed chairs centered around the wood-stove and lots of plants. The walls were hung with colorful quilts, and a sewing machine stood in an alcove, the table next to it heaped with scraps of fabric. Iona Fowler pointed me toward the chairs and went to fetch us coffee from the kitchen at the opposite end of the house. When she came back, I was warming my hands at the fire.

"You have a lovely place here," I said as she sat on the chair across from me, pulling off her boots and curling up her long denim-clad legs.

"Thanks. I guess it was meant for me; came on the market the day I decided to get out of Fayetteville."

"How come you chose this area?"

"I had a couple of friends in Berryville. When my life fell apart, they suggested I visit and look at property."

"Your life fell apart? How?"

"That's right—you wouldn't know. Had to do with my series on Stirling Aviation. After the trials I was contacted by a New York publisher that was interested in having me expand the pieces into a true-crime book. When I told them there was more to the whole business than most people suspected and that I thought I could put it together and back it up with evidence, they were even more enthusiastic. We were negotiating the contract when the threats started: middle-of-the-night phone calls, petty vandalism to my house and my car.

"Now, I'm not the sort who scares easily, but next somebody deleted the Stirling files from my office computer. No big problem, I always kept hard copy. But that night, before I could make extras and put them in a safe place, my house was torched and I lost everything. Not just the files but tapes of interviews and my notes of things that were said to me off the record. And two days later, when somebody took a shot at me in front of the friend's house where I was staying temporarily, I said the hell with it. I'd planned to quit my job to do the book anyway, so the day the insurance money came through, I was out of the *Democrat Gazette* and Fayetteville."

"Who do you think was behind all that?"

"Old man Stirling and his political cronies. I was after a story of corruption in high places, and I'd made no secret of it."

"You mean the father using connections to get the son freed on bond?"

"I truly believe that was only the tip of the iceberg."

"Oh?"

Fowler's gaze slipped away from mine. "Don't ask me what was going on; I don't know. I never got to do any serious investigating. Oh, I probably could've reconstructed a lot of the material, but the task seemed so overwhelming, especially as depressed as I was."

Something wrong there. Something she wasn't telling me.

"You know," she added, "I came up here and sat around doing nothing but feeling sorry for myself for two solid years. Then one day I woke up to spring sunshine and told myself, 'Woman, it's time you got yourself a life, so take yourself into town and sign up for those classes in cattle-raising and quilt-making.'" Her wide mouth quirked up. "Now I've got all those beeves and all that fabric. I've even got a live-in gentleman friend. You'll meet him, if he ever decides to come in from Manly World."

"Manly World?"

"The barn. He holes up there when he wants to contemplate... whatever it is he contemplates. Sits by the electric heater and carves heads." She paused, her brow furrowing. "I don't know, if I did wood carving, I don't think I'd carve *heads*. But that's his thing, so more power to him. But let me ask you this: why're you interested in an old crime like the Stirling operation?"

In hope of getting her to feel she could trust me, I gave her a truthful, although abbreviated, account of my investigation, stressing Zach's predicament. She listened without interrupting, then stared somberly into her coffee mug, clearly disturbed. Finally she said, "Well, under those circumstances, I'll be glad to help you. What d'you need to know?"

"Let's start with David Stirling. Is he still alive?"

"Yeah, the old fool. Lives in the same limestone mansion down in Alda, and I hear he's made it into a kind of shrine to his drug-dealing, murdering son."

"Even after what Dunc did?"

"The old man's into denial; I think that auto accident messed up his head as well as his body. He never did believe any of it went down, at least not the way Ash Walker said, and as far as he's concerned, Dunc could do no wrong. Managed to convince his political buddies of it too—why else would Dunc've gotten out on bail? Here's the prime example of how deluded the old man is: even though Stirling's a publicly held company, he's the majority stockholder, and he's put his shares in trust for Dunc, in case he surfaces and is exonerated."

"Interesting. These political buddies—who are they?"

"Behind-the-scenes heavies, people with money."

"Names?"

"Charlie Vernon—he's big in the poultry industry. Ken Rule—electronics. Calder Franklin—former president of the state bar and Stirling's personal attorney."

Calder Franklin—the man who had been piloting the Silver Ranger registered to Stirling Aviation when it landed in Los Alegres.

"What're my chances of getting to talk with them?"

Fowler considered. "Not good. An outsider mentions the Stirlings, and the protective wall goes up."

"I'm particularly interested in Calder Franklin. You say he's David Stirling's personal attorney. Did he also represent Duncan?"

"Hell, no—no love lost between the two of them."

"Why?"

"Who knows? Even when they were kids they didn't get on."

"What's Franklin like?"

"I can't really say. Was a time when we all thought he was going to be state attorney general, but after the Stirling mess, that went away. He wasn't involved, but no politician worth his salt was going to have anything to do with anybody connected with the Stirlings. Since then Franklin's stayed far behind the scenes, but he controls things, no doubt about that. Has a hand in everything, and nothing—if you know what I mean."

"Can you give me an example?"

"Nothing specific comes to mind."

Pressing her further wasn't going to get me anywhere. I'd have to figure out a way to talk with Franklin himself. "Okay," I said, "what would you say my chances of talking with David Stirling are?"

"Now, that's another story entirely. You might be able to get to him if you can come up with the right story."

"Such as?"

"Well, if you could convince him you might know where Dunc is, for example. I hear he's seriously ill—cancer—and wants to see his son before he dies."

The idea of giving a dying man false hope didn't sit well with me—until I reminded myself that in all likelihood his blindness to his son's crimes had led to Matty losing her life. "Let's get back to Duncan for a minute," I said. "What can you tell me about him?"

"You mean, what kind of man is he? Complex and contradictory. There was a time, before he got into the heavy stuff, when he and I ran in the same circles. Back then he was... well, the word 'secretive' comes to mind. Always disappearing without any warning and reappearing without any explanation of where he'd been. You'd ask, and he'd just smile cryptically."

"For how long and how often?"

"A week or two, maybe every other month. I gather it happened more frequently later on, although for shorter periods. The pressures of running a drug-and-arms smuggling ring can take a lot out of a person, you know. Anyway, when he came back, he was always more relaxed—relaxed for Dunc, that is."

"He always went alone?"

"Uh-huh. He'd jump into his Silver Whisper, one of Stirling's small jets, and be gone."

"Okay, you said he seemed relaxed for Dunc. I take it he was high-strung?"

"Very."

"A cocaine user?"

"Well, you'd see him snort a few lines at parties, but I seriously doubt he was the cokehead that some of the press portrayed him as. Dunc's thing was self-control—rigid—but it didn't take much to shatter it. Little things would set him off, and then he'd turn into a screamer."

"Paranoid?"

"Yeah."

I pictured the photographs of Stirling that I had in my file: high-browed, with patrician features and the kind of dark eyes that might have been soulless or might have contained shards of light from fragmented and violent emotions; the poor quality of the photos made it impossible to tell.

I asked, "What else do you remember about him?"

Fowler thought, running the tip of her tongue over her lips. "He liked guns a whole lot, always carried one. Once I saw him shoot a hole in the ceiling at a party. He used women for sexual purposes but didn't like them much, might've even been afraid of them; I had the feeling he'd be just as happy to do without but felt a responsibility to keep up a studly appearance. He liked to take shortcuts, do everything the easy way—which is why, I suppose, he turned to crime rather than working to build the company. He romanticized himself: He was an adventurer, a risk taker, a renegade hero."

"You seem to have quite a handle on him."

Fowler's mouth twisted painfully. "I ought to: the woman he had murdered because she knew too much—Cindy Kershner—was my best friend. And don't believe what some of the papers said about her blackmailing him; Cindy hadn't a clue about what was going on at Stirling. She loved Dunc, poor fool, and wanted a commitment—that was her crime."

"I'm sorry." I sipped cooling coffee and checked my tape, giving her time to regain control. "What about Winthrop Reade? He was a test pilot for Stirling; now he's CEO."

Something flickered in Fowler's eyes—a spark of emotion that quickly died. "Yeah, he's turned the company around, made it a top contender again. And now Stirling and his political buddies have picked him to be groomed for the U.S. Senate. Reade's got charisma, is shrewd and savvy; if he's elected, he'll get things done. I don't always agree with his politics, but I admit that Win'll go a long way in Washington—maybe all the way to the top."

Now Fowler frowned, as if concerned about the type of legislation Reade might push through. Well, the man's politics weren't my concern; I was after the nature of his relationship to the Stirlings.

"What prepared him to become CEO? I mean, a pilot's license isn't the same thing as an M.B.A."

"He learned from a master: during the years when Dunc was running the company into the ground, Win was the old man's personal assistant and liaison to the so-called management at the plant."

"Reade was playing both sides, then?"

"...He testified that he didn't know what was going on. The way it went was like this: Dunc had known Win all his life; they'd practically been raised as brothers. So Dunc knew how sharp Win was and how strong his loyalties to the old man were. Dunc set it up so that Win dealt only with him and was allowed limited access to the plant. And Dunc had the production reports and financials falsified for him. By the time Win realized what Dunc was doing, it was late in the game, and the feds were already building their case. He went to the old man, tried to tell him, but Stirling didn't want to hear about it. So Win just rode it out and let Dunc hang himself. And then he picked up the pieces."

"He could've gone to the FBI; Ash Walker did."

"Walker had been gathering evidence; he had something to trade for immunity and protection. Win didn't have tangible goods to give them."

"But he did cooperate eventually."

"Of course. Win was out to save his own fanny, and he did."

"You speak as though you know Reade well."

"Hell, everybody knows everybody down in Alda. Win and I grew up together. I do believe he gave me my first kiss, during a game of spin the bottle."

"What's Reade's relationship with Calder Franklin?"

Fowler looked startled. "What *is* it about Cal that interests you so much?"

"I'm trying to put together a picture of the people who're involved with David Stirling, that's all."

"Well, I don't know as there is any relationship. Cal's done some work for the company, so naturally he's had dealings with Win. Win may use him as his attorney; he and the old man are like family, so it stands to reason."

"The two of them get along?"

"I suppose."

"And Reade—what's he like personally?"

"Well, even after all the years I've known him—and that includes going steady for about two weeks in high school—it's hard to say. He's a chameleon. Can be charming, of course. Ruthless when it comes to business. A loner, like Dunc—he's never married—but doesn't lack for social graces. You can set him down anyplace, and he fits right in. Highly intelligent and, as I said before, shrewd. You can't put much over on him. Loyal—that goes without saying. He's stuck by David Stirling through thick and thin. He once told me that he looks upon the old man as a substitute father. And now, I suspect, the old man considers him a son."

"I'd like to talk with Reade too."

Fowler smiled. "You get to the old man

227

with your story about knowing where Dunc is and you'll meet Win. No way he'd be excluded from that kind of conversation. Act convincing enough and you'll be having tea at the Stirling mansion with both of them this very afternoon."

Sixteen

Tea it was. Poured from a silver pot into fine bone china. Cream, sugar cubes, little rounds of lemon, and thin vanilla wafers were offered around before the uniformed maid departed David Stirling's rosewood-paneled library.

Since he'd fallen ill with cancer, the wheelchair-bound old man told me, maintaining his daily rituals was vital to him. "If you let go of them," he explained, "you make it too easy for death to have its way."

The determined jut of his jaw told me he fully intended to give death a run for its money, but the cancer had made visible inroads: Stirling's eyes were sunken and his skin papery, the fine bones seeming about to tear through it. But even huddled beneath a Hudson Bay blanket, moccasined feet propped on the footrests of his chair, Stirling had a commanding presence. While he might be into denial on the subject of his son's crimes, otherwise he was alert and in full possession of a keen intelligence. The old man would go down fighting, and until he did, no one would hold an edge on him.

I was glad I'd taken the trouble to refine the story I was about to tell him, fleshing out details and making it close enough to the truth that I could lie confidently. It would stand up to a vigorous cross-examination as well as to any checking he might have done.

Stirling had said that his chief executive officer would be joining us, and he was reluctant to discuss the subject of my visit until Winthrop Reade appeared. We made small talk: First visit to Arkansas? Yes. What do you think of our state? Charming. I looked around the library of the big limestone house on Alda's main street; where the walls weren't covered with built-in bookcases containing volumes on aviation, they were hung with framed photographs—the shrine to Duncan Stirling that Iona Fowler had mentioned.

"May I have a look?" I asked, motioning at the pictures.

"Please do."

I stood and moved to the far wall. An eight-by-ten showed both Stirlings posing together in hunters' garb, rifles to hand. "What were you after here?" I asked.

"Deer. That was our last hunting trip together before my accident. You know about my accident?"

"Yes."

"Damned useless legs! It's a hell of a note, being crippled by an idiot redneck drunk at nine in the morning. A plane crash—now, that would've made sense. I flew fighters in Korea, personally tested every type of aircraft we manufactured; if I'd known I'd end up this way, I'd've flown a Silver Star over the Gulf of Mexico and gone out in a blaze of glory."

Silver Star—Matty's plane. The way she'd

gone out was no blaze of glory. Still, I understood Stirling's railing at the half-life he'd been condemned to. I'd often wondered what kind of person I would become if I couldn't do my work, fly, or enjoy my other pursuits. Not gracious, accepting, or compensating, I feared, and definitely a pain in the ass for those who cared about me.

"I hear what you're saying, Mr. Stirling. Where was this picture taken?"

"Northern Michigan, at one of our favorite hunting camps. We went every year for the opening of deer season."

"Did you and your son share many activities?"

The question seemed to disconcert him; he pushed out his lips, frowning. "Well, hunting. And I taught him to fly as soon as he could reach the rudders. Otherwise..." He shrugged, not meeting my eyes. "Duncan had his life, I had mine. That's healthy and normal."

Depends on what those lives contain. "His mother—"

"Died when he was a baby. I raised him myself, with the help of several nannies. It wasn't easy; I became a father for the first time at the age of forty."

"He's an only child?"

"Yes."

"And he never married?"

"Eventually he would have. The women were always flocking around."

"Before you turned control of the company over to him, he worked in the marketing department?"

"Yes. It was his area of specialization at the university."

"The university at Fayetteville?"

"Yes, my alma mater. He—"

The door opened, and a stocky man in a blue suit strode in. Winthrop Reade looked exactly as Gray Selby had described him: broken-nosed and scarred on the chin, with a thick mane of silver-gray hair. Under the well-tailored suit his muscles bulked powerfully, as though he worked out with weights. His eyes, which Selby hadn't been able to see through his sunglasses, were a strange light gray that matched his hair; when they moved, they seemed to shimmer.

David Stirling's face became animated as he greeted his CEO. "Win, thank you for coming. This lady is the California private investigator I told you about, Sharon McCone."

Reade turned to me, taking in my appearance in one quicksilver glance. He extended his hand, clasping mine in a grip so firm it hurt. "Ms. McCone, I'm glad to meet you." Releasing me, he dropped heavily into a brown leather chair. The maid appeared, poured tea; Reade took a lemon slice and waved away her other offerings.

To Stirling he said, "Sorry I'm late, David. Got caught in a meeting with Production, a problem with the new 380. But that's resolved, no need to go into it." After sipping tea he turned his attention to me. "David says you may have a line on Dunc. Tell me about it."

"In a minute, Mr. Reade. First we should discuss terms."

Reade and Stirling exchanged quick glances. Reade said, "You want a finder's fee."

"You could call it that." I sipped my tea,

which the maid had refreshed, set the cup in its saucer. "I make it my business to keep up with the wanted circulars, in case I run across a fugitive in the course of my work. However, I've read up on Duncan's case, and I believe he was unjustly indicted; I was reluctant to notify the authorities as to his whereabouts, even though there is a substantial reward for information leading to his apprehension, posted by the family and friends of a young woman he was accused of having murdered."

Stirling exclaimed, "My son never had anyone murdered! Filthy lies—"

"Take it easy, David. Ms. McCone is on our side."

"Woman's got good sense."

Reade's smile was fleeting. "The reward, I believe, is twenty-five thousand dollars. We'll double it."

"For information leading to Duncan? Or for his safe delivery?"

"You can deliver him?"

"I think so. But it will involve considerable effort and expense on my part."

"We'll triple the reward," Stirling said, "and cover your expenses."

Reade's eyes flashed like moonlight ripples on a lake, but he held his own counsel.

I pretended to think over Stirling's offer, then nodded. "All right, the situation is this: A few weeks ago I was hired to find another missing man. His live-in woman friend wanted him back; he didn't want to go. He bartered useful information for my silence—that he'd run across Duncan in his travels."

Stirling leaned forward eagerly. "Where?"

232

"I can't say."

"Can't or won't?"

"Mr. Stirling, I have to protect my interests."

He frowned but said, "I understand. Did you verify what this man told you?"

"I did. It's quite likely that the man he met is your son. But Duncan keeps on the move; by the time I got to the place where he'd been living, he'd disappeared again."

A disappointed sigh escaped Stirling's dry lips.

"However," I added, "I gathered enough information there to begin to sense a pattern to his movements. With your help, I'm sure I can pick up on his trail."

"Just tell me what I can do."

I glanced at Reade; his mouth was twisted ironically now, but still he kept silent. "I need to know about Duncan—anything you can tell me. Even the smallest piece of information may lead me to him. In addition, I'll need to be put in touch with his former friends, both male and female, if you can persuade them to talk with me. And I also would like to speak with your personal attorney, Mr. Stirling."

Both men frowned. "Why?" Stirling asked.

"I work under retainer for a prominent San Francisco attorney; he hired me to investigate for one of his clients—the case that led me to learn of your son's most recent whereabouts." It was only half a lie. "Professional courtesy dictates that I touch base with your counsel."

Stirling nodded and looked at Reade. "You'll handle that?"

"I'll call Cal immediately and see if he can

meet with Ms. McCone when we're finished here."

Stirling asked me, "Shall I give you a retainer?"

Now Reade began to frown, obviously opposed to money changing hands. I didn't want to push my luck, so I said, "No, that won't be necessary; I can see you're a man of your word. All I need from you at this point is your complete cooperation."

According to his father, Duncan Stirling had been a quiet child, preferring his own company to that of others. He was happiest when engaged in solitary pursuits: model-airplane building, reading adventure stories, fishing at the family cottage on Table Rock Lake in Missouri.

He'd taken naturally to flying and was an excellent pilot, but shared none of David Stirling's passion for it. To Duncan, a plane was merely a convenient mode of transportation. His Silver Whisper had disappeared with him and was never spotted again, in spite of the FBI having circulated its number throughout the country and to Interpol. Sold to an unscrupulous buyer or junked, Stirling said with a grim twist of his lips. One of his greatest disappointments was that his son had absolutely no reverence for fine aircraft.

As Duncan grew into manhood he became increasingly distant from his father. Hunting and fishing trips were all they shared, and during them Dunc spoke very little. He was a good tracker, an excellent marksman, and harbored no sentimentality about his prey. Nor did he take pride in his kills; animals and fish were meant to be food, not trophies.

According to Winthrop Reade, Dunc had abandoned the country-club set in his early twenties, gravitating instead to a rougher crowd who frequented the Razorback Tavern in downtown Alda. The men were blue-collar and outdoorsmen like Dunc; the women worked at low-end jobs and liked to party. Although the Razorback was known as a place to score drugs, Reade didn't think Dunc became a habitual user; he took his pleasure seriously and was careful never to lose control. "It was like he had to work at having fun."

Both men agreed that during the years he'd been at the helm of Stirling Aviation Duncan became increasingly secretive; the trips he took alone in his Silver Whisper were a subject off-limits to everyone. He made Christmas plans with his father before he was indicted but inexplicably failed to appear, even though he knew David was counting on him. When David questioned him upon his return, he made light of the lapse, then flew into a rage when pressed. "That was when I knew I was losing my boy— maybe losing him for good."

As he showed me out of the library, Winthrop Reade handed me an envelope containing photographs of Duncan and said, "You're to meet Cal Franklin at the Old Post Office restaurant at five-thirty. You know where that is?"

"Yes, just down the street from my hotel."

"Good. He said to tell you he'll be wearing a brown leather flight jacket. I've briefed him on the situation. Now, I'll try to set up appointments for you with what few of Dunc's friends I still know how to contact, but I can't promise anything. Will tomorrow be all right?"

"Yes. I'm going back to California tomorrow evening." Sunday was Matty's memorial service at Bodega Head—no way I would miss it.

"Well, I'll see what I can do and call you later at your hotel."

We reached the front door, and the maid appeared with my jacket. Reade helped me into it, and I turned to face him. "I notice you didn't voice any opinion in there"—I motioned toward the closed library door—"as to Duncan's guilt or innocence."

He shrugged. "Personally, I think he was guilty as sin on all charges, but David doesn't want to hear that. I've spent damn near a dozen years shielding him, and I'll keep on as long as is necessary."

"Are you sure that's a good thing?"

"Who's it going to hurt? You saw David; he's a real sick man. The only thing that's keeping him alive is believing he'll see Dunc again and somehow be able to make everything right."

"You must care a great deal for him."

"Damn right I do. My daddy was one of David's pilots, bought the farm testing one of our early aerobatic models. When they found out that the crash was caused by structural failure, David started sending my momma monthly support checks—out of his own pocket. He personally taught me to fly, said he didn't want me to miss out on the thrill of it on account of what happened to my daddy."

"He sounds like quite a guy."

"You bet he is. When I needed extra money for college, he was there with it. When my sister was in the hospital with breast cancer, he paid what the insurance didn't cover. He tried to be a father to both of us, and I'll tell you this—we've been better kids to him than Dunc ever was."

"And now you've undone Dunc's damage and turned Stirling Aviation around."

"I figured I owed it to David."

"You must've benefited too."

"Well, sure I have. I've got stock, I've got a good salary. But I could've had that with any firm. No, I did it for David, and now I'm gonna make sure he dies happy. If that means bringing Dunc home and keeping him under wraps till the old man's gone, I'll do it. But afterward the law can have its way with that lousy excuse for a human being."

"What if Dunc manages to beat the charges? On a technicality, for instance?"

"How's he gonna do that?"

"Well, the primary witness for the prosecution, Ash Walker, has been missing for over ten years."

"That's not a problem."

"Seems to me it is. And I understand Mr. Stirling has put his company stock in trust for Dunc. What would happen if he got off and took control again?"

"I tell you, he won't. That boy is guilty as sin, and everybody knows it."

"But without Walker's testimony—"

"I said it's not a problem. Now, why don't you take yourself back to Fayetteville and

237

meet with Cal while I try to line up some of these other folks?"

No, I thought as I went down the front walk, Reade wouldn't consider Walker a problem; he'd spoken with him as recently as two weeks ago. He thought he knew exactly where he was. What he hadn't taken into consideration was the sight of Cal Franklin sending Walker on the run again.

Calder Franklin's appearance did indeed betray Native American bloodlines, but if he noted any similarity in mine, he chose not to mention it. Seated across a polished oak table from me, his angular features blunted by the dim light from the Old Post Office's vintage sconces and chandeliers, he seemed aloof and somewhat amused. Once our preliminary greetings were out of the way and our glasses of wine had arrived, he cut to the heart of the matter.

"I want you to know that I don't believe the line you handed the old man."

"You mean you don't believe I can locate Duncan?"

"No, I think it's possible you can. But I don't believe this crap about thinking Dunc was innocent."

"Why not?"

"Because Win told me you seem like a bright woman, and from what little I've observed of you, I'd say he's right. All you have to do to know Dunc was guilty is read the newspaper accounts. You're in this for the money, nothing better than a bounty hunter."

"So why didn't you advise your client not to deal with me?"

"When it comes to his son, David Stirling listens to no one."

"And why did you agree to meet with me?"

"I have my reasons, and I'll get to them in a minute. But I do want you to be aware of what I think of your attempt at petty extortion."

"Extortion?"

"What else would you call showing up here and taking David's money—"

"Mr. Franklin, do you know of a San Francisco attorney named Glenn Solomon?"

His scornful expression altered subtly. Glenn Solomon was one of the more respected criminal defense attorneys in the country—and a friend of Hank's from law school; he'd recently referred a number of cases to me.

I added, "Do you really think a man of his caliber would retain an extortionist? And remember—no money has changed hands between Mr. Stirling and me."

He hesitated, dark eyes glittering as they shifted in calculation. "Do you mind if I check with Mr. Solomon?"

"Feel free. His office number is—"

"On second thought, that won't be necessary. Now, let's assume you do locate Duncan and can deliver him home. What possible good can that do?"

"David Stirling—"

"Is a fool where his son is concerned. And as for Win Reade's plan to keep Dunc under wraps till David's gone—well, it's unworkable. Dunc will be taken into custody, tried, and convicted of capital murder. And that will kill David, if the cancer hasn't already."

"So you're trying to talk me out of pursuing this."

Franklin leaned back in his chair, studying me, fingers playing restlessly with his wineglass. "Not at all. You see, when I say Win's plan isn't workable, I mean *he* can't make it work. He's a good man and a good CEO, but he... well, I won't go into that. Suffice it to say that I can handle the situation much more effectively."

"How?"

"That doesn't concern you. What I'm proposing is this: I'll double your fee if you locate Dunc, lead me to him, and allow me to take it from there."

"How?" I repeated.

Again the analytical gaze, this time over the rim of his glass. "Ms. McCone," he said after a minute, "ten years ago a lot of things got ruined for a lot of people around here. First Dunc destroyed Stirling Aviation; jobs were lost, careers went down the drain. Then his so-called friend Ash Walker"—he spoke the name as if it were an epithet—"stepped forward and ruined other lives, lives of people who were going somewhere, going to accomplish things."

"Accomplish things by dealing in drugs and arms—and murder?"

He moved his hand dismissively. "The murder-for-hire business was a small element in what went on. As for the rest—hasn't our own government participated in similar trading? Not that I condone what happened," he added

240

quickly. "I'm just trying to impress upon you that some very valuable people were dirtied in Ash Walker's rush to save himself. The public is only now beginning to forgive our guilt by association."

I recalled what Iona Fowler had said about Franklin's chances at the state attorney generalship going away; the use of "our" was probably intentional.

"So you're afraid that if I deliver Duncan and he does stand trial, all the dirt will be stirred up again."

"It's a distinct possibility."

"Well, I don't suppose Walker will resurface to testify. From what I was able to find out, he's gone to ground."

Franklin's gaze grew remote; he was probably remembering the scene at Los Alegres Airport. After a moment he said, "No, I don't suppose he will."

"You still haven't answered my question about how you intend to handle the situation if I lead you to Duncan."

"No, and I see no reason to."

"It seems to me there's only one action you could take: kill him."

Franklin started and glanced at the nearby, mostly unoccupied, tables. "Good God, are you insane? And keep your voice down. All I intend to do is spirit Dunc away someplace where he can't cause any further damage."

"Where?"

"I haven't gotten that far in my planning."

"Any measure you might take seems extreme, simply to avoid him going to trial."

"You don't understand what's at stake here, Ms. McCone. For one thing, Win Reade is headed straight for the U.S. Senate next election. He's young, energetic, bright, and very charismatic. We need leaders like him, who can go the whole way."

"To the presidency."

He nodded.

"With a lot of you riding his coattails. 'Attorney General Calder Franklin' has a nice ring, doesn't it?"

To my surprise, he smiled faintly. "I suspected you'd researched me. Well, why shouldn't I ride Win's coattails? That's the way things are done in this country, isn't it?"

"Oh, yes, it certainly is." I finished my wine and stood. "Thank you for meeting with me, Mr. Franklin. I'll think about your offer."

"An immediate reply would be preferable."

"I can't give you one. I make it a policy to discuss decisions of this sort with Glenn Solomon."

Franklin didn't like that one bit. He knew Glenn by reputation—had to be aware that on the ethical compass, they were a full hundred and eighty degrees apart.

Outside the restaurant I set off on foot to think over what I'd learned in the course of the day. The night was cold and starshot; wind sent dry leaves skittering and rattling across the pavement; in the distance I heard music, the wail of a steel guitar. I turned right at Post Office Square, walked along with my hands in the pockets of my jacket, looked at the displays in the lighted shop windows, and thought of my long list of unpurchased gifts.

Was it possible Christmas would come this year as it almost always did, in a bustle of activity and then a rush of peace? Or would it be snatched from me as Thanksgiving had? What I'd previously thought of as the Christmas Eve from hell now seemed a highly desirable event; family, friends, even the most ill-behaved and wounded of the Little Savages were what I needed—

Footsteps behind me, treading lightly.

I glanced over my shoulder, caught a slight motion, as though someone had ducked into a shop entry. Then nothing.

I kept going, stopped a few doors down before a window displaying an eclectic assortment of artifacts. Pretended to study a carton of gilded eggs while holding the sidewalk in my peripheral vision. No more motion. After a moment I continued walking softly, listening. The footsteps started again.

Sloppy tail job. Clearly an amateur.

The shop to my right had red velvet draperies tied back with green bows to either side of its entry. Velvet draperies—and no one had stolen them. In San Francisco I'd have given them five minutes, max. I glanced at the window next to them, saw the reflection of a large figure darting between two buildings.

What now, McCone? Confront whoever it is? No, you're five-six; he or she is at least six-two and hefty. When unarmed, don't tangle with people who are bigger than you.

I turned back toward the hotel. All the way there I heard footsteps behind me. When I was half a block from the Hilton they stopped as suddenly as they'd begun.

My room had been searched.

Nothing so obvious as the trashing of John Seabrook's house, but subtle signs were there: a zipper undone on the toiletries bag I'd hung in the bathroom; a rearrangement of the folders in my briefcase; a minute shift in the position of the audiotapes next to the cassette player I often use to lull myself to sleep. Subtle signs, but they added up.

So who had done it? Someone in the employ of David Stirling and Winthrop Reade or perhaps Calder Franklin. They'd want to find out more about me, verify my story. And the person who had followed me at Post Office Square? Someone working with the searcher, keeping tabs on me.

Quickly I inventoried the contents of the briefcase; nothing had been taken, and I'd left at home any papers naming either John Seabrook or Matty. The only file I'd brought along was on Stirling Aviation, and it backed up what I'd told the two men. No harm done.

The discovery made me edgy, though. I hooked the chain on the door before I went to the phone and called my home number, hoping to reach Hy and make arrangements for flying to Bodega Head on Sunday. No answer there, only my taped voice. "Shut up, McCone," I told it after the beep.

My phone quest for Hy widened without success over the next few minutes, and when I called his ranch and heard only his recorded message, I felt a wrenching so severe that I made a little pained noise. This time I hung up before the beep.

The 757 droned through the dark evening sky between Dallas and San Francisco. I leaned back in my seat, thinking over the day's interviews with former friends of Duncan Stirling. They'd fleshed out my image of the man but left me curiously unsatisfied; I didn't feel as though I really knew him, and I hadn't a clue to his present whereabouts. Finally I pulled out my recorder, put on the earphones, and began replaying the tape, skipping from section to section.

Emily Forrester, former girlfriend: "For the first six months things were good with us. Then Dunc started to scare me."
  "In what way?"
  "Well, it was the guns. He started keeping them all over his house and under the bed at my apartment. Why? I asked. Cautious, he said. Paranoid, I thought."
  "Did anything else frighten you?"
  "Long silences. He'd sit and not talk for hours, and I'd catch him staring at me like... well, like I was one of the pieces of sculpture he had in his living room, and he was wondering whether to move me or get rid of me or... well, or just take me out on the patio and smash me."

Paul DeSoto, former poker buddy: "Sure, Dunc did coke—grass, too. Doesn't everybody? But I never saw him wrecked. Not once. No way. Dunc's weirdness was real inside stuff, not the kind that comes from getting too much of a load on."

"What exactly do you mean by 'inside stuff'?"

"The kind of shit that comes from deep down here, in your gut. Something was twisted inside of that boy. Had to've been, to do what he did."

"You knew what was going on at Stirling?"

"Suspected. Most of us did. Even the local cops knew, but after the chief tried to talk to old man Stirling and was told to back off, they stayed out of it on account of his political clout. If it wasn't for the state cops, ol' Dunc'd probably be operating out there at the field to this day."

"Did you also suspect about the murders?"

"Absolutely no fuckin' way! You think I could've sat across a poker table from him if I did? That Cindy Kershner, the one they say was blackmailing him, she was a nice lady. I think Dunc had her blown away because he got tired of her. And that makes him the lowest of the low. The absolute lowest."

Tim McCorkle, former Stirling Aviation designer: "Dunc and I went to school together, kindergarten through college. He was a real straight arrow up until the summer after our junior year at the university. Then he started to change."

"How so?"

"He didn't come around anymore, either to the country club or to parties. I heard he was running with a rough crowd that hung out at one of the local bars. It was the same at school; he dropped out of the fraternity, rented a run-down house, spent a lot of time in the bars. Not drinking—at least not much. Just... I don't know. Soaking up the atmosphere? One thing I've got to credit him with—he always made his grades."

"And then he went to work at his father's company?"

"The same year I did. In marketing. He was good, he had what it takes, but you could tell he wasn't really into it. Every now and then we'd have lunch, for old times' sake, I guess. He'd talk about how bored he was. The job was a piece of cake, he wanted a real challenge. Well, he created one for himself, wouldn't you say?"

"Were you aware of what he was doing?"

"No. I was one of the first to be let go. Dunc knew me, you see. I'm a straight arrow. My wife claims I'd be miserable if she didn't make the laundry put extra starch in my shirts."

"What excuse did Duncan give for letting you go?"

"No excuse whatsoever. He just looked me cold in the eye, said I should pick up my final check and severance pay, told me they'd supply good references. When I asked him why, he turned on one of his famous silences. So I walked out the door and never spoke to Dunc Stirling again."

"Do you know Winthrop Reade?"

"Hell, yes. Everybody knows Win."

"What was his relationship with Duncan?"

"Not close, but cordial. Exceptionally cordial, seeing as Win was one-sidedly competing for the affections of Dunc's father."

"Win was competing, but Dunc wasn't?"

"That's right. Win genuinely loves old man Stirling. Dunc didn't love anybody but himself."

Carol Wizner, manager of the Razorback Tavern: "That's right, Dunc wasn't a drinker. He'd nurse a beer for an hour or more, sitting right down there at the end of the bar and acting aloof and mysterious. Personally, I think it was an act to get women. And he got them. Lord, how he got them!"

"Did you know Cindy Kershner?"

"Now, she was a sweet little thing. Nobody believed she was blackmailing him. Nobody. But then, nobody believed he would've had her killed, either. So much for what people think."

"I guess you also knew Ash Walker?"

"Of course I did. He was about as close to a buddy as Dunc ever had. He'd come in, sit right next to Dunc, watch him perform. We all thought he was a—what d'you call them? Wanna-be. Wanted to be like Dunc—quiet and dangerous. Now, of course, we all know why he was watching him so close."

"Ash worked as Dunc's pilot for a while, I understand."

"Only a short time, when Dunc wrecked his knee. He couldn't fly, so he had to depend on Ash."

"Did Dunc go on any of his mysterious trips during that time?"

"Now that you mention it, I think he did. We were all curious about those trips, and I remember one of the regulars complaining that he'd asked Ash where they'd gone, but he wouldn't say. Wonder if that was because he was going to testify about them at the trial?"

I turned off the recorder and thought about what the tavern manager had said. Exactly what kind of testimony from Ash Walker had the prosecution's case against Dunc Stirling consisted of? After a moment I took out my credit card and address book and used the in-flight phone to call Craig Morland's home in Bethesda, Maryland. The FBI agent's machine picked up, and I left a message.

"Craig, it's Sharon McCone. Sorry to trouble you again, but I need to know how to go about getting some information about that matter we discussed on our date the other night. Call me at any of my numbers anytime. And thanks very much."

Morland would know that I wanted to take him up on his offer of accessing Justice Department files, and I supposed that my message constituted a nudge toward the invisible line across which he seemed so eager to step. But I'd worded it in such a way that it left him an out. Now the decision was his.

Seventeen

Sunday afternoon:
Bodega Head, California

"...She kept me up there when I was ready to quit. One time she actually came to my house and coaxed me to the airport. Her teaching never took a backseat to her aerobatics; the two meshed perfectly."

The water off Bodega Head was deep indigo, and white foam spewed high as the waves crashed on the rocks. Seabirds wheeled above it in celebration of the fine day. Those of us who had flown to Bodega Bay to honor Matty had climbed down the sandy trail from the parking area, and now we stood in a circle on a bluff halfway to the beach. Sightseers and hikers seemed to sense our serious purpose and kept a respectful distance.

Not all the reminiscences were solemn, however. As Mark Casazza, Matty's fellow instructor, spoke, people smiled.

"Rainy days we'd sit around the FBO and hangar-fly and play poker. She always saved her best stories for when she was running a bluff—you all remember those Wildress bluffs—and it worked most every time because her stories were so hilarious that they'd totally distract everybody."

Hy, Zach, and I stood beyond a patch of ice plant, a little apart from the others; Hy and I hadn't been members of the airport family, and Zach seemed to need some distance. I'd found Hy at my house when I returned last night, and he'd explained that Zach had called and asked if we would take him along to the service. The boy, he said, had seemed remote and somewhat nervous—only natural, since it would be the first time he'd flown since Matty died. Hy had already booked a Cessna 172 so there would be room for him.

When I asked where Hy had been while I was

gone, his explanation was so simple that it made me ashamed of my feelings of panic and alienation. He hadn't wanted to see people on Thanksgiving, so he'd flown to his ranch and spent most of the time there outdoors, riding and helping his hands mend fence. The high desert, he told me, was exactly what he'd needed to clear his head.

And now we stood above the sea under a beautiful early-winter sky, saying good-bye to Matty.

Bob Cuda, somewhat pale from his first flight, spoke. "What can I say? She finally got me off the ground." He looked skyward and added, "Are you proud of me, Matty?"

"I'll bet she is," Steve Buchanan, the head mechanic, said. "Matty always gave credit where it was due, and if you were slacking off, she told you, but in a nice way. Reminds me of the primer on the old 150. It was balky; no matter how often I fixed it, sooner or later it stuck. Matty's signal that it was overdue for maintenance was to tell the students to pretend to push it in with their feet. Whenever I saw a student curled up like a pretzel in the cockpit, I knew I'd better get to work on the primer."

I was looking down at Matty's yellow-and-red scarf, which I'd worn tied around my neck in tribute to her. It rippled and flowed on the air currents—as gracefully as she'd moved on the currents of life. When I raised my head several of the people I'd known from my flight-training days were watching me.

Into the silence I said, "Matty believed you learned from your mistakes. One time after I did the run-up she said to me, 'What have you forgotten?' I grabbed the list, went over it; I'd checked everything, from the magnetos to the controls. Then I looked at her; she was sitting there with a wicked grin on her face—and no seat belt! Since that day I have *never once* neglected to make sure a passenger's seat belt is fastened."

Hy squeezed my hand and moved forward. "Matty was one of my best friends, but I admit we had our differences. She called me a tree-hugger; I called her a shortsighted reactionary. Once, when I was arrested after a save-the-redwoods protest at the Russian River, I phoned her, and she refused to bail me out of jail. Said I'd gotten exactly what I deserved. I'd been in jail before, though, so it didn't particularly bother me. And I remembered that at the time I really needed her, when it counted, she'd been there for me."

On my other side Zach squared his bony shoulders and cleared his throat. In a thin, shaky voice he said, "The first time my dad and I went to an air show? I was scared for Matty. Afterward she told me it was okay to be scared. She said courage doesn't mean you're not afraid. It means you can act effectively even when you *are* afraid. I'm always going to remember that, and I'm going to try to live that way."

There was another silence. Gray Selby coughed, and all eyes moved toward him. He bent his head, kicking at stones underfoot, then looked up and began to speak, focusing mainly on me.

"I guess you all think I've got a nerve being here today, much less saying anything. Well, I'll tell you, I've learned a lot in the past week. I miss Matty. I admit it. She kept me on my toes, kept me honest. Last summer, for instance, I'm strolling through the tie-downs and she's taxiing in with a student. I'm in a bad mood, so I decide I'm in no hurry, and I slow down and block them. Then all of a sudden the plane's taxiing faster, seems out of control, coming straight at me. Man, do I run! As it goes by, I see her laughing; she's on the controls, has everything in hand. Afterward I yelled at her, and she told me that's what I got for acting like an asshole. Well, deep down I knew she was right."

This time the silence spun out for minutes. Finally Jim Powell, Matty's aerobatics instructor, spoke. "Matty worked harder than any student I ever taught, but she played harder, too. She'd take that Pitts she trained in way up high and just have a ball. She told me she'd laugh and talk to the plane and even sing—the only time she ever sang because she couldn't carry a tune, and there was nobody up there to hear her. I'm not a religious man, but I like to think that right now she's someplace on high, pulling those G's and singing up a storm."

It was the perfect closing tribute. After a moment Art Field, the airport manager, said, "Matty Wildress was a joy to fly with and a joy to know, and she had very little tolerance for sadness. So what say we take this on home to the Seven Niner Diner? Beer's on me."

As the others started up the trail, I turned

toward the sea. Above it gulls wheeled in the free and natural flight that we humans can only struggle to imitate.

"Sharon, can I have a word with you?" Steve Buchanan was waiting for me on the deck outside the diner.

"Sure." I motioned for Hy and Zach to go on inside and followed the mechanic next door to the shop, where small planes stood in various stages of disassembly. As we came inside, a slender dark man with a wispy mustache withdrew his arm from an engine cowling and moved toward us, wiping grease-streaked fingers on his dark blue coveralls. "Shop's open on a Sunday?" I asked Steve.

"Yeah. Students keep busting the trainers. Flight school's down to two, so we need to get the rest back in service. This here's Juan."

I held out my hand to the other mechanic, but he waved it away, showing me his dirty fingers.

Steve said, "Tell her about Matty and the guy in the Silver Ranger."

Juan nodded. "Steve told me you were asking about those guys, and I remembered that the pilot spent some time talking with Matty."

"Just the pilot, not the passenger?"

"Right. The passenger was already inside the diner when the pilot brought the Ranger into the shop. After he talked with Steve about it, he started over to the diner, too. A couple of the other guys and me, we were eating at one of the outside tables, and Matty was at the next one, alone. The pilot stopped for a few minutes, and they talked about their planes and the company that manufactures them."

"What exactly did they say?"

"Well, I wasn't paying much attention, but they traded performance stats, that kind of stuff. And then the guy asked if she'd heard about the mess Stirling Aviation'd been mixed up in. She said of course she had; a friend had told her all the details, including some that were never made public. The guy seemed real interested in that, but right then somebody came out of the shop and called for him to come back there. And a few minutes later Matty split."

I looked at Steve. "Did the pilot ask you about Matty before or after that?"

"After."

"And you're sure you didn't tell him John Seabrook's name?"

"Positive. What's so important about Matty talking to that guy, anyway?"

Plenty, but I couldn't quite grasp it.

I said to Hy, "Could John Seabrook have told Matty about his past? About Stirling? And if he did, why did she lie to us?"

"I doubt he told her anything. The aviation community's really pretty small; most people know about what went down at Stirling. And Matty had a lot of friends. She could've discussed it with anyone."

"But the inside details—"

"Say it was somebody who used to work for the company or who works there now. Or somebody who was trying to impress her by claiming to have inside knowledge."

We were standing on the deck outside the diner, facing the field. A restored Tiger Moth was doing a touch-and-go, but I was too preoccupied to give it more than cursory attention.

"Okay," I said, "Calder Franklin saw Matty with the chief prosecution witness in the Stirling trials. And he misinterpreted her comment about the company to mean Walker had told her everything that happened, including details few other people knew. But so what? He also saw the way Walker ran from him; that wasn't the behavior of a man who was planning to resurface if Dunc was ever apprehended and brought to trial."

"And at the time, Dunc being apprehended was a remote possibility; it only became a probability when you went to Arkansas and talked with David Stirling."

"I wish I knew why Walker panicked when he saw Franklin but not when he exchanged words with Win Reade. Franklin may still be angry at Walker for coming forward and casting guilt by association upon him and his political buddies, but it doesn't make sense for Walker to be afraid of him."

"Something just snapped, I guess. When you've been in hiding for that long, your reactions aren't always in proportion to the situation."

"Maybe."

Hy was silent, lines gathering at the corners of his eyes as he watched the Moth turn downwind for another touch-and-go. "You know, I understand that Franklin and Reade showing up here was the catalyst that caused Walker to disappear, but I don't see what it has to do with Matty being taken out."

"Well, I don't suppose that the two of them went home and kept silent about seeing Walker. What if someone they talked with in Alda is still in touch with Dunc, could get a message to him as to Ash's whereabouts? And what if Dunc decided to finish what he started when he killed Andie Walker?"

Hy nodded grimly. "But by then Walker was gone. That left only his woman for Dunc to take revenge on."

I thought for a minute, tapping my fingers on the deck rail and watching the Moth as it lost speed and altitude. "Okay, Walker and his son had been safe for over ten years; he had a woman he loved, was flying again. He knew Reade and Franklin would talk about seeing him and that somebody might get word to Dunc. So he decided to get to Dunc before Dunc got to him."

"He decided he wasn't going to let Dunc destroy his life a second time. He was going to put an end to things once and for all. You know, McCone, one thing really bothers me: there was nationwide coverage of Matty's crash on TV and in the papers. If Walker saw it, he'd've worried about his son being alone and in danger. Wouldn't he have come back for him?"

"I would think so. If he was able to."

"So it doesn't look good for his survival. Poor Zach."

I glanced back at the diner, saw the boy

staring through the window at us, sorrow molding his features into a little old man's. A hollowness expanded under my breastbone; the cold wind that always blew here on winter afternoons made me shiver. Hy slipped his arm around my shoulders.

I said, "The only way we're going to know what happened to Walker or to experience any sense of closure about Matty is to go after Dunc Stirling ourselves."

"There's nothing I'd like better, but how the hell are we going to locate him?"

"I don't know, but I think we should take another look at the Seabrook house."

We borrowed Bob Cuda's car and dropped Zach off to visit with Wes Payne at the tree farm. Then we drove to the house and I let us in with the key Payne had loaned me. Inside, it was cold, and the house harbored dampness from last week's rain; except for faint grumbles from the old refrigerator, silence enveloped us. As we stood in the hallway I felt my grief and anger rekindle.

Matty would never again stride down this hall and carelessly fling her mail on the kitchen table. She would never again turn up the sound system in the parlor and tunelessly sing along when nobody was home to hear. She would never again fill the place with the aroma of her famous garlic bread. Or laughingly but affectionately relate the latest foibles of her students. Or pack Zach a school lunch with a special treat. Or...

Or all those things that I'd never witnessed but knew she must have done.

"So where do we start?" Hy asked.

"My theory is that, when in doubt, turn to the right."

The room to the right was the one containing Matty's desk, aviation library, and exercise equipment. We stepped inside and I touched Hy's arm. "Just stand and look. Aside from the disorder, does anything strike you as unusual?"

He did as I told him, then shrugged. "I never visited here; I can't tell."

"There's got to be something somewhere in this house that'll give us a lead on where Walker went." I kept studying the room, blocking it out into segments. When I came to the cluttered table, I noted a stack of food magazines, some Christmas catalogs, a basket full of thread and other sewing gear, a pair of jeans with the legs pinned up to be hemmed, a throwaway type of camera, and Matty's course plotter—

Quickly I went over and picked it up, taking care not to change the circular piece with the arrows that indicate true magnetic course. I'd noticed it the other day when I was here and thought nothing of it, but now Matty's voice echoed in my mind: *I haven't been on a cross-country to unfamiliar territory in ten months; I've probably forgotten how to plot a course.*

She hadn't been a tidy housekeeper, but I doubted she'd tossed the plotter on the table and left it there for over ten months. And I also doubted that she would have bothered to use the instrument had she needed to plot a course. Plotters are mainly used by student pilots—or by someone who hasn't been current for many years. Someone, perhaps, who is also nervous about getting where he wants to go.

John Seabrook, a.k.a. Ash Walker.

I studied the clear plastic instrument more closely. A purple stripe lay along the straight edge. I rubbed it and sniffed the residue that came off on my hand. Grease pencil, the same color Wes Payne had been using to mark price tags at the tree farm. I checked the heading: 10 degrees if one planned to fly northeast, 190 degrees if one planned to fly southwest. A tick mark along the straight edge, also in purple grease pencil, indicated a distance of 46 nautical miles.

"Ripinsky, I think Ash Walker used this plotter to mark up a sectional." I showed it to him, explained the significance of the purple. "My guess is he borrowed the plotter, took it to his office, then brought it back and left it here. Matty probably kept it in the bookcase with her flight computer; maybe he meant to return it there but got interrupted. Anyway, he's left us a lead."

"McCone, he'd been taking flying lessons; he'd've had a plotter of his own."

"Maybe not. When I took lessons, money was short, so Matty loaned me this one—her computer, too. Besides, he wouldn't've kept one here or at the tree farm; she might've found it, and that would've spoiled the surprise."

"Okay, that's possible. And he might've still been rusty at navigation, so he'd've needed one. But we haven't the foggiest notion which sectional he used, what the area's magnetic deviation is, or in which direction he planned to fly."

"So where would he have gotten hold of a sectional? One of Matty's? No, he wouldn't've risked her noticing it was gone. The Prop Shop at the airport? Somebody might've mentioned him buying one to her. Over at Petaluma? More likely. But what if..." I scanned the table, pawed through the Christmas catalogs, then went to the bookcase. On top of some aviation magazines lay the latest mail-order catalog from Mickey's One-Stop Pilot Shop, a large supplier of everything from training videos to electronic flight computers. A label with Matty's name and customer number was affixed to it. I put it and the plotter into my bag.

"Let's collect Zach and head back to the city," I said. "I think I'm on to something."

Eighteen

"I hate Sundays! Nothing's open, nobody's there. And now I can't get hold of either Mick or Charlotte. Where the hell are my employees when I need them?"

"Give it a rest, McCone."

"And why hasn't Craig Morland returned my call? I left a message *last night,* for God's sake."

"He'll call. And Mick and Charlotte will surface. And Mickey's One-Stop will open for business in the morning."

"And in the meantime those political cronies of old man Stirling's have refused to talk with me."

"Like I said, give it a rest. Right now I'm hungry."

"This sounds like a reprise of last Tuesday night, but I don't feel like pizza."

"Chinese?"

"Ugh. I had a perfectly dreadful Chinese chicken salad at Dallas–Fort Worth yesterday. So where the hell can they be?"

"The Chinese?"

"Mick and Charlotte!"

"Okay, you don't feel like Chinese or pizza, but I still think we need Italian. Consider eggplant parmigiana."

"I'm not... The Gold Mirror?"

"Salad, sourdough, eggplant, and a bottle of that good Chianti."

"I suppose I *could* give it a rest. For a few hours, anyway."

"Mickey's One-Stop Pilot Shop. How may I help you?"

"My name is Sharon McCone; I'm the attorney settling the estate of one of your customers, Matty Wildress. I wonder if you would check to see if there's an outstanding balance on her account?"

"Ms. McCone, I can't tell you how saddened we at Mickey's were at the death of your client."

"Thank you."

"I'm accessing the account now. No, I show no outstanding balance."

"Are there any recent orders that we should be expecting? Perhaps one that's already been paid for?"

"The most recent was placed nearly two weeks ago."

"I don't think it's arrived. Will you give me the details?"

"It was placed by her employee, Mr. John Seabrook. He referenced her account number, then changed his mind and charged it to his personal credit card. Frankly, I don't know why I didn't set up a separate account for him. Possibly because it went to Ms. Wildress's address."

"When?"

"That same day—Federal Express, priority overnight."

"And what was the merchandise?"

"Two sectionals—Green Bay and the Twin Cities."

"Okay, Mick—Wisconsin or Minnesota. What airlines fly there?"

"Northwest probably has the most direct flights."

"How long do they keep passenger manifests? And who will they release them to?"

"I don't know."

"Well?"

"Well?"

"Find out!"

"Rae, while Mick's contacting the airlines, I need you to call around to the long- and short-term parking lots for SFO and find out if Seabrook left his truck at one of them. Here's the make and license-plate number."

"What if they won't give out that kind of information?"

"You're a wanna-be writer. Make up a story so compelling that they'll break their rules and scour the lot for it."

"And if that doesn't work?"

"Drive down there and start scouring yourself."

"Jeez, what an assignment. Well, if I do have to cruise the lots, at least I'll cruise in style."

"Oh?"

"Brand-new yellow Miata convertible—my Christmas and birthday present from Ricky for the next thirty-seven years."

"What is it, Ted?"

"A message that I just took—"

"I told you to hold all my calls and not to bother me."

"But this guy—"

"Who?"

"Calder Franklin. When I said you were unavailable, he made me write his message down word for word."

"So read it to me."

"'Since you apparently are not going to accept my offer, I feel I must warn you: further probing into the Stirling matter could place you in extreme danger.'"

"A melodramatic threat, that's all."

"Maybe you should take it seriously. I didn't like the way he sounded."

"How did he sound?"

"As though he meant every word of it."

"How're you coming with the airlines, Mick?"

"I've got calls in to reservations supervisors at every one that flies from here to that area. No replies so far."

"Try my travel agent, Toni Alexander. She knows everything."

"I got lucky with the parking lots on the third try, Shar. Seabrook's truck is at PCA."

"So he did fly commercially to the Midwest. I suspected as much. How'd you persuade the people at PCA to look?"

"Anybody with a heart would, after they heard that my poor diabetic husband mistakenly left the bag containing his insulin supply in his truck and flew off on a long trip, forgetting which lot he'd parked in. I'm to show up with my spare key to fetch the stuff so I can express it to him."

"Jesus, when you don't, they'll probably panic."

"Shar, I may spin a yarn or two, but I'm not insensitive. In about twenty minutes I'll call and say he was able to get a temporary supply from the hotel doctor in Caracas."

"Caracas?"

"I've always wanted to visit Venezuela."

"No callbacks from the airlines, and your travel agent's in a meeting with an important client."

"Important client? Who's more important than—"

"Large corporate client."

"Oh."

"Mick, I've been thinking. Homicide can always squeeze information out of people. Maybe Adah Joslyn—"

"I've already thought of asking her to call the airlines, but she's taken the week off."

"You try her apartment?"

"Left a message on the machine."

"Why are people always missing when I need them?"

"Dammit, Ripinsky, we're so close!"

"Yeah, we are, and time's wasting. There's got to be a way. Let's see what we know: he paid for the sectionals by credit card and had them Fed Exed; marked them up the next morning—"

"Credit card! Two weeks... possible."

"Huh?"

"Where'd I put the number for the tree farm? Here."

"What—"

"Just wait a minute... Wes? Sharon McCone. I'm very close to a break in my investigation, and I need to ask you to do something not quite kosher.... Good. Does John receive his personal bills there at the office?... Will you look through them and see what's come in since he's been gone?... Thanks.

"He's checking, Ripinsky. Keep your fingers crossed that the billing cycle's right. Yes, Wes.... Okay, the American Express and Visa— will you open them and read me the charges?... So Mickey's is the only charge on Visa. What about AmEx?... Northwest Airlines. I'll need the card number, the ticket number, and the date of the transaction.... Thanks. I'll be in touch."

"Yes, that's the correct ticket number.... John Seabrook, that's right.... Really? There must be some error. Will you give me the flight numbers and dates, please?... . Thanks. I'll speak to my employer and get back to you."

"Well, McCone?"

"Eleven-thirty a.m. flight to Minneapolis–Saint Paul, arriving four fifty-four. Connection on Northwest Airlink to Chisholm-Hibbing, Minnesota, arriving eight fifty-five p.m."

"Let's go."

The red-eye to Minneapolis was almost empty. Shortly after we reached cruising altitude the attendants stopped their restless activity and dimmed the cabin lights; the turbines throbbed as we moved along the dark airways on a sure course. Below us the continent lay remote and unfathomable.

Hy and I leaned close together, sharing a brandy because neither of us had wanted a whole one. And in the intimacy of that seemingly endless night I was finally able to ask the question that had lived inside me for three years.

"What was Matty to you?"

"A friend."

"More than that."

"...Yeah. I loved her."

I waited.

"She was Julie's friend first. Best friend. They grew up together in Kern County. After high school they more or less drifted apart. Matty didn't approve of Julie's environmental work; she thought it shameful that Julie funded liberal causes with the money her conservative father had left her. But when Julie was dying, Matty was the friend who came to be with her and help me out.

"Julie died at home. I guess I never told you

267

that. She didn't want to be in a hospital, surrounded by strangers, and I didn't want that for her, either. At the end, Matty was holding her hand. She'd sent me outside to that bluff overlooking the lake; Julie wasn't recognizing either of us anymore, and Matty knew I couldn't bear to watch her slip away. It was a warm, clear July evening; I remember the sunset fading to purple and dying on the water.

"After it was over, Matty came and told me. She made the arrangements for Julie and helped me call the people who should know. And later—toward dawn, after they'd taken Julie away and there was nothing left to do—Matty came into my bed and made love to me. And it didn't seem wrong to us, any more than it would've to Julie.

"It only happened the once, McCone, could never happen again, and we knew it. But Matty got me through both ends of that terrible night. That's why I owe her and always will."

What he said didn't surprise me; maybe on some level I'd known. I felt no jealousy, only a rush of gratitude toward Matty. I took Hy's hand, held it silently until I caught his anxious, questioning glance.

In reply I said, "I'll always owe her, too."

Three Years Ago

"Coming up on your checkpoint, McCone. You spotted it yet?"

"No. I can't believe this is the same territory I've driven across time after time."

"So look at your sectional. You know Highway 101's to your right. What landmark did you pick out to your left when you planned this flight?"

"Lake Sonoma, and I can't— There it is, ahead. We're ten miles due south of Cloverdale."

"You got it."

"I've studied this sectional for a solid week, but everything looks so different from up here."

"That's because you're picturing it the way it looks from the ground. Often what's easy to spot on the ground isn't easy to spot from the air—and vice versa."

"And it's so easy to get lost...."

"Well, you're not lost now. Just watch your instruments and check for other traffic and relax. Cross-country flying's supposed to be fun, you know."

"But there's so much you've got to pay attention to."

"Such as the fact you've let your altitude drop to eleven hundred feet. Where's your emergency landing place?"

"Right over there."

"No way at this altitude that you could establish a glide that would get you there. Like as not, you'd end up in that creek bed—a clear case of pilot error."

"God."

"You know, McCone, pilot error's the cause of nearly every fatal aviation accident. So what you have to do is both avoid and correct for it. No harm in making a mistake, provided you correct for it right quick."

"I'm correcting. Time to let Cloverdale traffic know where we are."

"Cloverdale's closed."

"What? Why?"

"Because I say it is. So where're you going to go?"

"Dammit, Matty!"

"You've got to start thinking in terms of alternatives. The situation often isn't what you expect it to be."

"All right! Okay. Lampson in Lake County is due east; I've got more than enough fuel to get there."

"So what're you waiting for?"

"Matty, I've been thinking about this business of pilot error. In a way it's comforting."

"You're catching on."

"When I've got my license, I'll be completely in control. I'll have to follow the rules and use my head in order to make sure my passengers and aircraft are safe. And if an emergency comes up, I'll have to deal with it. The situation'll be in my hands and nobody else's."

"So what does that tell you about people who fly?"

"We may be crazy, but we sure aren't afraid to take responsibility for our own actions."

Part Four

December 3–5

Nineteen

Tuesday morning:
Chisholm-Hibbing Airport, Minnesota

A stuffed black bear that must have weighed five hundred pounds stood on a low pedestal in a corner of the small terminal. At close to nine-thirty after a night when I'd slept little, the sight was positively surreal. I moved to get a closer look while Hy went on ahead to ask about the local fixed-base operator. The bear was the genuine article, all right. I shook my head, turned, and located Hy talking to a woman at the rental-car counter.

We met in front of the doors to the parking lot. "FBO's called Aeroventure," he said. "Let's take a walk over there while they offload the bags. You want to do the talking, or should I?"

"I will; I've worked out a scenario. You be prepared to jump in if I say something stupid."

"McCone, I've heard you say strange things, but stupid? Never."

The glow that his words kindled warded off the cold as we went outside. The temperature must have been in the twenties. It had snowed recently, and while the parking lot was plowed, many of the cars were draped in white, like stored furniture under sheets. The chill stung my face and nostrils, made the jeans and jacket that had been more than adequate in

California seem insubstantial. I longed for the heavier things in my suitcase. Too bad we'd had to check our bags, but on commercial flights, firearms have to be packed in baggage that goes in the hold. And given the circumstances, we'd been reluctant to leave our guns at home.

We crossed the lot toward a large hangar with an attached one-story building. The planes in the nearby tie-downs shivered and creaked in the cold wind; frost covered their wings and fuselages. Frost: relatively easy to remove, but a killer if you don't—as well as a warning of potential icing conditions. And ice, whether of the rime or clear variety, can be deadly to fliers. Thank God Hy was used to cold-weather piloting, his ranch being located in the often snowbound high desert.

He grabbed my hand and we ran the last few yards to the FBO. Inside, the air was warm enough to steam the windows. The smell of freshly brewed coffee made me sniff like a hunting dog; I'd carried a large cup onto the plane in Minneapolis, but my weary system craved more caffeine.

A tall man with dark hair and wire-rimmed glasses smiled at us from behind the counter. "Ten-cent donation'll buy you a cup," he said. "Help yourselves, if you like."

Hy declined, but I went ahead, adding sugar for energy and dropping a dime into the chipped mug by the urn.

"You folks off the Twin Cities flight?"

"Yes," I said, quickly running through my mind the scenario I'd constructed. During the long night I'd had to firmly resist embroidering it to the point of preposterousness—something

274

I'd often warned Rae against. Warned her with little success; baroque fictionalizing is as natural as breathing to her, and one of these days she may actually realize her dream of becoming a writer and quit the agency—my loss.

I said to the man behind the counter, "We're hoping you can help us. A friend of ours, John Seabrook, was supposed to meet us down at Minneapolis, at Flying Cloud, yesterday. He was VFR, didn't intend to file a flight plan since we were expecting him, but never arrived. He was coming to this area"—I spotted a poster on the wall and improvised—"to tour the Hockey Hall of Fame, then planned to rent one of your planes and fly around to visit friends. He would've rented somewhere in the neighborhood of November fourteenth."

"Seabrook... yeah, I remember him." He reached for his rental log and paged through it. "It was the fifteenth. The blue-and-red Super Cub. Six-eight-three-seven-Lima. He called about it a couple of days before. A month's rental; we took a big cash deposit and ran his Visa card through to be on the safe side. How come you didn't notify Search and Rescue when he didn't show?"

"Uh, well... you see, John's impulsive, and he's got... an eye for the ladies. Doesn't he, dear?"

Hy stared at me as if I'd lost my mind; never in our time together had I addressed him in such a manner. After a beat he said, "Yes, he does—*honey*."

I suppressed a smile. "Did our friend actually plan on keeping the plane a month?"

"He wasn't sure, said he'd let us know."

"Did you ask where he was going?"

"Of course. International Falls, Fargo, Pierre, Sioux City, Twin Cities—quite a tour."

Hy said to me, "You know something? I bet he's at Judy's."

Now it was my turn to stare.

"You know—that woman from North Dakota he met last year in Jamaica."

"Oh, her."

To the man Hy said, "I'm not worried anymore, and you shouldn't be concerned for your Super Cub. It'll be returned in good condition—unfortunately for you, without too much chargeable time." He added to me, "You know, I think we should rent a car, drive up there, and interrupt his tryst, to get even with John for inconveniencing us. What d'you say?"

"Sure, why not."

He thanked the man, took my hand, and led me outside without giving me time to toss my empty cup in the trash basket.

"Now what?" I asked.

"Well, we can't rent a plane here. I'd have to show my logbook and I.D., give him a credit card. I don't want that guy to be able to identify me as somebody who was asking after Seabrook. We don't know what might've gone down when he caught up with Duncan Stirling."

Or what might go down if and when *we* caught up with him.

"Good thinking," I said. "Better not to rent a car here, either. I noticed that the Hockey Hall of Fame is nearby, in someplace called Eveleth; that means motels. Why don't we grab a cab and find a place to hole up and make some phone calls?"

I looked up from the sectional that I'd spread on the table of our room at the Holiday Inn on the outskirts of Eveleth. "He could've used either the Green Bay or Twin Cities chart if he planned to fly northeast, but Twin Cities is the one that works for both directions."

Hy stopped prowling around inspecting the room—an old habit born of too many years of dangerous living—and joined me.

"Here's Chisholm-Hibbing." I jabbed at the magenta circle with my index finger. "Forty-six nautical miles is about this much." I measured with my thumb and middle finger, then placed them on the chart at a course of approximately 190 degrees.

"Nothing there," Hy said.

"I may be a bit off."

"You could be off by twenty degrees either way, and there still wouldn't be anything there."

"Unless he planned to make an off-field landing. I doubt he would've concerned himself with whether they're legal in the particular area or not."

"No more than I would. But I suspect he plotted his course to some recognizable landmark, and as you can see, there's none there. Try the other direction."

I measured again. "Well, would you look at that: Arrowhead Airport, up near this prohibited area."

Hy scanned the sectional, then flipped it over

and studied the explanatory material. "Superior National Forest, and the Boundary Waters Canoe Wilderness. Flight below four thousand feet is continuously prohibited."

"You know anything about that area?"

"An old environmentalist like me? Sure. The Boundary Waters is over a million acres chockfull of rivers and lakes. It sits on top of a plain of rock called the Canadian Shield, tucked up against the border. It's been a protected wilderness since 1930."

"Do people live there?"

"You mean, could Dunc Stirling live there? No. I've only heard of two longtime settlers, and the Forest Service had to appoint them special assistants in order for them to stay on."

"Then we're looking for someplace close to but outside the wilderness area."

"Right." He glanced at his watch. "It's after noon already. I better get started on locating us a plane to rent. Two-seater?"

"I'm thinking four."

"McCone, you can't really believe we'll be bringing Ash Walker back with us."

I shrugged. "You never know. And then there's Dunc Stirling."

Our eyes met and held. Then we both nodded. No, Stirling would not be coming back with us.

Quickly Hy looked down at the sectional. "Okay, the nearest airport of any size is here in Eveleth. It's bound to have an FBO."

I pulled the phone book from the nightstand and paged to the heading for aircraft rentals. "Iron Range Aviation," I told him, and read off the number.

While he called, I opened my travel bag and pulled out a knit hat, gloves, and down jacket. Then I removed the hardcover case containing my .38, which I'd declared at the Northwest ticket counter at SFO, and sat down to load it.

Hy spoke for a minute, scribbled on a notepad, and hung up. "They've got a Cessna 172, but it's rented and not due back until well after nightfall. I don't mind flying up to Arrowhead at night, but we'll need daylight to find Stirling's place."

"So let's fly up and spend the night there."

"I doubt there're any motels; that's pretty wild territory. And I definitely don't want to sleep in a chair at the FBO—not after last night."

"Well, does Iron Range have any other four-seaters available?"

"Not today. The guy gave me the number of the FBO at Orr Regional, though. That's forty-some miles north of here; we could rent a car and drive there." He dialed, listened, and hung up. "Orr's closed, due to frost buckling the runway."

"Damn!" I consulted the sectional. "How about Ely? It's about the same distance from here."

He went through Information, dialed the FBO at Ely, and spoke at length. "Nothing available that you're checked out in."

"You're going to pilot, so what does it matter if—"

"I may need you to take over. As you recall, it's happened before."

But that had been because he was ill—a sit-

279

uation in which he normally would have grounded himself, had not lives other than our own been at stake. In this case, if he was unable to pilot, it would mean—

"I'm not anticipating anything, McCone," he said gently.

"The hell you aren't!"

My exclamation shocked him—shocked both of us. For a moment the only sounds were our mingled breathing and the whine of a vacuum cleaner on the floor above. Then he said, "I'll call the guy at Iron Range, tell him we'll take the 172 tomorrow."

"Wait—we can drive to Ely and you can check me out in whatever they do have."

"No, McCone. By the time we rented a car, drove there, made arrangements for the rental, and you got familiar with the plane, it'd be getting dark. We've already got this room, there's a restaurant right here in the motel, and we're both tired. Let's have a relaxing evening and wake up fresh for whatever we find up north."

He was right, of course. "Okay, call Iron Range back," I said, and began to unpack a few things while he dialed.

When he finished his conversation, he came up behind me, put his hands on my shoulders, turned me so I faced him. "All set."

Our gazes locked again, open and steady, and I knew the half-truths and evasions of the past two weeks were ended. Hy and I had always possessed the uncanny ability to communicate without words, and often at great distances. Now, as we faced each other in this impersonal motel room far from home,

I felt the connection more strongly than ever.

McCone, you're still with me.

Yes, I am.

Whatever happens, we'll be in it together.

"Yes," I said, "we will."

He nodded, unsurprised, and pulled me close.

Twenty

You mind if I turn off the cabin heat for a while?" Hy asked. "It's making me sleepy."

"Go ahead, no problem." I continued staring out the side window of the 172.

We were flying across an icebound lake that contained dozens of small islands. Bristling with snow-dusted pines and lean, long-limbed white birches, they resembled pieces of an unfinished jigsaw puzzle cast on a glass table. The ice reflected the gray of the sky.

We'd gotten a late start, as the previous renter had squawked a problem with the Cessna's radio that required immediate maintenance, and already it was after noon. Hy had requested both an outlook and a standard weather briefing from the local flight service station, and no adverse conditions were reported, although a cold front was moving in from the west. Still, the day had turned gloomy, threatening an early nightfall, and cold fronts are changeable and can move fast. I turned my head and studied the horizon on Hy's side of the plane, noting stacked-up clouds that could be thunderstorms preceding the actual front.

I said, "I don't like this weather."

"Neither do I. Take a look at that sectional, would you? How far are we from Arrowhead?"

"...We just passed over Island Lake, and I see a chain of little lakes to my right, so I'd say about seven miles southwest."

"Thanks."

"So what're you planning to do?"

"Pinpoint the airport, then check the lay of the land while I get an en route briefing. Weather's changing too fast for my liking."

"And then?"

"Depends on how things look, what Flight Watch tells us. No matter what, it makes sense to land at Arrowhead, chat up the folks there."

"You mean because Ash Walker may have stopped there or they may know of Dunc Stirling."

"Right. I've been thinking about Stirling: he used to fly up here in that Silver Whisper, and in that type of plane you wouldn't want to attempt an off-airport landing. I'll bet he flew into Arrowhead."

"Maybe. Tricky to talk with people who might know him; if we arouse their suspicions, they'll alert him to us."

"One of us'll think of a way to finesse it. That's the least of our problems. There's the airport; let's see what's around here."

Twenty minutes later I'd decided we had more chance of identifying one particular pine tree among the millions we'd flown over than we did of locating Dunc Stirling's hideaway. The territory was vast and rugged, thickly forested and frosted in white. Small icebound lakes lay scattered in among the trees like broken pieces of slate. We spotted the occasional logging road, but nothing resembling an airstrip or even a good place for an off-field landing. The en route weather briefing Hy had requested from Flight Watch wasn't reassuring, either; the cold front was moving faster.

"You about ready to give up and turn back for Arrowhead?" I asked him.

"Yeah. What's the unicom there?"

I consulted the sectional. "One twenty-two point eight."

He put the Cessna into a turn, rolled out, and started back along a different course than we'd come. We were flying low, only a few hundred feet above the treetops, and I continued scanning the terrain. A logged-off area stretched ahead of us, stumps protruding through a light snow cover; the prevailing winds had blown the narrow access road free of snow. My eyes followed it to where it disappeared into the forest—

"Ripinsky, check this out."

He glanced at where I was pointing. "Something blue-and-red tucked under those pines."

We flew over, but whatever it was remained an indistinct splash of color. Hy put the plane into a gliding turn, and we descended lower. Now I made out the distinctive shape of a wing.

"A plane," I said. "Stirling's place?"

"Not unless he's taken up logging." Hy brought the Cessna around for a second look. "But it's a plane, all right."

"Ash Walker's, then. The guy at Aeroventure said it was blue-and-red."

"He didn't crash into those trees; it'd be tangled among them, not in underneath. Probably he made a forced or deliberate landing on the road and pushed it under to conceal it."

"How's it look for us landing there?"

"Piece of cake."

Low-hanging branches draped over the Super Cub; so well did they conceal it that I might not have spotted it had the branches on the windward side not been pinned behind an upraised aileron. We approached cautiously, our weapons drawn. The woods were silent except for the soughing of the wind in the pines. Hy slipped around to the opposite side of the plane, and we both peered through its windows.

Empty, although an open duffel bag sat on the seat—the large expandable blue duffel that Matty had described to me. Hy yanked the door open and examined it.

"He must've put on layers of clothing," he said. "There's not much in here."

"Do you suppose this was a planned landing?"

"Can't tell. This is interesting, though." He pointed to the place where the magnetic compass normally is; it had been removed. "He took it so he wouldn't get lost."

Hy withdrew from the cockpit and checked the fuel tanks. "Nearly dry. He may have put down because he exhausted his fuel supply, or else he siphoned it into something and took it with him, in case he needed to make a fire. Is he a smoker?"

"Matty wasn't, and I don't recall any tobacco odor in their house."

Hy continued examining the plane. "Uh-huh. The battery's missing too. It can be used to ignite fuel if you don't carry a lighter or matches. Man's got good cold-climate survival skills." He came over to me and rested his hand on the strut, frowning. "Okay, he lands, hides the plane, strikes off on foot. Question is, did he die in the woods or make it to Stirling's?"

"No way to find out till we know where Stirling is. Let's fly over to Arrowhead and see if we can find that out."

Snow had been plowed into two-foot mounds along the runway and taxiway at the small airport. Even so, when I stepped down from the Cessna, my foot slid on a patch of ice and I had to grab the strut for support. The chill wind brought tears to my eyes as I looked around.

Not much there—just a gas pump, hangar, and a double-wide trailer with smoke drifting from its venturi chimney. A few planes were tied near the hangar, including a derelict Cherokee missing its prop. Forest ringed the field on all sides, the tops of the trees silhouetted against the gloomy sky. Even the wind sock—once orange but now bleached to a drab brown—looked cold and dispirited.

I helped Hy secure the Cessna, and then we hurried toward the trailer. Inside, it was cozy and smoky and warm—more of a home than an airport office. A heavyset woman sat in front of the woodstove reading a paperback; she held up a finger, finished a paragraph, and shut the book. "Help you?"

"Hope so." I began telling my story about our irresponsible friend John who had failed to meet us at Flying Cloud, ending—with the jolt of inspiration that Hy had earlier predicted—that we'd come to Arrowhead because John had planned to visit a friend in the area. They had, I added, a tendency to get into the bottle when together, which probably was why he hadn't called to say he wouldn't be making his ETA down south.

At that point Hy threw me the same cautionary glance that I give Rae when she starts to overelaborate.

"What's your friend look like?" the woman asked.

"Big and brown-haired. He was flying a blue-and-red Super Cub, six-eight-three-seven-Lima."

"Oh, sure. He flew in a couple of weeks ago. Topped off the tanks and asked how to get to the hermit's place, said he'd been there before but had forgotten the landmarks."

"The hermit?"

"My name for him. My husband says that one of these days I'm gonna slip and call him that to his face, and then he'll stop fueling here." She laughed. "No way. The guy's too caught up in his own world to notice."

"What's his real name?"

"J.D."

"No last name?"

"Uh-uh. Even the occasional supplies he has flown in here from Ely come addressed like that."

Hy asked, "He owns a plane?"

"Nice little Maule."

"How come you've never looked up its registration to find out his whole name?"

The woman frowned. "Mister, you don't understand. People like J.D., my husband, and me—we're here for a reason. To get away from what goes on outside, to get away from so-called humanity. We don't ask questions, and we don't pry. The guy who used to run this place told us all about J.D. that we need to know."

Quickly I said, "We're not prying, we're worried about our friend. When he and J.D. get to drinking, there's no telling what might happen. Believe me, we've heard horror stories."

"Well, yeah, J.D. does have a lot of guns. And drunks're always wandering off in the snow and freezing to death. The hermit doesn't strike me as the type to do anything foolish, though; he's been a woods survivalist for at least ten years now. Guy who used to run this place told us J.D. used to come up from somewhere in the South, in a private jet, no less. Spent time on the land, building the cabin and clearing trees for his dirt strip. Then he came for good. Stays out there most of the time, except for the occasional trip into Ely. Hunts, fishes, lives off the land."

"Lives alone?"

"Yeah. As far as I know, he never has visitors. In the seven years we've been here, your friend's the only one who's ever come around asking about him."

I glanced at Hy and sighed. "Well, I guess it's up to us to fly there and drag John home."

"I guess." To the woman he said, "Will you tell us how to get to J.D.'s place?"

"Sure. He's at Pickerel Lake, owns all the land around it—big tract. You have a sectional?"

Hy had brought the chart from the plane, and now he spread it on a nearby table. The three of us leaned over it, the woman pointing out landmarks along the way. "The strip's on the north side of the lake, easy to pick out because the trees come right down to the water everyplace else, and there's a small hangar. Cabin's over here to the west. There's an old logging road here"—she pointed to the southwest—"next to this little slough."

"Sounds as though you've been there," I said.

"Once, years ago. J.D. ordered some building supplies that he couldn't haul in the Maule, and he asked my husband and me to fly them out there. After we offloaded, he had us to the cabin, gave us coffee. He's that kind—southern gentleman, raised right. Still, he couldn't wait for us to leave."

Hy started to fold the sectional. Paused. "You know," he said to me, "I'm sick of rescuing John from these scrapes he gets himself into."

I knew where this was leading—brilliant stroke. "But, dear—"

"No, honey, I mean it this time. Let him sit out there in the woods and drink all winter, if that's what he wants to do."

"But what if—"

"No what-ifs. Let John take care of himself for a change. Besides, it's not a good idea to show up unannounced. This lady said J.D.'s got a lot of guns."

I pretended to think that over. "Well, you're probably right."

"You know I am." To the woman he added, "Thanks for your time. If John comes in to fuel after he sobers up, will you tell him that Mick and Charlotte from Minnetonka are royally pissed at him?"

"I sure will, mister."

The wind was blowing more strongly when we stepped outside the trailer. Once in the shelter of the Cessna, Hy looked up the number of the nearest flight service station in his Airport/Facility Directory and called on my cell phone. I glanced toward the northwest—the direction in which we'd have to fly to get to Pickerel Lake—and noted more cumulus clouds stacked up on the horizon.

When Hy broke the connection he said to me, "Winds aloft have picked up, and ceilings and visibility are near minimums. There've been some pilot reports of moderate precipitation to the west, but the front's not likely to pass through here for at least an hour. They aren't saying VFR not recommended. It's your call, McCone."

"You're pilot in command."

"I'm bowing to your better judgment on this. As if you didn't know, I'm sometimes inclined to fly reckless."

I considered, my eyes on the clouds. "We could check out what's at Pickerel Lake, then turn back for Ely before the front arrives. We could spend the night there, make our plans for when the weather improves."

"It's a go, then?"

"It's a go."

Twenty-one

Pickerel Lake was shaped like a fish, its fins and tail and snout formed by sloughs whose dead reeds protruded through the ice. Trees grew down to the waterline, except at the north end, where Dunc Stirling had cleared the land for his airstrip. Next to the strip stood the hangar; there was no plane in sight.

When I commented on that, Hy said, "Probably in the hangar; in this climate you want to park inside, if possible." He took the Cessna far down and flew along the strip; the hangar's double doors were shut.

Climbing, he continued flying along the lakeshore, west and then south. For a time we saw only trees and ice; then a second clearing appeared to the right. A log cabin with a tin roof stood in its center, surrounded by a welter of objects that mainly looked to be junk. A boat was upended against the railing of the cabin's tiny front porch, and a battered snowmobile crouched next to it.

I said, "From a stone mansion to this."

Hy put the Cessna into a glide.

I grabbed his arm. "You don't want him to realize we're checking the place out."

"Use your eyes, McCone: nobody's home; there's no smoke coming from the chimney, and he'd freeze without a fire going."

He circled the clearing twice, but no one came

out of the cabin. Then he put on full power and turned back toward the lakeshore.

"Where're we heading now?"

"The logging road the woman at Arrowhead mentioned. If it's in good shape, I'll put down there, conceal the plane, and we'll walk in. It's a good time to take a look around, while the place is deserted."

The logging road looked to be in terrible shape.

"Ripinsky, you can't!"

"We're set up for a perfect short-field landing; even the wind direction's right."

"But that's a field of *boulders!*"

"Watch this."

I closed my eyes as the Cessna descended toward the rocky, rutted road. Gripped the edge of my seat as Hy pulled back on the yoke.

Opened my eyes and said, "Show-off."

The logging road soon dwindled to a rough track hacked out of the wilderness. White birches leaned over it on either side, their limbs meeting above us like bleached beams in the nave of a cathedral. Even on this gloomy late afternoon their bark gleamed; I felt as if I were walking down a strange, light-filled aisle. Snow had drifted here, and our footsteps crunched. The cold was bitter enough to penetrate the thermal leggings I had on under my jeans.

Hy pointed out two sets of animal tracks bisecting the path. "A deer," he said, "and maybe a fox."

He often revealed new facets of his knowledge, but it never failed to surprise me. "Since when are you a tracker?"

"Since my daddy first took me hunting."

"I didn't know you hunted."

"I haven't in a long time; I'm not much on blood sports."

We walked in silence for a few minutes. The track narrowed even more, the birches and jack pine and cedars having reclaimed it. I smelled the pines' fragrance, thought once again of the Christmas-tree farm, and Matty. My sense of loss was blunted now, because Hy and I were taking action—for her, for Ash Walker, for Zach.

He put his hand on my shoulder, stopped me. We'd come to the edge of the clearing. The cabin was a small one, with a narrow front porch where a metal garbage can stood, lid weighted with a rock. A shed and outhouse that hadn't been visible from the air, as well as a food cache perched high on stilts against the incursion of animals, stood several yards behind it, and all around between patches of snow lay the junk: oil drums, a stovepipe, sawhorses, a ladder, scraps of lumber, a broken-bladed ax, bottles and cans, a rusted outboard motor.

Hy had taken out his gun; I did the same. He raised an eyebrow at me, and I nodded. Quickly we picked our way through the junk to the cabin, mounted its steps, flattened ourselves against the wall to either side of the door. I reached around and turned the knob; it yielded, the door swinging inward. With his left hand Hy fumbled out the flashlight he'd brought from the plane and shone it around the cabin's interior. Then we stepped inside.

The cabin was frigid and smelled of old fires and cooking. The rough board shutters of the single room were closed and the logs firmly chinked against the elements. Its furnishings were few and plain: a plank table and straight chair; a narrow bed covered in heavy woolen blankets; a woodstove; a metal footlocker; an ice chest. Clothing hung from pegs on the wall near the bed; dishes and utensils and supplies filled three long shelves by the stove; fishing poles and guns were lined up in a rack on the rear wall.

Hy got the oil lamp on the table going, and I went over to check the footlocker. It contained fishing paraphernalia, ammunition, and mail-order catalogs for such products as hardware. The labels on the catalogs gave the name J. D. Wilson and a post-office box number in Ely. When I shut the locker and turned, I saw Hy sniffing an empty glass that had sat next to a stack of books on the table.

"Sour mash whiskey," he said, "the southern gentleman's drink of choice."

"Wonder what he reads while he sips?" I crossed to the table and felt the temperature of a gallon jug of milk that had been left there; no need to put it in the ice chest.

Hy made a strange sound. I looked up and saw he was holding one of the books. Wordlessly he turned it face out for me to see. It was on the ecology of the Mammoth Lakes area of California, and its introduction had been written by Julie Spaulding. His eyes were so pained that I had to look away, scanning the other books on natural history, geology, and the environment.

Hy said tightly, "The son of a bitch ordered her best friend's death, and now he's going to pay for it."

When we stepped outside the cabin, we found night had fallen. The only sound was the distant whine of a plane's engine, probably above the four-thousand-foot level prescribed for transversing the canoe wilderness area. I said flatly, "We're stuck here till morning. No way you can risk taking off from that road in the dark."

"Then we'll check around some more before camping out in the cabin. It might be our only opportunity. I want to take a look at that hangar."

I peered up at the sky. The dense overcast had lifted, blown away by the strong winds preceding the front. A three-quarter moon shone brightly, and cumulus clouds piled on the other side of the lake.

"That hangar's a long walk from here," I said, "and the weather's bound to change fast. If we're going to attempt it, we'd better borrow some survival gear."

He nodded and we went back inside. I relighted the oil lamp and searched the shelves, coming up with trail mix and jerky and bottled water. Hy stripped blankets from the bed and appropriated extra jackets. I found a small pack, put the food and a box of matches into it, then went looking for kerosene.

"McCone, take a look at this."

I turned, kerosene container in hand; Hy was pointing to the floor close under the table. I went over, saw the stains. "Looks like dried blood."

"Hard to say how old, though. Or whether it's animal or human." He moved the flash around, evidently looking for signs of violence. There weren't any, but that, like the bloodstains, didn't prove anything either way.

A sense of unease stole over me. "We'd better get going."

Hy went to the rear wall, pulled a rifle from the rack, and checked its load. "Won't hurt to take along some extra protection."

I knew animals weren't the only predators on his mind.

We struck out, following the shoreline. It was cold enough to make me shiver in spite of the extra jacket. The moon laid a bright path across the frozen lake, made the ice shimmer. And the piled clouds sank lower, moved closer.

Hy didn't speak. It was as though seeing Julie's name on that book in Dunc Stirling's cabin had brought him full circle, to the place where he'd been the night after Matty's crash. Back to the same remote and reckless state of mind as when we'd flown to the Sonoma County airstrip to confront Ed Cutter.

I took his arm, to let him know I was still with him.

The storm hit before we reached the strip, with gale-force winds and heavy, wet snow. It clung to our clothing, stung my cheeks, turned Hy's mustache and eyebrows white as an old man's. We pressed on, leaning into the wind, struggling to maintain our footing. Once I slipped and went down, and he almost fell on me, trying to help me up. It had grown very dark, and the flashlight's beam seemed absurdly feeble.

"Enough of this, McCone. Let's get in under the branches of this cedar, pull the blankets over us, keep each other warm. I'm sorry about dragging you out here; we should've stayed at the cabin."

"Should-haves don't count. We'll get through it."

"How cold do you think it is, Ripinsky?"

"Way below zero."

"Fronts like this are narrow and pass quickly, though."

"Usually."

"How far to that hangar?"

"McCone, I don't know. If this doesn't pass soon... well, I just don't know."

So far these blankets are keeping our combined heat in, and these snow-covered branches are sheltering us from the worst of the wind. But I'm beginning to understand how people freeze to death. God, I don't want to find out what it's like to die this way. ...

"Storm's mostly past, McCone. Let's go."

"...I'm so sleepy."

"Don't do this to me."

"Do what?"

"Come on, get up. Wind's died down some,

snowfall's light, and it can't be far to the hangar."

"Can't I sleep for a while?"

"Just *get up!*"

He grabbed me by my arms and hauled me to my feet. I had to help him. Once I got moving I'd be okay.

And someday we'll laugh at this. Maybe.

I leaned against the hangar's outside wall, breathing hard. In spite of the cold, my body was coated in sweat, my hair damp under my knit cap. The blankets that Hy had earlier insisted I wrap around my shoulders flapped and billowed.

He took out his gun and moved toward the double doors, but I put my hand on his arm and whispered, "Give me the flashlight. I'll open one side and shine it around. You cover."

"Are you sure you're okay?"

"Yes. I told you before, all I needed was to get moving."

His eyes still concerned, he pressed the light into my hand and stepped away, took up a shooter's stance. I grabbed the unlatched hasp on my side and pulled back on it, shielding most of my body with the door but leaning around so I could aim the light inside. Strangely, the air that came through the opening was warm.

A plane stood in the center of the hangar. Dunc Stirling's Maule. The floor around it was covered with tools and parts—as much of a chaos as the junk in front of the cabin.

Hy had moved up beside me. Now he nudged me inside, shut the door behind us. "He's been working on the plane. From the look of it, I'd say it's not airworthy."

"Then where—"

I heard a noise, moved the light to the right. Heard another and shone it to the left.

A man emerged from behind the Maule. In his hand was a pistol, aimed our way.

Twenty-two

"Ash Walker!"

He looked as startled at my exclamation as I imagined Hy and I did at the sight of him. Then his face tightened with fear, and he went into a crouch, finger trembling on the gun's trigger.

My first impulse was to throw down the flashlight and go for my gun, my second to hurl myself at Hy and knock him out of a bullet's trajectory. Then Hy said calmly, "Let's not panic." And I said, "Matty sent us. I'm Sharon McCone, one of her former students. This is her friend, Hy Ripinsky. She must've spoken of us."

Walker remained in a crouch, saying nothing, but his finger relaxed some on the trigger.

"I'm a private investigator, Ash. Matty hired me to find you."

"How do you know my real name?" he asked. "Matty doesn't." Then he added, "Don't come any closer."

"When Matty asked me to find you, I backtracked into your past."

"That doesn't explain how you knew I was here."

"It's a long story, and I've talked with a lot of people. You remember Iona Fowler, the reporter for the *Arkansas Democrat Gazette?* She thought you were courageous. Your neighbor in Gulf Haven, Mr. Simmons? He still thinks kindly of you. And then there's Wes and Karla Payne. And Zach, of course."

Walker lowered the gun slightly, looking overwhelmed and disoriented. A little shaky, too.

"Ash, where's Stirling?"

He ignored the question, seemed to pull himself together. "Matty and Zach—are they okay?"

I glanced at Hy. His face was grim; he shrugged.

"Are they okay?"

"Zach is, but Matty... Look, can't we put the guns down and talk?"

"What's happened to Matty?"

No way to avoid or soften what had to be said. "She's dead."

For a moment Walker stood very still; then he shuddered and let his weapon fall to his side. His face—raggedly bearded now—twisted, and he closed his eyes. "How?"

"She crashed during her routine at the air show. Her plane was tampered with."

"But I left her a letter—"

"She got it, but she refused to do what you told her. She said she didn't want to give up her whole life, her flying."

"Oh, Jesus... And my son? *Where's my son?"*

"With friends of ours in San Francisco. They have a good security system, and Hy put a guard on the house as additional protection."

Walker stood with his head bowed, fighting

for control. When Hy and I moved deeper into the hangar, he offered no resistance.

"Zach must be going through hell," he said thickly. "He loved Matty."

Hy said harshly, "We all did."

Walker looked up, his eyes wet. "You blame me for her dying."

Hy stared stonily at him; then his expression grew conflicted. "It's more that I'm angry. Angry at you for putting her in such a position. Angry at myself for not dragging her kicking and screaming from the airfield. Hell, I'm angry at *her* for being dead."

I said, "None of us is to blame. We all can name the guilty party."

Walker's lips tightened. He stuck his gun into the waistband of his jeans.

Hy asked, "You have any idea where Stirling is?"

Walker shook his head and seemed about to speak when he was seized by a coughing fit. Up close he looked pale and haggard, and his brow was damp.

I asked, "Are you okay?"

"Caught cold... out in the damned woods. Haven't been able to shake it." He turned his back and moved into the shadows.

I glanced at Hy; he nodded agreement. From the sound of those coughs, Walker's cold might have gone into pneumonia.

A moment later an oil lamp flared. A sleeping bag and backpack lay on the floor next to a kerosene heater; Walker shook out the match and sat down there.

I took off my cap and gloves and then the blankets that were still draped around my shoulders. After I folded them, I laid them down like cushions, and Hy and I sat.

Walker asked, "How's Zach dealing with Matty's death?"

I said, "He's grieving. He'll need time to get past it—time and your help."

Walker didn't respond. His gaze grew remote, focused on a dark corner of the hangar.

I let it go for now. "You still haven't answered Hy's question. What about Stirling?"

"He was gone when I got here."

"Gone? Where would he go without his plane?"

"Hunting, maybe. There's not much meat in the cache behind the cabin; he probably needed to lay in a store for winter."

"How long have you been here?"

"What is today?"

"December fourth."

He shut his eyes, calculating. "Okay, three days to find my way through the woods means I got here November eighteenth.

"You think he's been hunting for seventeen days?"

He shrugged.

Something wrong here—very wrong. "And you've been waiting for him all that time?"

His eyes flashed angrily. "What the hell else was I supposed to do? The piece of crap that I rented lost its engine, and I had to put it down on a logging road. I got so turned around trying to get to this place that I'll never find the plane again."

"We found the Super Cub. But what about Stirling's Maule?" I motioned at its dark shape.

"As useless as the other. It was torn apart when I got here; even the radio's shot. I've been working on it, hoping to get it airworthy enough to fly to Arrowhead, but I'm not really a mechanic."

Hy had been staring silently at the flickering oil lamp. Now he said, "It's possible Stirling hiked out or drove a snowmobile; we don't know that the one at the cabin is the only one he owns. But you know? What if this J. D. Wilson isn't Dunc Stirling after all? We didn't show the woman at Arrowhead a photograph, since that wouldn't have fit the story we gave her."

"I know for a fact he's Stirling," Walker said. "I searched the cabin and found a favorite rifle of his—a fairly uncommon Enfield, distinctive because his initials are etched into the barrel." He took it from behind the backpack and gave it to Hy.

Hy turned the rifle over in his hands. Ran his fingers over the initials and grimaced. "There's also the possibility that he's abandoned this place."

"He wouldn't leave without that rifle. Besides, when I got here the woodstove was still warm."

"That doesn't mean he's coming back soon, though. He might even have gotten out of here for the winter. Seventeen days is a hell of a long time."

Walker started coughing again; when he stopped, his breath came in bubbly wheezes from deep in his chest. I said, "You need to see a doctor. We'll fly you to Ely first thing in the morning."

"But Stirling—"

"We'll notify the FBI where their fugitive's been living, and they can take it from there."

Walker's lips twitched and he looked away from me, clearly not liking the idea. Hy was staring at Stirling's rifle; he seemed unaware I was watching him, as if he were hypnotized by the weapon. When he finally spoke, it was to Walker.

"You give up on the Maule?"

"A few days ago, when I started to feel really lousy."

"What've you been doing for food?"

"I brought some, and when that ran out, I pilfered from Stirling's stores. Last time was yesterday, and I knew I couldn't make another trip. Thank God you guys showed up."

"How come you didn't move into the cabin? It'd be more comfortable."

"...Well, in case Dunc came back, I didn't want him to be forewarned that somebody was here by smoke from the chimney. The woodstove's the only heating at the cabin, and this kerosene heater's too heavy to lug that distance."

"I see."

Something definitely wrong here, I thought, and Hy feels it too.

Walker was shivering now. Hy got up, unfolded the blanket he'd been sitting on, and handed it to him. Walker nodded thanks and wrapped it tightly around his upper body.

"Give me that pack, would you?" Hy said to me. I passed it over, and he took out a pint bottle of whiskey that I hadn't noticed him appropriate from the cabin. "Have some of this." He extended it to Walker.

Walker took it, twisted off the cap, and

drank, his teeth chattering against its mouth.

Suddenly I felt bone-tired. I wished I could lie down, slide into dreamless sleep. But that wouldn't do—not in this desolate place, not at the midpoint of this endless, frozen night.

I said to Walker, "We know that Winthrop Reade and Calder Franklin spotted you at Los Alegres Airport. What did Reade say to you?"

"He said he'd wondered what had happened to me. I told him I had a new life, had no intention of ever going back to Arkansas. I asked him not to mention seeing me to anyone, and he promised he wouldn't."

"But then you saw Cal Franklin..."

"And I just plain freaked. I thought I could trust Win not to say anything, but I knew Cal would use the information to hurt me, maybe even manage to locate Dunc and let him know where I was. Anyway, the sight of him sparked old terrors. The way my wife died—do you know about that?"

I nodded.

Walker took another swallow of whiskey. "The way she died kept flashing through my mind. It was like watching a movie: Andie waving to us, Andie falling. And then the previews of coming attractions started: Zach, Matty. I couldn't let that happen to them." He heard his words, and pain crumpled his face; half of it *had* happened. Before he went on, he tipped up the bottle.

"It'd been ten years. A whole *decade*. I felt safe. I was *happy,* dammit! And when you feel that way, your defenses come down, and the memories you've been fighting off creep into your dreams. A couple of weeks before Cal and Win showed up, I'd had this dream where Dunc and I were landing at a surreal, futuristic airport. He cautioned me against using his name in front of the people there. 'Here I'm somebody else entirely,' he told me. 'If you have to call me anything, make it J.D.' And then I dropped him off and took the Whisper southeast to a city of bridges and rivers, where I wandered in a maze, feeling frightened. Zach had been telling me the plot of one of his sci-fi novels at dinner the evening before, so I put the dream off to that." He drank again.

"After I saw Win and Cal at Los Alegres, though, I realized that the dream was based on an actual experience. The airport was a thinly disguised Arrowhead, where I flew Dunc one time when he had a knee injury. The city of bridges was Minneapolis, where I stayed while Dunc did whatever he did—he claimed he was seeing a woman—up there. I remember doing a lot of walking in Minneapolis, feeling confused and scared because I knew I was going to take my evidence to the FBI soon. Why, a dozen years later, I was so sure this was where he'd run to, I don't know. Anyway, it was the only idea I had, and a place to start. I made my plans and flew commercially to Chisholm-Hibbing, because the FBO there was the only one with a Super Cub—the plane I'm most comfortable in— that was willing to rent long-term to a stranger. And... well, you probably know the rest."

"Weren't you afraid of what you might find here?" I asked. "Didn't it occur to you that Dunc might be running the same kind of operation he had in Arkansas?"

"Of course. I planned to check the place out

carefully from the air. But he's not running anything from here, is he? From the looks of it, he's gone to ground."

Walker drank again; half the pint was gone and his eyelids were sagging. Quickly I asked, "What'd you plan to do to him, Ash?"

He coughed, drank again, looked away from me.

"What were you planning?"

"I told myself I'd track him down—here, someplace else, wherever he might be. I thought about turning him over to the FBI, told myself it was the right thing to do. But then I thought, Look what happened the last time. Look what it did to Andie, to your life. So instead I decided I'd use leverage: my silence in exchange for him leaving my new family and me alone. I decided a lot of things, but..."

"But what?"

He shook his head. After a long silence he said, "All I wanted was for the fear to end. All I wanted was to be able to stop looking over my shoulder, waiting for the other shoe to drop. I wanted to give Zach and Matty and myself a chance at a life."

Hy spoke, his voice rough with anger. "Tell me, Walker, when you arranged for the transfer of funds to Matty's account and wrote her the letter, were you really thinking of her? Did you once think about what she'd be giving up? How she'd feel when she found out you'd kept all of this from her? Did you think of your boy? How it would be for him, maybe growing up without a father and without so much as a photograph of his mother?"

Walker flinched and drew back; the bottle slipped from his fingers. For a moment he and Hy faced each other down, Hy's eyes shining with fury, Walker's dull with illness and pain. Then Walker flopped sideways onto the sleeping bag, turned his back to us, and curled up into a fetal position.

Hy made a disgusted sound; when I looked at his face I saw it was as much for his own behavior as for Walker's. "Jesus, McCone, hold me," he whispered, and pulled me against his chest.

We remained that way for a time, listening to Walker's breathing deepen, bubbling and rasping as he sank into sleep. Finally I got up, went over and slipped the gun from his belt. Hy lowered the flame on the lamp, and we moved next to the double doors, sharing the blanket, our backs to the wall.

Hy said, "He may have told himself all those things—about turning Stirling over to the feds, using leverage—but he came here for the same reason we did. He planned to kill him."

"Yes."

"So what's wrong with the picture we're looking at?"

"Something, but I can't pin it down. I'm too tired to think clearly, and I'm glad he passed out. He won't give us any trouble that way."

"Still, we better watch him. He didn't like the idea of notifying the feds about where Stirling's been living and... I don't know. I don't trust him, or like him."

"Me either."

"We'll sleep in shifts, then. I'll take the first, wake you later."

I yawned and leaned my head against his shoulder. "And at first light we'll be out of here."

We were silent for a while. I closed my eyes, but the flickering from the oil lamp played against their lids. My mind moved sluggishly from one detail of the day to the other, connecting none of them.

After a bit Hy asked, "What about this revenge thing, McCone? If we'd come face to face with Stirling, would we have killed him?"

"Probably."

"What does that say about us?"

"I'm not sure what it says about us. Maybe that we're human, but our experiences have made us colder and harder than most people. I do know what it says about our feelings toward the Dunc Stirlings of the world—and about our feelings for the Mattys."

Twenty-three

I woke feeling an urgent need to pee. The oil lamp was guttering and the hangar was cold. I still leaned against the wall, but Hy curled on his side, his arm cradling his tousled head. So much for sleeping in shifts, I thought. Ash Walker's breath rasped loudly.

I moved off my section of the blanket and wrapped it around Hy. He didn't stir. When I stood, my cramped joints protested, so I stretched this way and that to work the kinks out of them. Then I went to check on Walker. His brow was damp and hot, his hair and clothing soaked. Pneumonia, or close to it.

When I opened the hangar door, I saw it was

still dark, but to the east the tops of the trees were black against a purpling sky and a morning star hung high above them. We'd almost reached the other end of the long night, and the day showed promise of clear air and unlimited visibility. If the Cessna wasn't too deeply mired in snow, we'd be able to fly out early, to whatever airport was closest to an emergency medical facility. And after we delivered Walker there, we'd phone the FBI—

Wait a minute. There was an easier way to get the medical attention he needed.

By the time I'd half frozen the more tender portions of my anatomy, I'd formulated a plan. While Hy and Walker slept, I'd trek around the lake to the logging road and use the 172's radio to call Arrowhead's unicom. They could have a medevac chopper sent directly to the airstrip, and I'd be back there by the time it arrived.

The idea made the prospect of a long, cold early-morning walk through the snow seem almost tolerable.

I went back inside the hangar and carefully extracted the plane's key from Hy's jeans pocket. Checked Walker again, picked up the extra jacket I'd worn away from the cabin last night, and piled it on top of him. Then I found a pad of paper and a pen in a seatback pocket in the Maule and scribbled a brief explanatory note, which I weighted down with a wrench on the floor next to Hy. On the way out, I grabbed the flashlight, some jerky, and a package of trail mix.

The snow was dark gray in the predawn light, and in places it had drifted as high as my waist. The wind had stilled; silence hung heavy around me. I struck out for the trees that indicated where the shoreline was and kept to the left of them. My flashlight made the snow cover glisten; the hard crunch of my footsteps told me it was many degrees below zero, but the extreme cold didn't bother me. I felt curiously alert for one who had slept little, curiously optimistic for one who had feared she wouldn't live to see the end of this icy night.

With optimism came hunger. I opened the package of trail mix and, even though I'd never been fond of such stuff, enjoyed my breakfast. I bit off a piece of jerky and gnawed happily, not at all minding that I resembled a cow chewing its cud. The eastern sky became stained with violet, then ruby. By the time I reached the clearing where the cabin stood, I was enveloped in murky predawn gray.

I'd meant to go straight to the logging road, but the sight of the cabin stopped me. The same feeling of wrongness that had stolen over me at the hangar was back, stronger than ever. After a moment I scrambled up the lake's bank, not knowing what I was looking for but unwilling to go on until I'd looked around some more.

I lighted the oil lamp and searched the small room again. All was as we'd left it. I shone my flash down at the bloodstains under the table, followed a trail of small drops to the door.

Proves nothing, McCone.

Nothing, in and of itself.

I blocked out the room into segments, as I often did when examining a scene. Studied each slowly and thoroughly. When I scanned the table, I spotted a sticker on the spine of one of the books in the stack: "Ely Public Library."

I went over there, picked up the volume containing the introduction by Hy's dead wife, and opened it. A slip of paper fell out. The book had been borrowed on November 20.

The glass that Hy had said smelled of sour mash whiskey caught my attention. I picked it up, smelled the hard-caked residue; a faint odor remained. How long would it retain its smell after the drink was consumed? A week? Maybe. Over two? Doubtful.

He'd been here. Been here recently. Maybe been here the whole time.

Before I stepped out of the cabin I took my .38 from the deep pocket of my jacket. A solid weapon, and I was a good shot, but it seemed scant protection against a skilled marksman and hunter like Dunc Stirling. All the advantages were on his side, including knowing these woods.

On the narrow porch I paused to look around and listen. The branches and limbs of the trees around the clearing moved in the wind off the frozen lake; shadows were clotted among them. He could be right over there, watching me. He could be aiming a high-powered rifle, lining me up in the crosshairs....

Fear made my skin prickle and my heart beat faster. Without half trying I'd succeeded in spooking myself. The adrenaline rush sent me down the steps and around the cabin's side wall at a trot. There was no whine of a bullet, no boom of a shot, but the trees over here were as dense as the others. He could—

Drone of a plane in the distance. Suddenly I realized that it was possible Stirling owned another aircraft. I craned my neck around the cabin's corner, saw it banking on the far side of the lake, turning this way. Ski-plane, the ultimate in escape vehicles for fishermen and hunters wishing to reach isolated camps in winter—but this one might be piloted by a very different kind of hunter.

I sprinted around the cabin, headed for the large rough-board shed that I knew couldn't be seen from the air. Under cover of forest I stopped and looked back at the plane. It was light blue, a single-engine two-seater, but I couldn't identify its make. It circled the clearing, descending.

I ducked into the shed.

Pitch-dark in there and cold as a meat locker. The roar of the plane's engine increased, became deafening; it had to be dangerously low by now. I put my eye to a knothole and tried to spot it, but could see only treetops backlit by the glow of the rising sun.

The sound of the engine changed abruptly; the pilot had put in power, was climbing. I let out my breath in a sigh of relief; probably sportsmen, wondering if this was the camp they were looking for. Not Dunc Stirling.

So where *was* he?

I slipped my .38 into my pocket and took the flashlight from another. I'd stay inside until the plane gained altitude; no point in being spotted, no matter how innocent its occupants. Shining the beam around, I saw the shed contained shelves of supplies and a makeshift worktable cluttered with tools and hardware, a lantern and a heavy coil of rope. A newish-looking outboard motor sat beneath the table, and—

"Oh my God!"

A man's body lay prone on the earthen floor only inches from my feet. He wore jeans and a parka and hiking boots. His legs were splayed, his arms at his sides, and the blond hair at the back of his skull was clotted with what looked to be blood.

I squatted down and shone the light closer. Bullet wound, large and ragged, probably an exit wound. I put my hand on his shoulder and tried to turn him over.

He was frozen solid.

I set the flash down and grasped him with both hands, tipped him on his side and let him thump over on his back.

Duncan Stirling.

"Jesus!" I exclaimed. My breath was hot, my voice loud in this cold, silent place of death.

Stirling had been shot once in the forehead—a clean kill that had left only a small wound. His eyes were open, and in death they were much as I imagined they'd been in life: dark, empty craters leading deep into nothingness.

He *had* been here all along—dead.

And only one other person had been here all along—alive.

I was halfway through the minefield of junk in front of the cabin, on my way to wake Hy and tell him what I'd found, when I heard the plane again.

I scanned the sky from the east, where it had

flared into a near blinding display of color, to the south. The blue ski-plane was descending behind the treeline, probably toward the logging road where we'd landed in the 172.

Who? Anyone who knew Stirling would put down at the strip, and strangers wouldn't attempt a landing on unfamiliar terrain in the snow. Unless someone had spotted the Cessna and notified Search and Rescue? But wouldn't they use a helicopter?

The pilot had throttled back, but now I heard a burst of power. Looking to land, deciding against it. Full throttle, clean up the plane, climb out. Maybe go around, try again—

Oh no, not this time! No second chance.

Ripping and tearing and even from here I can tell limbs are being sheared from trees and I can hear the shriek of the stall horn as if I were in the cockpit.... The crash, how could anything hit the ground that hard?

I veered to the right and began running toward the crash site, icy air lacerating my lungs with every frantic breath.

I stood panting from my long run and staring in horror at the wreckage. The ski-plane had plowed through the trees at the far end of the logging road and lay crumpled on its passenger side on the road itself. Its right wing was sheared off, its left pointed skyward, and the pilot's door had sprung open against the strut.

I took a tentative step toward it. Hisses and pops came from the heap of mangled metal, and something was dripping. Fuel.

Extreme danger of explosion and fire, but if someone was trapped alive in there...

After a moment I went close enough that I could see through the shattered windscreen. No one on the pilot's side; he or she had been thrown clear. There was a body in the passenger seat, but that side had been so badly crushed that whoever it was couldn't possibly be alive.

More hisses and pops. I backed off and circled the wreckage, looking for the pilot. In the snow I picked up a trail of footsteps that meandered toward the trees beyond where Hy and I had concealed the 172 under a clump of jack pine. It now appeared that rather than being thrown clear on impact, the pilot had climbed from the cockpit and was wandering in the woods, dazed and disoriented. Before I searched any farther, I'd get on the radio to Arrowhead's unicom, ask them to send medical help and notify the FAA.

The Cessna's key stuck in the door lock. Frozen? I jiggled it, applied more pressure. It turned. I opened the door and without climbing in, hit the master switch; the electrical system whined—

Footsteps crunching behind me, coming fast. Hy had heard the crash and rushed here too. "Thank God," I called to him as I reached for the radio's switch. "The pilot's somewhere in—"

He grabbed me by the shoulders, pulled me back.

It wasn't Hy.

I grasped the yoke with both hands and kicked backward with my right foot, turning my head to get a look at him. All I saw before my left foot slipped on the ice and went out from under me was that he wore a black ski mask.

He yanked harder, but I clung to the yoke, my upper body pressed against the side of the seat. He moved in until he had me pinned there, then tried to pry my fingers free with big gloved hands.

I brought my left leg up onto the strut and lunged forward, trying to bite him. My teeth collided painfully with the yoke. He'd almost gotten one of my hands free when I gained enough leverage on the strut to kick my right leg back and up as hard as I could.

My attacker howled in pain and let go of my fingers. As he reeled backward, I reached across the instrument panel and put on full flaps. I twisted, prepared to do him further damage. The flaps rumbled down as he was coming up; they whacked him on the back of his head. He pitched forward, his body slamming into the wheel pant.

As the man lay moaning on the shattered fiberglass of the wheel cover, I heard Hy calling to me from a distance. *About time,* I thought—and then felt ashamed of my stress-induced reaction. "Over here," I yelled, taking my .38 out and training it on my attacker.

Hy came running along the logging road and, when he saw what was happening, drew his own gun and covered while I stripped the prone man's ski mask off. When I saw his face, I reeled back in shock. He wasn't who I'd thought he was.

"Who the hell's that?" Hy asked.

"Winthrop Reade—David Stirling's substitute son and undoubtedly second in line to inherit his controlling interest in Stirling Aviation. The man who has most reason to want Dunc dead."

"Jesus," Hy said as we watched the second medevac chopper clear the trees, "with all the questions we're going to have to answer and the statements we're going to have to sign, we'll be lucky to get home by Christmas."

"What can we tell anybody, really? Ash Walker came here to plead with a dangerous federal fugitive to leave him and his new family alone, found the man long gone, and got stranded. When he didn't return on schedule, we came to rescue him."

"And Win Reade?"

"We know nothing about him. And you can be sure he won't tell anyone about the arrangement he and David Stirling made with me." I turned and walked toward the Cessna, sore from my struggle with Reade and worrying with my tongue at what I feared was a cracked front tooth.

Hy followed. "How's Reade going to explain what he was doing here?"

"Who knows? But his kind always comes up with something." I stepped up and sat on the pilot's seat, turned toward him. "And as for his reason for attacking me, he'll probably claim he was in a deranged state brought on by the crash."

Hy leaned in and put his arms around me. "You going to be okay?"

"I'm okay now, but it's nice to have you hold me."

He smoothed my hair with his gloved hand, then pulled my cap lower. "You know," he said after a moment, "Reade must've been having you followed ever since you left Arkansas. Whoever he hired saw us check our bags through to Chisholm-Hibbing at SFO, and Reade and the poor bastard who died in the crash were there before we arrived. Easy for somebody we didn't know to overhear when I asked for a weather briefing for Arrowhead before we left Iron Range Aviation."

"And he and Reade probably waited out last night's storm chatting with the folks at Arrowhead about the people from Minnetonka who came in asking after their irresponsible friend John and the hermit."

"Who was the guy who died, anyway?"

"I heard Reade identify him as one of the company's security men, but I'll bet he was a pro brought along to kill Dunc. People like Reade never do their own dirty work, even if they like to watch it done."

Hy pulled away from me, looked me in the eyes. "Everybody's expendable to people like Reade, McCone. Look at how the plane crashed: There's a crosswind from the south to this road; he would've been turning his left wing into it. Yet they came down on the *right* side."

"He applied opposite aileron to save himself."

Grim and disgusted, Hy nodded. In a crash situation any good pilot—any decent human being—does all he or she can to ensure that the passengers survive.

For a while we were silent, looking at the wreckage that would remain here till the

NTSB investigators could examine it. Then he said, "Reade must be one hell of an arrogant guy to think he could land a ski-plane in that kind of crosswind. I doubt he'd had much opportunity to practice in Arkansas."

"Arrogance and stupidity bring them all down—literally."

"You know, there's still no closure here. Dunc Stirling's free and out there someplace, and has gotten away with murder."

I bit my lip.

"What?"

"There's something I haven't told you."

We stood in the shed over Duncan Stirling's frozen body.

Hy said, "Single shot, probably with Dunc's own rifle, the one Ash had with him in the hangar. Neat and efficient. An execution."

"Maybe, maybe not. It happened in the cabin. Dunc might've surprised him while he was searching it. There might've been some sort of confrontation."

"Sure."

"Look, I know you don't like Walker. I don't either. Frankly, he's not a very likable man. But there's a good side to him; you know that as well as I do. For one thing, he couldn't bring himself to sleep in the cabin where he'd killed Dunc."

"Maybe he preferred the kerosene heater in the hangar; burns cleaner than a woodstove and doesn't require as much tending."

"Come on, Ripinsky. Why d'you think he had to take a drink—maybe several—when he came back for supplies?"

"You mean that glass on the table?"

"Yes. Think about it."

"Okay, maybe he feels remorse—"

"The same as you or I would."

He didn't reply, his eyes on the body.

"Do you really think we'd have acted any differently if we'd confronted Stirling?"

More silence.

"Zach needs his father, Ripinsky."

"...Okay. What do you want to do?"

"Finished." Hy let go of Dunc Stirling's arms, and the body thudded onto its back in a thick stand of birches some hundred yards from the cabin.

I glanced at the sky; it was rapidly becoming overcast again. "The storm that chopper pilot warned us about is moving in tonight. It's supposed to be a major one, the first of a series; they may not find him till the spring thaws—if ever."

He took the Enfield from where he had it slung over his shoulder and laid it down next to the body.

I said, "We'd better be going. It'll be hard enough to take off on that road, without a storm to contend with."

"Don't you worry about that, McCone." He came over and put an arm around my shoulders. "This old warhorse can handle it. I'm a hell of a lot better pilot than Reade ever was."

For a moment we stood looking down at the body. Then Hy said, "Duncan Stirling: criminal, fugitive, and recluse—dead by misadventure."

"Amen."

"And case closed."

I didn't reply to that. Hy was tired and not thinking clearly. I wondered how long it would be before he realized that Stirling hadn't killed Matty—and that nobody else involved had had reason to.

Three Years Ago

"*Pull up to the hold line, McCone, and wait a minute.*"

"*What're you doing? Put that seat belt back on!*"

"*Uh-uh. Two perfect takeoffs and landings today. It's time for you to solo.*"

"*You are not getting out of this plane!*"

"*Oh, yes, I am. And you are going to fly a perfect pattern—all on your own.*"

"*Matty—*"

"*Pick me up here when you get back, and we'll take a run out to the coast, see if there're any whales hanging around today.*"

"*Matty!*"

"*Just do it, McCone. You don't need me anymore. It's time to let go.*"

PART FIVE

December 7–25

Twenty-four

I couldn't sleep.

I was lying in my own bed, and Hy had drifted off at least two hours ago, but I couldn't sleep. I tried to focus on my list of Christmas gifts, on the fact that I badly needed to make a hair appointment, on all the paperwork that had piled up at the office. Hell, I even thought about it being Pearl Harbor Day. But scenes from Minnesota kept pushing the safe and mundane aside: walking along the eerie light-filled aisle of white birches; Ash Walker stepping from the shadows behind the Maule; Dunc Stirling's frozen corpse; the mangled blue ski-plane; Winthrop Reade's stunned face...

Both Hy and I had been operating on our very last reserves of energy for the past day and a half, and consequently he had yet to discover the logical flaw in our assumptions about the murder of not only Matty but Andie Walker, Cutter, and Matthews as well. So far I had allowed him to remain unaware, but the problem gnawed at me, disturbing my sleep and my waking hours, and I knew I'd have to discuss it with him before long.

Quite simply put, Duncan Stirling hadn't committed any of those murders. It was clear to me that he'd gone to ground immediately upon being released on bond and had no further contact with anyone from his former life. He couldn't have known where Ash

Walker was, much less that he was living with Matty, and I doubted he'd nursed a desire for vengeance throughout all those years in the wilderness. Besides, the timing of Matty's death was wrong; in all likelihood Walker had shot Stirling days before the air show.

That left Winthrop Reade the obvious suspect—except that he'd had no motive to kill either woman. Reade wanted Dunc Stirling out of the way so he could assume his place as David Stirling's heir, but there was no reason for him to have anyone else killed. I'd toyed with other possible suspects: Calder Franklin, because he'd perhaps been involved in the drugs-and-arms operation and needed to silence Walker and his women. But that didn't wash; Franklin had long ago proven himself unconnected to what went on at the aircraft company and had, in fact, suspected Reade was having me followed and tried to warn me by phone the afternoon before Hy and I left for Minnesota. The attorney had informed me of that in a brief but heated conversation earlier this evening; his last words to me were "If only you'd listened to me, that fiasco up in Minnesota could've been avoided. A lot of damage control is going to have to be done before Win begins his senatorial campaign." Finally, desperate to believe the case was actually closed, I'd even taken a good hard look at Ash Walker as a suspect, but much as I didn't like the man, I'd had to conclude that I was constructing a ridiculous scenario.

The case seemed destined to be one that would nag at me for many years to come.

As I'd predicted, Winthrop Reade had facilely

explained away his presence at Stirling's hideaway: He'd remembered the Minnesota property and had flown there with one of the company's security men as a bodyguard, on the off chance that was where Dunc had fled. His plan, he claimed, was to persuade him to give himself up in order that he might be reunited with his dying father. The authorities bought his story, and I agreed to drop assault charges against him. Purposeless and potentially dangerous to pursue it.

During the day and a half that Hy and I answered questions and made statements, both to the local jurisdiction and the FBI, the predicted series of blizzards arrived. For a while they had to close the Twin Cities airport, but our flight to SFO was one of the first to leave once they reopened it, and we made sure to be on board.

At the airport we had a late lunch with Zach, Hank, and Habiba, who were waiting for their delayed flight to Minneapolis. As the boy's attorney, Hank had volunteered to accompany him east for a reunion with his father and to stay on with him until Ash Walker was well enough to travel—a matter of days, the doctor had told me. At the last minute Habiba begged to go along, and Hank agreed. He wanted, he said, to foster the growing friendship between the two kids; Habiba was a strong, steady little girl, and Zach would be able to lean on her during the painful adjustments both before and after his homecoming. Even though Wes and Karla Payne planned to put the farmhouse to rights, it would surely seem vast, empty, and without a center when Zach and Ash returned.

With such memories and thoughts of the future preying on my mind, was it any wonder I couldn't sleep?

Finally I reached for my cassette player, back in its usual place on the nightstand. I'd dragged it with me all over the country and never used it once, but tonight it would ease me into oblivion. I couldn't remember which tape was in it, but I guessed the one with the sappy music and sea sounds that I listened to when I was homesick for Touchstone. I slipped the earphones on, fumbled for the play button, and lay back.

A woman's voice came on: "Off-the-record interview with Quentin Ramsey—"

What was this? More to the point, who was this?

"...former controller of Stirling Aviation—"

Iona Fowler, the Arkansas reporter who had told me all her research tapes about the Stirling case had been destroyed by fire. I clicked the player back on, listened to the date and other explanatory material.

Okay, it was Fowler and this was a tape from before the indictments were handed down. But how—

Oh, right. The night after I'd visited her, someone had followed me during my walk around Post Office Square in Fayetteville. And later I'd noticed that a number of things in my hotel room—including the stack of tapes next to the player on the bedside table— had been disturbed. It hadn't been someone sent by David Stirling and Winthrop Reade or Calder Franklin; it had been Fowler, and she'd probably deputized her live-in friend to keep tabs on me while she contrived to get into my room and leave me this gift of evidence.

Too bad I hadn't felt the need to play my soothing tapes until now. If Fowler had gone to that much trouble, the contents of this one must be very interesting. I pressed the play button again.

"You promise this is off the record, Iona?"

"I guarantee it. Anything you tell me will be strictly on background. If I use it, I'll dig up my own facts to support it. Now, when you were controller at Stirling, did Dunc ask you to do some creative accounting?"

"Well, sure. He couldn't've covered that operation without my help. But if you repeat that—"

"Relax, Quent. We've been friends for a long time. I wouldn't do that to you. You took your orders directly from Dunc?"

"Uh-huh."

"Nobody else higher up was involved?"

"...Nobody."

"Quent, I've heard rumors that somebody else had a hand in that operation. Somebody with good political connections."

"...Look, what I know has already put me in a dangerous position."

"You know you want to tell me. Otherwise you wouldn't have agreed to this interview."

"Yeah, I want to tell you. Those indictments are coming down any day now, and I know one of them's got my name on it. But the bastard's untouchable. He's got connections clear to Washington, D.C."

"Who, Quent?"

"...Win Reade."

"Win? Come on!"

"I mean it. He was the man behind that operation. Oh, sure, Dunc handled the actual running of it, but Win was behind the scenes pulling strings the whole time. Dunc doesn't have the brainpower to finesse deals on that scale; he just thinks he does. And Win was clever and manipulative enough that Dunc half believed he was running the show."

"You know all this for a fact?"

"I do. One time when Dunc was telling me how to cook the books he slipped and said, 'Win wants—' He covered quick, but it made me wonder, and I started nosing around. Got corroboration from a very reliable source as to who was involved."

"You willing to name names?"

"I don't know.... Hell, yes I am! If I'm going down, I want to see the guys responsible go down, too. My source was Bobby Ames—you know him, the company's chief counsel. Bobby told me about Dick Norwood, head of sales and Win's best buddy—he was in on it from the beginning. Charlie Vernon, of the poultry Vernons, was getting a cut of everything. So was Ken Rule, the electronics magnate."

"What about David Stirling?"

"No, ma'am. Win, Charlie, and Ken kept him and his attorney, Calder Franklin, in the dark. By the time David had recovered from his accident enough to think straight, they had everything well oiled and running smooth."

"What about the murder-for-hire sideline?

I can't see the Win I grew up with involved in something like that."

"Iona, the Win you grew up with is a figment of your imagination. That man's corrupt, through and through. He's as guilty of at least three of those murders as if he'd personally pulled the trigger."

"Jesus. Are you sure?"

"Ask Bobby Ames, if he'll talk with you. Chances are he won't. None of those guys I've named are going down."

"They would if you'd go to the FBI with what you know."

"You think I'm crazy? I want to live. And Win's promised to pay my attorneys' bills."

"What about Dunc? Won't he turn on them when he's indicted?"

"No way. Win and Dunc cut a deal. Dunc takes full responsibility, is indicted, but never stands trial."

"How's that going to happen?"

"A corrupt judge, bail, and Dunc's Silver Whisper fueled and ready—with five million dollars in cash and bearer's bonds inside."

"Lord, this goes even higher than I suspected! I could be breaking one hell of a story."

"Well, you just see if you can prove any of this, honey. In the meantime, you never talked to me. And you take care, you hear? You're up against some mighty tough players."

There was a break in the tape. Then Fowler's voice came on again.

"Sharon, after you listen to what I have to say, take the first portion of this tape and do whatever you can with it. Erase this part. I admit I lied when I said all my tapes were destroyed in the fire; this one survived because I always kept it with me in my purse. You see, I couldn't prove a thing Quent told me, but Dunc's bail-and-vanishing act *did* happen, so I kept hoping I'd come up with somebody who would corroborate his story.

"I kept probing in all the wrong places, and then the good ol' boys started coming after me. When they burned me out and took a shot at me, I called my old friend Win and played this tape. Made my own deal: they'd leave me alone if I'd back off and get out of town, forget all about the book project. And I've kept my part of the bargain all these years because I wanted to preserve the peaceful little world I've created for myself here on the farm.

"After talking with you, though, I've realized I can't keep on withholding this kind of evidence. The federal statute of limitations has probably run out on the drugs-and-arms charges, but there's no limit on capital murder, and Quent was definite about Win being involved in that. Plus there's the possibility of new charges being brought against Reade; it's obvious to me that he, not Dunc, had your friend killed—and God knows what else he's involved in.

"Feels good, getting this off my conscience. Win Reade's always been a dangerous man, and now that he's the political machine's fair-haired pick for the U.S. Senate, he's dangerous to the country as a whole. So use this tape, please. Don't tell anybody where you got it, though, because I'll just deny it. But if and when the time comes, I'll confirm the conversation with Quent to the authorities, testify, do whatever it takes. And good luck to you."

So there it was: the prospect of closure ringing in my ears.

Win Reade had had a motive to have Andie Walker, Matty, Cutter, and Matthews killed after all. He'd tracked both Dunc Stirling and Ash Walker through Hy and me. And if he hadn't crashed his ski-plane, he'd have given the order for all of us to be killed.

But now, thanks to Iona Fowler's conscience, I had the evidence I needed to ensure that the man who had ordered Matty's death would not go unpunished. And I knew exactly how to go about it.

Craig Morland sprawled in one of my clients' chairs, more relaxed in jeans and a ratty sweater than I'd ever seen him. A suede jacket, as disreputable as the one Hy had recently—and reluctantly—consigned to the trash bin, lay on the other chair.

"So," I said, "when I left my message indicating I was willing to help you compromise your integrity and betray the Bureau's trust, you'd already drafted your letter of resignation and run off with Adah to that Mexican paradise she's always talking about."

He nodded, grinning and chewing on a toothpick; he and Joslyn had eaten a late breakfast at Miranda's before coming to the pier. "On Thanksgiving morning, when I volunteered all that information to you about Walker and the Witness Protection Program, I knew I was over the top. It was time to get out."

"What does the future hold?"

"Other than a move to San Francisco? I'm not sure. Nothing professional for a while. I've got enough money put aside that I can afford to take some time off, think about my options."

"While you're at it, you might consider McCone Investigations. I can use someone with your skills and connections. Of course, I can't offer you the salary or benefits you're accustomed to."

He looked around my office, eyes narrowed speculatively, then focused on the Bay vista beyond the big arched window behind me. "Life's full of trade-offs. But I take it a job offer wasn't what you had in mind when you asked me to stop by."

"No, it wasn't." I'd been trying to locate him for nearly a week, ever since I'd discovered Iona Fowler's tape. This morning Joslyn had finally answered the phone at her apartment and informed me of the startling developments in Craig's—and her—life.

I asked, "Do you recall anything about the Stirling Aviation business?"

"I refreshed my memory when I did that little job of research for you."

"Then I want you to listen to this." I pressed the play button on my office recorder.

"Where'd you get hold of that?" he asked as I hit the rewind.

I shook my head.

"Okay, then, what do you plan to do with it?"

"That depends."

"On?"

"Whether you'll help me. Even though you're no longer with the Bureau, I assume you know people there who will do you a favor."

He waited, his expression noncommittal.

"I need this tape and an anonymous report on more current events to fall into the right hands at the FBI—by a trail so long and convoluted that their origin will never be traced."

"That can be done."

"Will you facilitate it?"

He considered, gazing once more at the Bay. "You know, when we met in D.C. that night, I told you I didn't give a shit anymore. I still don't, but only as it applies to the system. In the smaller areas where the individual still can make a difference—such as what you propose— I still believe. So, yes, I'll do it—and in a way that neither the tape nor the report can be buried by somebody who can be bought."

"Craig, thanks." I took the tape from the machine and the report from my desk drawer and handed them over to him. "You'll keep my offer in mind?"

"Most certainly."

I walked him to the next office, where Joslyn was chatting with Rae, then watched the unlikely couple—she, half black and half Jewish, with parents who still hoped for the triumphant return of the Communist Party; he, WASP to the core, with a father whom the Bureau had once charged with tracking down those self-same Commies—leave the pier hand in hand. Then I went back to my office and collected my things. I had a lunch date in Los Alegres.

Gray Selby and I sat in a window booth at the Seven Niner Diner. It was Friday, normally a busy day at small airports, and the cloudless sky had brought fliers out in even greater measure. I watched a Cessna 152 make a clumsy arrival on the runway, thought with satisfaction of the near perfect landing I'd earlier made in the Citabria. Then I turned my attention back to the flight instructor.

"So that's what happened," I said. "Matty was murdered, and the man who ordered it will soon be under investigation by the FBI. I'd appreciate it if you would tell everybody else here; you'll probably all be contacted by them or the local authorities, and hopefully they'll be able to build a case against him."

"I'll be more than glad to. You're one hell of a detective, McCone."

I examined his face for traces of sarcasm, but saw none. "Thanks, Selby."

Silence fell between us. We'd said all that needed to be said, but neither of us wanted to get on with the business of the day. After a moment he glanced at my plate, spotted an uneaten dill spear, and raised an eyebrow.

"Take it." I glanced out the window. The 152 that had earlier landed had taxied into one of the flight school's tie-downs; Mark Casazza got out of the right seat, and a few seconds later Bob Cuda stepped down from the left.

338

"Do I see what I think I'm seeing?" I asked. Selby grinned. "Yep. Cuda's taking lessons."

"You're kidding."

"Uh-uh. Mark tells me he's doing okay, even though he keeps threatening to make Cuda hold an egg between the yoke and his death grip."

"You know what? I bet Bob'll do fine, once he gets over being nervous."

"Probably. And guess who else has been flying a lot? Your old buddy Ash Walker. He's up there right now in the Super Cub he just bought."

"He's not my buddy." Since Walker's return from Minnesota I'd spoken with him only once, to tell him about Iona Fowler's tape. He'd promised to take precautions till Win Reade was behind bars, but said he had no intention of uprooting Zach from their life in Los Alegres. He and Zach—who had opted to retain the first name he'd used for most of his life—needed to remain in the farmhouse and work things out between them, Walker had added. I hadn't asked what he meant by that, because Habiba had filled me in: Zach was justifiably angry with his father for his deceptions and still grieving badly for Matty.

Selby said, "Don't be too hard on the guy, McCone."

"Since when did you turn into a fan of his?"

"Since I realized he thinks his life is over, just like I did when I came back from my war."

"Is it?"

"His or mine?"

"Both."

"No, not by a long shot."

After I left Selby, I detoured to the terminal to pay my parking fee and found Zach sitting on the steps to its deck, huddled close to Max, Art Field's old Lab.

"Sharon," he said, "why're you here?"

"Having lunch with a friend." I sat down on the other side of Max; he leaned against me and licked my cheek sloppily. "Doggy breath, Max," I said. "Get away from me."

As if he understood, he got up and wandered over to the patch of lawn.

"So how're you doing?" I asked Zach.

"Oh... okay."

"Your dad flying today?"

"Yeah. I still haven't gone back to school, so he made me come along. Said I had to get over being upset around airplanes."

"And?"

"It's not the planes that upset me. I just don't want to be around *him*."

I waited.

"Look, Sharon, Dad lied to me about *everything*. A month ago I thought I was twelve years old; now all of a sudden I'm fourteen. I thought I was Zach Seabrook, but I was really Roger Walker, and now I'm Zach Walker because Roger reminds me of fuckin' Roger Rabbit. My dad told me over and over again that I didn't see my mom get shot. But now it turns out I did. He said he loved Matty and me, but he ran off and left us and she got killed, and even then he didn't come back for me. And yeah, I know why he didn't come back, but that doesn't stop me from wanting to... I don't know what. Maybe run off on *him*."

And he had, in an emotional sense. "Have you told your dad how you feel?"

"Would he listen?"

"You never know till you try."

The Super Cub was on final; Zach turned his head and watched it, his face a study in mixed emotions. After it touched down, he let out his breath in a long sigh. "Then maybe I will try," he said. "Can't hurt, can it?"

"How's it going?" I asked as I passed Ash Walker in the tie-downs.

"Better. The flying helps ward off the more painful memories." He moved around to chain the tail section, clearly uninterested in further conversation. I went on toward where I'd parked the Citabria.

Memories...

When I reached the plane I stopped, my hand resting on its high wing, and looked across the tarmac at the fuel pumps. For a moment I could see Matty leaning against the counter, hands thrust into the pockets of her jacket, long hair blowing in the crosswind. Then for the last time I laid the image to rest and took out the key to the Citabria. It was going to be a beautiful ride back to Oakland.

When I stopped by Pier 24 1/2 to check in, I found Ted leaning on the railing outside his office and staring morosely at the array of Christmas decorations.

I went over and leaned next to him. "Brooding again?"

He glanced at me, lines between his eyebrows bunching into a scowl. "I do not brood."

"You brood."

"I *never* brood."

"Do so."

"Well, look at all that stuff! I opt for the traditional, and they choose to express themselves."

As far as I was concerned, Ted's scheme of garlands and little winking lights, red velvet ribbons and silver-and-gold ornaments was masterful. Was it so creative of the documentary filmmaker downstairs to spray-paint whatever had ended up on the cutting room floor in iridescent Christmas hues and then fashion a wreath from it? Were the architects' blowups of photographs of recent projects really enhanced by the tiny magazine cutouts of decorations and holiday revelers that they'd glued to them? Was the Santa's village in front of the financial planner's office anything more than a costly fix for a potentially time-consuming problem?

Was this ridiculous decorating contest such a big deal, anyway?

I glanced at Ted's woebegone face. Yes, to him it was, so I'd keep my fingers crossed.

I asked, "Who's doing the judging, anyway?"

"Three hunky hetero guys from the fireboat station."

"I'm sure they'll find ours the most aesthetic."

"Firemen? They wouldn't know aesthetic if it bit them on the ass!"

"Well, cheer up. The suspense'll be over on Friday." I started for the stairway.

"Hey, where're you off to so early?"

"Macy's, F.A.O. Schwarz, and the Gap—

among others. I've got to prepare for the Christmas Eve from hell."

Twenty-five

Hy and I were drinking champagne with Rae and Ricky amid the glorious post-celebratory wreckage in their living room. Empty boxes were strewn everywhere; crumpled wrapping paper drifted against the furniture; bows were stuck to lampshades. A huge tree— a gift from Seabrook's Christmas Tree Farm— stood in the window overlooking the Golden Gate, and prominently displayed on it was a white porcelain dove that my sister and her new husband had presented to Ricky when he collected the kids at the airport. Except for one aspect, the visit was going better than expected.

Rae said, "You know, Mick and Chris set the tone for the others."

I nodded. They'd apparently made the decision to act like pleasant adults, and had even hugged Rae when they left for Mick's condo, where Chris had opted to spend the night.

"They set the tone for everybody but Jamie," Ricky muttered, staring glumly into his champagne flute.

Quickly Rae said, "Molly and Lisa really liked their presents. And Brian even unbent and smiled a lot. He's coming around."

"Jamie isn't."

I tried to steer the conversation away from the behavior of Ricky's middle—and favorite— daughter. "Seems like we all got what we

343

wanted for Christmas. Even Ted took first place in the pier decorating contest."

"Jamie hasn't even opened her presents."

None of us cared to comment on that. Rae patted Ricky's hand; Hy went to tend the fire. And I found myself becoming seriously pissed off at my niece. I stood and said, "Be back in a minute."

Upstairs I knocked at the door behind which fifteen-year-old Jamie had been sulking since yesterday evening and, when there was no reply, simply walked in. She was curled up on the bed listening to her Walkman: a slender young woman with tiny features that were overwhelmed by ferociously permed brown hair. When she saw me, she glared and turned up the volume.

I glanced around. The room could have been in a hotel; it contained absolutely no trace of its occupant except for a largely unpacked duffel bag on the bureau. When I looked back at Jamie, she was ostentatiously ignoring me, so I went over and yanked the earphones off her head.

"What the hell d'you think you're doing, Aunt Shar?"

I wanted to scream at her for spoiling her father's—and her own—Christmas Eve. I wanted to grab her by the arm and forcibly march her downstairs and make her apologize. But neither action would have produced the desired results. Instead I studied her, trying to figure out which button to push.

Finally I said, "I came up to tell you good night."

"You're going to bed *already*?"

"Uh-huh. We all are."

"But—"

"What?"

"Oh, nothing." She shrugged elaborately.

"We had a great time tonight. Everybody liked their presents."

"Are they mad at me for not coming downstairs?"

"No, why should they be? It was your choice. Actually, I don't think anybody noticed you weren't there. Well, except for Chris."

"Chris? What'd she say?" Ever since her older sister had gone off to Berkeley, Jamie had entertained an intense—and one-sided— rivalry toward her.

"She asked if we could open your present from your dad and divvy it up among us."

"She *what!*"

"Relax, we didn't; it's still under the tree. Not that we didn't want to, but it's tailored especially for you."

"What is it?"

"I promised not to tell."

She pushed her lips out in a pout. Directed a flinty look toward me. Then she got off the bed, hitching up her jeans and tugging at her Hootie and the Blowfish sweatshirt.

"Oh, all right," she announced. "I'll go down there and open the damn thing!"

When we came into the living room, Ricky looked up, pleased and surprised. Jamie aimed her scowl at him, then transferred it to Hy, who said, "What did *I* do?" She didn't so much as glance Rae's way.

Rae said, "Hy, will you pour Jamie a glass of champagne?"

Ricky no longer looked pleased. He surveyed his daughter as if she were a stray cat looking to take up residence and said to Rae, "What the hell do you think you're doing, serving my kid alcohol?"

Completely unruffled, she replied, "She's a young woman, not a kid. Mick and Chris each had a glass; Jamie should, too."

He grunted.

Jamie took the flute from Hy, glancing tentatively and suspiciously at Rae. Rae flashed her a crinkly-nosed grin and winked. I went to the tree and fetched the present, a red envelope with a green bow. Jamie frowned as she took it, probably thinking it contained money and what was so specially tailored about that? But when she opened it and read the note from her father, she flushed with pleasure.

"Really, Daddy?"

"Really."

"Thank you!"

"You'd better thank Red. She pointed out the error of my ways and suggested I make amends. When I tried to send you off alone with my credit card during your visit in October, I was all caught up in my own life and being very insensitive. I'm sorry, and I'll make up for it on Thursday."

In his note he'd promised that the two of them would spend the entire day after Christmas together: buying things for her room, having lunch, and doing whatever else she wanted.

Jamie hesitated before looking at Rae. "Thank you," she said stiffly. Then she went over and flopped down on the couch next to her father, still looking at her. She might not like Rae yet, but she definitely found her interesting.

I yawned and held out my hand to Hy. "Let's take these people up on their offer of a guest room."

"Sounds good to me. We'll get up early, go to your house and feed Ralph and Allie their Christmas chicken livers, and be off to Touchstone."

The message light was blinking on the answering machine when I came into the cottage. I set Hy's Christmas gift on the coffee table and hit the play button; the tape was rewinding when Hy entered, carrying a black plastic garbage bag that had been in the back of the Citabria when he arrived from his ranch on the twenty-second.

"What," I said, "you're giving me your trash for Christmas?"

He smiled mysteriously, deposited the bag next to his present, and waited to hear the message.

Craig Morland: "Sharon, I can't track you down, so I'm leaving this on both your machines. Talked with a buddy of mine in D.C. this morning, and he says Justice is moving cautiously but quickly on the Reade matter. Deals have been cut with two people who can link him solidly to the murder-for-hire operation, and there's also a possibility charges can be brought for the murders of Wildress, Cutter, and Matthews. Looks like they'll go for an indictment on the Arkansas matter before New Year's. So how's that for a present? Merry Christmas!"

"Case closed," I said to Hy. "Really closed this time."

He got champagne from the fridge while I hung a gold filigree star in the window overlooking the sea. We toasted: to each other, to Matty, to closure. Then he said, "You want to open your present?"

"You go first." I slid the gaily wrapped package along the table to him.

Rip, shred, tear: Hy was as voracious as the Little Savages when it came to gifts. "McCone! New dual headsets! I can toss out those antiquated pieces of junk I've got now, and we won't have to scream to be heard anymore." He lifted the padded carrying case from the box, opened it, and pulled one unit out. "Jesus, these're light. Telex Airman ANRs! What'd you do—rob a bank?"

"You're worth it."

He put the headset on, sat there grinning happily. "Your turn now."

I opened the garbage bag; inside was a long tube wrapped in red foil. I did some ripping, shredding, and tearing of my own, pried the cap off the tube, and felt inside. A thick roll of paper.

I looked questioningly at Hy; he continued smiling.

I slipped the roll out and smoothed it on the table: an architectural drawing of a graceful wood-and-stone house that matched the style of the cottage. Quickly I flipped to the next sheet: floor plans.

"Our house?" I whispered. We'd often talked of the home we would someday build on the foundations of the one that used to stand on this property, but that had seemed a far-off event.

"Our house." He scooted over next to me. "An architect buddy of mine designed it, with plenty of input from me."

"It's beautiful." I ran my hand over the elevation of the front.

He began pointing out various features: a huge central area with a pit fireplace that combined living and dining rooms and kitchen. A bedroom wing for guests at one end and a bedroom-and-den wing for us at the other. The house was very like the previous one, which had been destroyed by explosion and fire. Although Hy had never visited there, I'd described it to him, and he'd incorporated its best features into the design.

"What's this?" I pointed to a circle in an area on the ocean side, off the master bedroom.

"Hot tub. I've seen those lustful glances you cast at Rae and Ricky's. Someday we too will be able to sit in one without our swimsuits and gaze at the Pacific. Of course, these plans're only preliminary; my buddy'll make any changes you want."

"No, it's perfect just as it is." Suddenly I felt overwhelmed. To build a house together was such a commitment.

He put his hand under my chin and tipped my face up toward his. "McCone, is this scaring you?"

"A little."

"Me too."

We both laughed.

"So what do you say?" he asked. "Is it a go?"

I pushed my fears aside. "I say, how soon can we lay the cornerstone?"

If you have enjoyed reading this large print book and you would like more information on how to order a Wheeler Large Print Book, please write to:

 Wheeler Publishing, Inc.
P.O. Box 531
Accord, MA 02018-0531